Praise for *Binding Energy* |

"In their range, and the articulation of styles, and in their balancing between self-aware referentiality and fist-clenched passion, Daniel Marcus's brilliant assemblage of stories could be seen as a kind of map for the future of literary SF."
- **Jonathan Lethem, National Book Critics Circle Award-winning author of *Motherless Brooklyn***

"Marcus has put together an outstanding collection -- emotionally taut, tough-minded, and beautifully rendered, these stories are models of compression and power."
- **Karen Joy Fowler, World Fantasy Award winning author of *Black Glass, Sarah Canary,* and *The Jane Austen Book Club***

"Raymond Carver crossed with William Gibson."
- **Salon.com**

A CRACK IN EVERYTHING

A CRACK IN EVERYTHING

Daniel Marcus

For David Marcus

Copyright © 2011 by Daniel Marcus
Cover design by Chris Manfre.

Published by Apodis Publishing Inc.
www.apodispublishing.com

ISBN: 978-0-9738047-5-1

Printed in the United States of America.

There is a crack in everything. That's how the light gets in.

Leonard Cohen

CHAPTER ONE

They were making the pilgrimage down from Philly for their three weeks on the Delaware shore – Gabe, his Mom and Dad, and his little sister Ariel, who had just turned six the week before. It was August and the sky was hazed with heat, mercilessly bright. Traffic was very bad, and Gabe's father kept cursing their foul luck, leaning on the horn and sticking his head out the window to yell things like "Drive it or park it, you son of a bitch!" or "Move, for Christ's sake, will you just fucking *move?*"

Every now and then, he reached into the styrofoam cooler between his wife's legs and grabbed another golden, sweating can of Ballantine ale. He would roll the can on his forehead and lean back in the driver's seat making an "aah" sound before he ripped open the top and held it up to his mouth, draining it in three or four gulps. Gabe could see his Mom looking over and biting her lip, wanting to say something, but she never did. When there was no more beer, Gabe's father opened the glove compartment and pulled out a thin, flat bottle. The car filled with the sick, sweet smell of peppermint. It reminded Gabe of Christmas.

It was mid-afternoon by the time they reached the Ocean View RV Park. Gabe's father had fallen silent when all the schnapps was gone and drove hunched over the wheel, the cords in his neck standing out like rope. They pulled in front of a long, battered trailer near the back of the lot,

1

raising a cloud of dust as they came to a stop. Gabe's father was renting it from someone he worked with at the restaurant back in Philly. Its white paint was chipped and scratched, the shiny aluminum showing through underneath. Beyond the trailer was a low dune scattered with clumps of tough grass, beyond the dune a service road clustered with fast food shacks, and beyond that, more dunes, the state beach, and the ocean, blue as a marble.

Gabe's father sat in the driver's seat, still gripping the steering wheel. His lips were moving but Gabe couldn't hear what he was saying.

"Come on, kids," his mother said. "Let's start bringing the bags in. Daddy'll be along." Her voice had a tight edge to it.

The trunk was full. There were suitcases, bags of groceries, and a loose collection of Gabe's stuff that he'd thrown together at the last minute – a basketball, a frisbee, some games, a bag of books. He'd brought a few Heinlein and a bunch of Edgar Rice Burroughs – all four Pellucidars and a half-dozen of the John Carter of Mars books. His Dad had turned him on to the Burroughs. He'd read them all before, but that didn't matter. He looked at the books bulging out of the brown Safeway bag and imagined the dizzying towers of Barsoom thrusting up out of the red desert sands, waiting to receive him. He itched to curl up in a dark corner somewhere and be taken there.

Ariel hovered about, trying to help and getting in the way. Gabe handed her a small bag to carry inside and she scurried off.

The trailer was very hot and had a sour smell, like dirty laundry and old milk. Gabe's mother turned on the air conditioning first thing and it started with a laboring clatter. Narrow windows let in shafts of light swimming with bright, slow specks of dust, but the light did little to illuminate the interior. There was a combination kitchen and living room, the whole thing not much bigger than Gabe's bedroom at home, and down a narrow corridor, the two tiny bedrooms and a bathroom. Gabe didn't mind sharing a room with Ariel even though she cried at night and sometimes wet her bed. It was easier to keep her out of trouble when she was nearby.

When Gabe went outside again to get more luggage, his father was standing next to the driver's side door, looking out at the ocean, his hand held up to his forehead shielding his eyes from the glare. His t-shirt was darkened under the arms with half-moons of sweat and the brisk wind coming in from the ocean lifted his wispy hair. Gabe imagined the wind picking his father up like a paper kite, lifting him above the trailer park, above the highway, above the ocean, carrying him off.

Gabe's father turned around and looked at him. Craggy brows angled in a frown over bloodshot eyes. He shook his head as if awakening from a trance. "Help your mother unpack, boy," he said.

"That's what I'm doing, Dad."

Something crossed his father's face, like he smelled something bad for a moment, then it was gone. Gabe tensed.

"Good," his father said slowly, nodding. "That's good." He kept looking at Gabe with an odd expression.

"Well, I have to help Mom," Gabe said, finally. He hated the squirmy feeling he got sometimes with his father. Especially when the old man was *loaded*, like now.

His father nodded. "Good boy, you do that. Hurry up and get those last bags out of the trunk. I have to go to the store."

Gabe knew that "the store" meant "the liquor store". He pulled a heavy suitcase out of the trunk and dragged it through the sandy dirt, up the aluminum steps, and through the dark doorway into the trailer.

He left the bag in his parents' bedroom. The door to his room was half open and he could hear voices – his mother's in quiet admonition, Ariel's whining in protest. He slipped quietly past and when he was at the bottom of the steps, he called out.

"I'm going exploring, Mom. Back in a while."

3

As Gabe hurried away from the trailer, he heard her voice calling from inside, something about "your sister," but it was lost in the wind. He saw his father's Escort up ahead, driving out through the entrance, fishtailing a bit as it turned onto Route 1. He headed in the opposite direction, down toward the beach, to his Place.

That's how he thought of it, with a capital 'p'. It was a hollowed out refuge deep in the middle of the sprawling bramble that bordered the beach. He found the entrance, a section of the seemingly impenetrable bushes that arched slightly above the sand. It was a little overgrown, but that was a good sign – it meant nobody had disturbed his sanctuary.

He got down on his belly and slithered through the space. The bushes opened up around him almost immediately and he could crawl comfortably. The path meandered through the heart of the bramble, seeming to find its own course. Then, suddenly, it opened up into a space about six feet across and almost big enough to stand in.

His Place. The light that filtered in through the tough, fleshy leaves seemed to resonate in the green part of the spectrum, but there was a softness to it, a kind of syrupy glow. Even in the dead heat of the middle of the day when the adults were all back in their trailers napping or watching television and all the dogs in the park were crouched in whatever shade they could find, their tongues lolling, Gabe's Place was cool and comfortable.

And it stayed pretty dry when it rained. Once, Gabe had weathered out a fierce thunderstorm here. His Dad had been drinking and smacked him for tripping over the television plug, pulling it out in the middle of a football game. Gabe bolted out the door before anyone could stop him and ran through the driving rain down to the bramble. He huddled in the hollowed space, the dim, gray-green light punctuated with flashes of electric brightness. Once, the lightning strike must have been very near. There was no discernible gap between the flash and the almost deafening roar, and the sharp smell of ozone filled his nostrils. Beneath

4

the rain and thunder, the waves crashing on the beach sounded very close. Gabe almost expected a foamy torrent to come roaring through the tangle of bushes.

When the storm was over and he got back to the trailer, his father was passed out in the back bedroom and baby Ariel was asleep in her crib. His mother got up from the kitchen table and put her arms around him, even though he was dripping wet. She made him hot chocolate and they sat together, not saying much. She didn't even scold him for running off.

A few people knew about Gabe's place. Every now and then, he found an empty whiskey bottle or a small cluster of cigarette butts jammed into the sand, sticking up at odd angles. Once, a few years back, he found a condom wrapper. He knew what it was because he'd stolen one from his father's dresser once. You were supposed to put it over your dick so you could make love to a woman without getting her knocked up. Gabe tried it on, but it didn't fit very well.

Gabe had a feeling that the people who shared the place with him respected its sanctity, too, even though some of them were slobs. He'd never actually run into anyone here, which was just as well.

He sat down with his back against a thick tangle of branches and closed his eyes. The branches made a kind of webbing and he leaned back into it, letting it support him. It felt good to just be there, the cool green light making a dappled pattern against his eyelids. He would set the place up, bring down some books, a stash of food and water. He dug his battered copy of Burroughs' *At the Earth's Core* out of his back pocket and opened it to where the page was folded back. Pellucidar. The world inside the world. Mountains, jungles, seas all hanging there on the inside surface of the hollow Earth, right under our feet, invisible.

Gabe started reading and felt his surroundings sloughing away like a layer of dead skin, felt himself sinking into that other place. After a little while, though, he put the book down. He wanted to explore, see who was around. He

5

crawled out through the bramble and walked back up to the RV park.

There were a lot of empty spaces, rectangles filled with bright, green weeds, surrounded by patches of sandy dirt. Scuffed footpaths led straight to the edges of the rectangles and stopped. Most of Gabe's friends from previous summers were already gone, back to Philly or New York or Washington or Baltimore. But at the other end of the lot, there was a trailer Gabe had never seen before. It was one of those old Airstreams, the whole thing shiny silver like an elongated drop of mercury, its sleek, rounded lines holding the deep blue of the sky in rippling curves.

Gabe could hear the exuberant strains of salsa music, getting louder as he approached the trailer. He walked around the back. There was a large patch of bare dirt, and two people sitting in lawn chairs, facing the ocean. Between them was a cooler, a pair of Cokes and an open bag of Doritos on the closed lid. The music blared forth from a medium-sized boom box on top of a wooden crate in front of them.

He stood there for a while, caught between curiosity and shyness. Finally, a low, booming voice, so deep Gabe imagined he could feel its rumbling sub-harmonics in the soles of his feet, called out from one of the chairs.

"Don't just stand there like a pillar of salt, come on over and introduce yourself."

Even more shy now, Gabe slowly walked around to the front of the chairs. Seated there were a man and a woman. His eyes were drawn immediately to the woman. Curly black tresses framed a perfect, oval face. Her cheeks were dark olive, smooth and clear, and her eyes were the shade of green that the ocean gets only rarely. For a second, they looked completely empty to Gabe, like there was nothing behind them at all but a howling darkness. Then she smiled and the darkness vanished, like fog when the sun hits it.

Gabe tore his gaze away from her and looked at the man. He had flowing white hair, the pure white of fresh snow, and a long beard of the same color that cascaded in ringlets halfway down his chest. His face was strong and handsome, with high cheekbones and a long, aquiline nose.

He looked exactly like the pictures of God Gabe had seen in Chick Comics, the creepy, fundamentalist pamphlets that Daisy Johnson next door back in Philly forced on him whenever she could.

"Hello, there," he said in that booming voice. "I'm Otto Nye and this is my wife, Mary."

Mary nodded, a quick, bird-like motion.

"And who might you be?" Otto asked.

"Uh, Gabe. Pleased to meet you."

Otto got up from his chair with a grunt.

"Gabriel like the angel, eh?" he asked.

Gabe took his hand. "Yes, sir," he stammered.

Otto produced a thick stub of a cigar from somewhere and jammed it into his beard. "Have a seat, Gabe. I'll go in and get another chair."

As Otto walked back toward the Airstream, Gabe saw on the cheeks of his Day-Glo pink bathing trunks a pair of smiling dolphins leaping in perfect curves out of a cartoon-blue sea.

"Drink?" Mary asked.

"Yeah, a Coke would be great."

Mary pushed the cooler lid aside, reached down, and pulled out a dripping can. She gestured to Otto's chair.

Gabe sat. The cross-hatched, plastic webbing of the lawn chair was still warm from Otto. Gabe felt unaccountably nervous. He hoped Otto would return soon – Gabe liked his gruff affability. But Mary was a spook.

He looked over at her. Up close Gabe could tell that she was *old*. A fine tracery of lines spread out from the corners of her eyes like cracks in a windshield.

Otto returned with another chair and unfolded it with a snap. He nodded his shaggy, white head in the direction of the boom box.

"Honey, could you turn that crap down? It's great

7

stuff, but it's starting to really get on my nerves." He looked at Gabe. "A Japanese band, can you fucking believe it? A bunch of Goddamn Japs doing salsa. Sound just like the real thing don't they?"

Gabe nodded. "Uh, yeah, I guess so..."

"What, you're a cripple?" Mary asked. "You can get up."

Otto looked at Gabe, shrugged, and winked. The music stopped suddenly. For an instant it seemed that everything was still, then the sounds came rushing in -- the periodic, white-noise sough of the ocean, the sharp cries of a pair of gulls circling overhead, the roar of a truck gearing down for the stop-light on Route 1.

"Goddamn box must be jammed again," Otto rumbled. "That's what we get for shopping on Fourteenth Street."

Mary rolled her eyes. Gabe had the feeling that something had just happened, but Otto started talking again before he could think about it.

"So, Gabe, you here with your family?" he asked.

"Yeah, we're down at the other end of the park."

"Where are you from?"

"Philadelphia."

"Whereabouts in Philly?"

The conversation had slid into that adult-child question-and-answer mode that Gabe knew well. He had the feeling that Otto knew most of the answers but that he was just trying to make Gabe feel comfortable.

"Hamilton, near 45th," he said. He could see it in his mind – the quiet, tree-lined street, a double row of brown-stones on the cusp between quaint and just plain old. They always seemed to lean in towards each other, nodding like the junkies that clustered on stoops in the neighborhood where Gabe's father worked before he got the restaurant job.

Otto nodded. "Good, good. A bit outside the student ghetto. The rest of that area's going to Hell in a handbasket, though. Yuppie scum from New York buying up land like it

8

was uranium mines, opening up cheese-steak boutiques, crap like that. Fucking shame."

Gabe didn't know what to say to that, so he didn't say anything. This Otto character sure cursed a lot. It sort of reminded Gabe of his father, but it was different. His father's curses seemed to rise like curls of grey smoke from around the door of a neglected oven turned on high. Otto seemed completely engaged with the world, his language a way of bringing it closer to himself.

"*Gabe*—" His mother's thin voice rose above the trailer park. It carried with it an edge of tension that made Gabe nervous. Otto and Mary looked at each other. Again Gabe had the feeling that something was exchanged, but he wasn't quite sure what.

"That's my Mom," he said. "I gotta go. Nice to meet you folks. Thanks for the Coke."

Mary nodded. Her eyes were large, revealing nothing.

"Come back any time," Otto said.

When Gabe walked into the trailer, his mother was on the phone. Ariel was hovering nearby, looking scared.

"—I don't know how bad it is," his mother said.

"No." She shook her head. "No. They took him to St. Paul's Presbyterian. Some sort of emergency surgery. The cop didn't say anything else, told me I had to talk to the doctor. They'll probably transfer him to Wilmington when he stabilizes. Yeah…through the front window of a Liquor Barn. Apparently he was trying to brake and he hit the gas by mistake…Of course he was loaded. Jesus Christ…I know, I know. Don't start, okay?"

She looked up. "Gabe just walked in. We gotta go. Yeah, I'll call you…Yeah, we'll just have to see what happens, but thanks. I love you, too. Bye."

She hung up the phone. "Gram sends her love to both of you…" Her voice trailed off and she just stood there staring off into space.

Gabe felt a cold knot in his stomach, his hands

tingling. He walked up to his mother and touched her arm.

"What's going on, Mom?"

She shook her head and put her arm around him, reaching out with her other arm and pulling Ariel close. Gabe leaned his head on her breast. He could feel it rise and fall with her breathing.

"There's been an accident," she said.

The hospital waiting room smelled of Lysol, tobacco, and something else that Gabe couldn't quite identify, a medicine smell. Old magazines – *Good Housekeeping* and *Highlights for Children*, mostly – were scattered across the low, formica tables that framed the battered couches lining three sides of the room. Household safety posters, corners peeling, hung from the cracked and grimy walls, warning about electricity and poison in faded pastel colors. A television on a metal cart was pushed up against the fourth wall next to the door. *Jeopardy* was on, the sound turned to a low murmur.

An old man in stained, flannel pajamas, cloth and skin both faded to a kind of colorless off-white, sat near the end of one of the couches. Grey stubble sprouted from his chin and ran down the leathery wattles of his neck. He leaned forward on a metal cane, peering intently at the television. Every now and then, a tremor passed through the arm holding the cane. Small at first, it increased in amplitude until the man's entire arm was flopping like a fish thrown on the deck of a boat. It gradually subsided, leaving the arm steady as a rock again. His attention never wandered from the television.

They had been there for four hours. Ariel was acting up at first, running back and forth in the little room, imitating one animal after another. Dog, cat, bird, monkey. She got this hyper thing going when she knew something bad was going on but she wasn't sure what. Gabe figured she needed attention, and she wasn't getting much from Mom, so from time to time he said stuff to her like "good one" or "do that one again."

Their mother was in a daze. She stared in the general direction of the television, emerging from her funk long enough to tell Ariel to hush, then sinking back down again. Gabe had seen her like this before, usually when she and Dad were going through an especially bad patch, but never this bad.

Finally, a doctor came in the room and walked up to her. He wore loose, green clothes, like pajamas, and his white mask was pulled down around his neck.

"Margaret Lambent?" he asked.

She nodded.

"Can we go talk in the hall?"

She nodded again and turned to Gabe. She looked very frightened. "I'll be right back," she said.

They disappeared around the edge of the door and Gabe could hear their hushed voices. After a few moments, his mother came back in the room.

"We can go see Daddy now," she said. There was an odd expression on her face. Later, when Gabe was thinking about it, he couldn't figure out if it was relief or disappointment.

Gabe's father was in a double room, but the other bed was empty. Wheeled machines surrounded him, trailing tubes and wires that snaked under the covers. Pilot lights and digital readouts glowed red and yellow. His head was almost completely covered in bandages; in a few spots, small, dark stains were visible, as if they were trying to push themselves out from beneath the swaddling gauze. There was a gap in the bandages for his eyes, but they were closed. The skin around them that Gabe could see was purplish-black and swollen.

Gabe's mother grabbed his shoulder when she saw him, her fingers digging so tightly into his skin that it hurt. He wanted to squirm away but he didn't, and after a moment, her grip loosened.

"It isn't Daddy. It isn't Daddy!" Ariel wailed, and began to cry in great, whooping gulps.

"Hush, Ari," Maggie said, and put her other arm around her, pulling her close. The three of them stood there looking at the bed. Maggie's lips moved; the sound came out softer than a whisper, but Gabe could still hear it.

"Gene."

Gabe looked at her. "What's going on, Mom? How bad is it?"

The question seemed to draw her out of herself, and when she answered him her voice was steady.

"He's in a coma, Gabe. The doctor couldn't really tell me anything. He's hurt pretty bad. They don't know how to wake him up."

"What are we going to do?" He didn't know what he meant, really – whether he was asking about the immediate future or the long term.

"Well, they're going to keep him here for observation for a couple of days, then send him to Wilmington. Either way, Lewes is a lot closer than Philly. Besides, we can't go home for three weeks anyway." They had rented out their house back in Philly to their neighbor's visiting cousins to help with vacation expenses.

He looked at the still form of his father, lying there in the bed. He could just barely see the rising and falling of his chest. The machines labored, pumping fluids, monitoring, recording. The small, mysterious sounds of their servitude filled the room.

CHAPTER TWO

Gene hovers in the darkness.

Above him the sky, opening up like a burning flower over the road. His throat is so dry. Strip mall like a jumble of alphabet blocks, bright flashes everywhere lancing off mirrored surfaces, tight turn pressing him against the door as he feels himself pulled toward the source, guided toward the light. He hears snatches of rock and roll, echoing like they're being played in a tile room – a phase-shifted Hendrix lick, a Clapton arpeggio. His foot punches the gas like it's not even a part of him but picking up a scrambled message from some other station and the window rises in front of him, growing in telescoping flashes, filling the sky and collapsing with a sound like ripping velcro, sparkling like dust, beautiful.

An instant of perfect silence just after the Escort wraps itself around a concrete post in the middle of the store. People frozen like statues, mouths open in identical 'O's. Gene almost wants to wave at them but he is flying, flying, and the top of his head meets the windshield in a gentle caress, pushing out the glass until something somewhere gives and he bursts through like a diver breaking the dappled surface of a pool from below.

Voices, lights, more snatches of music like a disjointed audio collage. Down, far below, a speck of light. He glides towards it and it grows brighter, resolves into a cone of

13

illumination around a hospital bed. In the bed, a body swaddled in bandages. Me, he thinks with a detached corner of his consciousness. *Me.*

Three people stand just at the periphery of the light. He glides closer.

Maggie. Gabe. Ariel.

He almost doesn't recognize them. The kids look so *big*. How the hell did that happen? It was as if he hadn't seen them for years. Gabe practically a man already, in the middle of that gawky, tentative stumble between puberty and adolescence, right before the hormones kick in like rocket fuel.

And Ariel, sweet Ariel. You were just a baby. He wants to reach out and touch her cheek. Tries to, but no hand materializes in front of him.

And Maggie.

God, she's beautiful. That waify look – big eyes, high cheekbones, careless shock of straight brown hair. She doesn't look much different than she did when they first met.

Then, as if he's reached the farthest extent of an elastic strand, he feels himself receding back, away from the cone of light, back up into that crushing, velvet darkness.

No! Too soon!

He wants to shout but there is no sound here, everything muffled as if by black cotton batting. There is another light ahead, a beckoning patch of illumination, and if he had arms he would spread them wide to steer himself towards it. He drifts closer, begins to tumble...

The new guy just wasn't getting it. He'd put jobs in all three of the microwaves and stand around waiting with his thumb up his ass, new orders piling up. Then he'd put them all out at once and they'd fry under the heat lamps while the waitrons ran themselves stupid trying to keep up.

"Look," Gene said, "there's a rhythm to this. You gotta stagger the ovens. Look at five or six orders at once. Put a job in, do a salad, do a setup, put in another job, do

14

another setup. By that time, your first job's done. Don't wait for the bell."

The kid looked up at him and nodded, eyes wide, strands of hair plastered to his forehead.

"Just relax." Gene patted him on the shoulder. "This is about as bad as it gets. You're doing fine." He didn't think he'd last the week.

Sharon, the head 'tron, hurried past the window, a huge tray balanced on one hand. She picked a tall drink from the clutter of plates and glasses and placed it in the window, to the left of the heat lamps.

"Later," she said, and continued into the dining room.

Gene picked up the glass and took a sip. One-fifty-one and Coke. It was his fourth drink that shift but he didn't feel a thing, sweating it out as fast as he consumed it.

Sharon's face reappeared in the window.

"Gene. Phone."

"Shit, this isn't a good time."

"It's Maggie." She gave him a knowing look.

"Don't say it, Sharon."

He picked up the kitchen phone and punched the flashing button.

"Maggie, damn it, where are you? It's World War Three in here."

"I'm sick, Gene, I can't make it. I feel like shit."

There was a faint, metallic echo on the line. In the background, he could hear Otis Redding singing *Dock of the Bay*.

"Where the fuck are you, Maggie? Are you in Hugo's? Jesus, I can hear the jukebox."

"I feel like shit, Gene," she repeated.

"You're pushing me, Maggie. I'll talk to you later."

He hung up the phone and took another sip of his drink. Fucking Maggie. He looked out into the dining room. Still pretty busy, but it had slowed down a little.

"You okay here for now?"

The kid nodded. He didn't look okay, but Gene

wasn't going to hold his dick all night long.

He went into the employee's bathroom next to the prep kitchen, locked the door, and sat down on the closed lid of the toilet. He took out a compact mirror, placed it on the flat part of the sink, and sprinkled a generous pile of cocaine from a small, brown glass vial onto the shiny surface. With a single-edged razor blade, he chopped at the powder until it was a fine, uniform consistency, then separated the pile into two long, parallel lines. He took a twenty out of his wallet, rolled it into a tight, thin tube, bent over the mirror, and did the lines, left first, then right. The drug left a bitter, chemical drip in the back of his throat.

He went back to the front kitchen, passing Sharon on the way. She looked at his face, stopped, and began to laugh.

"What's your problem?"

"If I were you, Gene, I'd go check out a mirror before getting back onto the floor."

"Why? What?"

"See for yourself."

He hurried back to the bathroom and looked in the mirror.

"Jesus Christ."

There was a crust of white powder around both nostrils. Small, cakey patches clung to his mustache. He rubbed his nose and mouth with the back of his hand, and licked at the streaky residue.

"Fucking waste," he said aloud. The words echoed in the little room.

He went back out front and helped with the backup. The kid was getting better, starting to pick up the rhythm of it, but he was still too damn slow. When they got down to five orders in Incoming and they were putting them out at about the same rate as new ones were coming in, he turned to the kid.

"Why don't you take five, grab a smoke or something."

The pace was manageable for one person, and he

16

wanted to work alone for awhile. The kid just nodded and left. Gene settled into a steady rhythm, his motions precise and economical.

Maggie. God damn it. He'd hired her when they'd just started going out. They thought it would be fun working together. Stupid. Actually, it *was* fun. Maggie was about the best restaurant worker he'd ever seen. After two months, she could work any job in the place, tend bar, cook, wait tables, lightning fast and *funny*. There was a window though, somewhere between three and eight drinks. Less than that and she was a bitch on wheels. More, and her I.Q. dropped sharply; she started making mistakes left and right and sometimes mouthing off at customers. It was a problem.

His partner Eric was playing some George Winston piano thing on the sound system. It sounded all wrong. Gene picked up the phone and punched the intercom to the bar.

"Save that Windham Hill crap for the Sunday brunch crowd. I'm all alone back here."

"You just coke up in the bathroom?"

"Just do it. Give me some Stones or something. Loud and stupid."

The George Winston cut ended and Gene paused, listening. The Ramones cover of *Needles and Pins* came on. He laughed out loud. The Ramones were just fine – he'd seen them down at CBGB's just a few weeks back. During the break, Joey Ramone threw a beer in someone's face and there was a fistfight. Ripples of violence spread through the tightly-packed crowd like waves on the surface of a pond until the club owner got on the P.A. and threatened to call the cops. Gene had a great time.

Sharon put up a huge order. Party of eight and half of them wanted the stuffed shrimp, which were a pain in the ass. He picked up the ticket and looked at the bar tab. Blender drinks. Pussies. He quickened his pace. By the time Sharon came back, the entire order was sitting under the heat lamps, steaming.

"Jesus Christ, Gene. Maggie told me you were fast, but I had no idea..."

"You know that Howlin' Wolf tune, *Sixty Second Man?*"

"I know something called *Sixty* Minute *Man.*"

"Fifteen seconds of huggin', fifteen seconds of kissin'..." He sang tunelessly.

She laughed and took down the food and he wondered, not for the first time, what it would be like with her. Shit, he had enough problems.

He could sense a presence behind him. He whirled around and the kid jumped back about two feet.

"Don't *ever* do that."

"What?"

"Sneak up on me like that."

The kid looked confused.

"Never mind. Forget it. You think you can handle it from here on out?"

"Sure. Okay."

"Good. You did all right tonight."

Gene took off his apron. As he left the kitchen, he wadded it up into a ball and pegged it at the linen box in the hallway. He walked back to the employee's bathroom, locked himself in, and did another couple of lines. When he unrolled the bill to put it back in his wallet, there was a thin line of dark blood across the top. He ran the cold water and put his hands under the faucet, letting the water run over his hands and wrists, soaking his shirt sleeves. He looked at his reflection in the mirror. His face looked as if it belonged to someone else. The light from the bare twenty-five watt bulb set in the high ceiling cast shadows that were so thick and purple they appeared almost luminous.

He walked back out front and sat down at the bar. Eric was flirting with a very young looking coed down at the far end. Amherst, probably; they had women now. Not Smith. Definitely not UMass. Eric saw Gene and said something to the girl. She threw back her head and laughed.

He fixed a drink and brought it over to Gene.

Gene took a sip. The rum burned his throat and made his eyes water.

"You card her?" he asked.

"You bet. Sixteen."

Gene laughed and shook his head.

"Some supper tonight."

"Yeah, we did all right, especially considering we were short. Maggie flaked again, huh?"

"You let me handle Maggie."

"Jesus Christ, Gene, that's the freaking problem. If you weren't boffing that bitch she would've been out the door weeks ago."

"Watch it, partner, you're on thin ice."

There was a long, awkward silence.

"You're right, but you're on thin ice..."

They both laughed. Gene took another sip.

"I'll have a talk with her," he said.

"Yeah, you do that."

Gene pushed back the stool and stood up.

"See you tomorrow."

"Take it easy, Gene. You look like shit."

"Thanks. You sound like my ex."

"Say hello to Maggie for me."

Hugo's was practically empty. A few of the regulars sat at the bar, watching *Star Trek* with the sound off. Willie was tending bar. He looked, to Gene, like a cross between Fred Flinstone and Alice Cooper. Gene had once left him a Percodan on the bar as a tip and he'd drunk for free for a week.

Maggie was sitting in the booth next to the jukebox, head down, face hidden by her long, brown hair. There was a jumbled pile of change on the table in front of her, and an assortment of empty bottles and shot glasses. *Dock of the Bay* was on the jukebox and she swayed back and forth, out of time to the music. Willie scowled at Gene when he saw him.

19

He opened a bottle of Rolling Rock and put it on the bar.

"Get her out of here. She's been like that all night, feeding quarters to the juke. Every other song is *Dock of the Bay*. If I hear that dead nigger whistle one more time, I'm gonna blow someone away."

Gene looked at him in silence for a long moment. Fucking caveman. He picked up his beer and sat down at the booth, next to Maggie. She looked up at him without recognition, an oily streak of tears down one cheek.

"The island...the islanders..."

Her eyes snapped into focus.

"Gene."

She leaned forward and put her head on his shoulder. He put his arms around her. Her body seemed to vibrate in his arms and he thought of a pet bird he had had as a child. He liked to take it out of its cage and hold it, cupping the small, trembling creature in his hands. How easy it would be, he remembered thinking, to crush the life out of it.

"Let's go home, baby."

He awoke to bright sunlight against his closed eyelids. There was a sharp, throbbing pain in his forehead, his nose felt numb and swollen, and his bladder was full. He lay there for what seemed like a long time, listening to Maggie breathing next to him. He could tell she was not asleep. He opened his eyes and she smiled at him. Her eyes were puffy and bloodshot.

"We have to stop meeting like this," she said.

He grunted, slid out of bed, and padded into the bathroom. The sensation of relief he felt as he pissed was so intense that it overshadowed for a moment the pain in his head. He had a rush of vertigo and steadied himself against the sink until it was past. When he got back to the bedroom, Maggie was gone. He could hear her rattling around in the kitchen. He threw himself at the indentation left on the bed from her body, curling up to her warmth, burying his face in the smell of her left on the pillow.

20

She returned with two bottles of Beck's and handed him one.

"Bless you, my child," he said, and held the bottle up to his forehead. He closed his eyes and pressed the cold, smooth glass against them, one at a time. He lifted the bottle to his lips, took a long pull, and shuddered. God, it was good.

"Does this mean we're alcoholics?" he asked, and they both laughed. It was an old joke between them.

"Actually," she said, "there are a lot of situations where alcohol with breakfast is okay."

"Tell me about it."

"Well, your standard WASP brunch, for example. Mimosas, coffee, croissants and jelly. You've got most of your basic food groups right there. Alcohol, sugar, butter, caffeine..."

She took a long sip from her bottle.

"One time," she continued, "I was coming back from visiting my family out in California. It was an early flight, and I was incredibly hung over. I remember looking out the window of the plane. We were just leaving the coastal range behind, flying into the sunrise. It was beautiful. I couldn't believe how shitty I felt. One of the stews starts pushing this cart up the aisle, pitchers of Bloodys and Tequila Sunrise. 'Would you like a drink before breakfast?' she's saying. 'Would you like a drink before breakfast?' Jesus, are the Kennedys gun shy?"

He chuckled softly. They were silent for a few moments. Absently, she traced figure-eights in the matted hair on his stomach. She looked up suddenly.

"*Vikings*," she said.

"Vikings?"

"Yeah, vikings. They were actually a very noble culture. I think they invented astronomy or something. They drank like there was no tomorrow. I can picture Leif Erikson getting up in the morning, knocking back a quart of ale out of an elk's horn, scarfing down some venison, and going off to discover Greenland. They were like Hell's Angels in boats."

21

"Uh-huh."

"Wait here. Don't go away."

She slid out of bed and hurried across the room to where stacks of record albums lay at odd angles in plastic milk crates. She squatted down, looking through them, and he admired the curve of her back, the cleave of her ass. She still looked damn good.

"You keep them in those things, your records'll warp," he said. "They're not quite big enough. I think the milk companies do that on purpose so they won't get ripped off as much."

She put a record on the turntable and crawled back in bed with him. The music was unfamiliar at first, but then he recognized it. Wagner. Something Valkyrie. He knew it from the movie *Apocalypse Now*. He could picture Robert Duvall in his cowboy hat, the helicopters like great, metal birds coming in low over the ocean.

" 'I love the smell of napalm in the morning,' " he said, quoting from the film.

"What?"

"Never mind."

They lay there holding each other, not moving or speaking, until long after the music was finished.

"I gotta go," he said, finally.

"You opening this morning?"

"Yeah, just prep."

When he was finished dressing he sat down on the edge of the bed next to her. He began running his hand softly through her hair, tracing with his fingers the outline of her jaw, her lips. After what seemed like a long time, he spoke.

"Do me a favor and stay out of Eric's face for a few days. You're right at the top of his shit list."

"Fuck him if he can't take a joke."

"Don't be late tonight."

She smiled at him, rolled over, and buried her face in the pillow.

Eric had left the coffee machine set up for him – all he had to do was flick the switch. There was something about being alone in the restaurant early in the morning, the silence, the light. He walked back to the prep kitchen and began setting up the Hobart, a kind of industrial Cuisinart.

He liked the way it changed things. You put something in the hopper and out it came, completely transformed. He started up the machine, quartered a head of cabbage, and began feeding the pieces to the spinning blades. He reached into the bin on the other side and grabbed a handful of the lacy, shredded stuff. His hand shook as he held it up to the light. It was like angel's hair.

CHAPTER THREE

Maggie hated the little rent-a-wreck, a scarred, dusty Chevette they had picked up from the garage down the highway from the trailer park. There was no air conditioning and the interior of the car smelled faintly of vomit. Something was wrong with the automatic transmission – at cruising speeds, it hopped between second and third, causing the car to surge forward and jerk back in random spasms.

Ariel didn't say a word most of the way home from the hospital. This was unusual for her; most car trips she kept up a running commentary, spelling out words on the road signs, talking about the other cars on the road. Today, she sat next to Maggie in front, staring out the window, mute as a post. Gabe sat in the back seat, reading.

The silence felt to Maggie like something that had fallen on the car like a blanket, covering them. But she couldn't bring herself to fill it, to do the Mom thing. She had absolutely no idea what they were going to do. Gene had some medical insurance from work, but she didn't know if that would get canceled somehow because of the D.U.I. they were going to slap Gene with if he ever woke up. Did it work like that? She didn't know. All she knew was that if Gene came out of this in one piece it was just the start of the shitstorm for all of them. Maybe this would be a good time to take the kids and get the fuck out. Just get out. She could get hired as a waitress anywhere. Just get out. Her mother was in

Oakland; maybe that would be a good place to start. There was a lot to think about. It was a little like the math she'd taken in college before dropping out – buried in the morass of choices was something unambiguous and precise. If only she had the key. The calculus of dependency, the geometry of need. With a start, she realized that she hadn't spared one thought for Gene himself, what kind of shape he was in, how he was going to come out of this. She smiled ruefully to herself. Maybe that was a good sign.

Finally, when they were in Lewes, driving along the main commercial strip past the fast food joints, auto part stores, and furniture showrooms, Ariel turned to Maggie.

"Is Daddy going to die?" she asked.

Maggie bit her lip. "Well, Ari, he's hurt pretty bad. He's…sleeping right now, sort of, trying to get better, but nobody knows how long it'll take."

"He's a fucking alky," Gabe said.

Maggie reached back to slap him, but he dodged away. The car swerved across the double yellow line into the oncoming lane.

"Look out!" Gabe hollered. Ariel gave an ear-piercing shriek.

Maggie grabbed the wheel with both hands and jerked it back to the right. The car started to skid – she could feel herself losing control. Then, almost miraculously, it caught hold and they veered back into their lane. The angry blare of an oncoming horn dopplered down as they passed each other. Ariel was crying, a high, wavering keening.

"God damn it, Gabe. How many times have I told you about that language?" She regretted the impulse to hit him, though. It didn't happen often, but sometimes it just came over her like a stranger taking over her body, moving her hands. The impulse to hurt.

"It's true, Mom," he said. "He's a total alky. Like *you*, only you don't drink anymore."

Maggie bit her lip. She knew she deserved that. She'd made up for a lot these last few years, but she couldn't rewrite history.

"He's…sick. Hush, Ariel." The words seemed to have no effect. Ariel's wails rose and fell in pitch like the ululation of a siren. "He's sick," she said again. "Sometimes he gets this bad feeling, and when he feels bad, he drinks. Ari, *hush*." Ariel stopped in mid-cry. Her eyes were wide and frightened.

Gabe gave her his 'don't bullshit me' look. "Well, he must feel bad an awful *lot*, then," he replied archly.

She didn't know what to say to that. They were silent the rest of the way back to the trailer park.

As she pulled into the driveway, she noticed a trailer down at the other end she hadn't seen before, one of those old, bulbous Airstreams. It reminded her of the Sixties – Kennedy, Dick Clark, moon rockets, Pop Tarts. They still made those – she'd seen them in the supermarket back in Philly. Space food.

She looked at the Airstream again and got a sudden bad feeling, a transient whiff of unfocused dread.

She put the car in park and turned to Gabe. "You keep an eye on Ariel for awhile," she said. "I've got some things to do."

He made a face.

"Help me out here, Gabe. What do you want for dinner?"

"You gonna cook?"

After a brief pause, she nodded.

"Let's send out for pizza."

The banter was a little forced, but she could tell he was trying. He was a good kid.

She smiled. "We'll see. Go on, get. Give me a kiss first. You too, Ari."

She drove into the parking lot behind Al's Garage and Wrecking, pulling up next to an old Valiant up on blocks. She felt a sharp stab of emotion when she saw the thing – a complicated mix of anger and nostalgia. It was just like a car Gene had had back in Massachusetts when they were first going out. A total drunkmobile – it seemed to run on fumes and Grace, surrounded by white light. She sat in the car for a minute, breathing, collecting herself, then she went into the garage.

Al was a squat, repulsive gnome who kept licking his lips and rubbing his hands with a greasy rag as he talked. She could practically feel his eyes sliding across her body, like oil on glass. His overalls were grimed to a splotchy greyish-brown, their original color betrayed by streaks of blue peeking through the filth.

"It's over here," he said. His voice sounded like he gargled with aquarium gravel. "Fucking totaled."

He led her through the office door into the main part of the garage. There were four bays. All of them were occupied with cars in various stages of disassembly, but she recognized the Escort right away. Its front end was crumpled like an accordion.

She walked closer. A web of cracks spread out across the windshield, radiating out from a spot in the middle of the driver's side. She thought she could see traces of blood still in the cracks, but that may have been a trick of the dim light. She could imagine the accident, his body sailing through the interior of the car like a rag doll. He never used a seat belt.

"Fifty bucks." The aquarium gravel voice sounded right behind her.

"Excuse me?"

"Fifty bucks." He worried the rag between his hands.

"I – the car's almost new. I should be able to do better than that."

He looked at her like she was crazy, then he laughed with a phlegmy bark. "Sister, I'm talkin' *you* pay *me* fifty bucks to junk the thing. Nobody's gonna give you any money for it. Look again. It's scrap metal."

Maggie felt numb. Christ, they were still paying for it. Insurance would cover something, but Gene always carried the legal minimum – the only reason he carried any insurance at all was because she had insisted. Suddenly, she just wanted to get out of there. She reached into her purse.

"Of course, we could make other arrangements." The man was giving her that look again. A pink nubbin of tongue peeked out from between his thin lips.

That was it. She let her purse fall back on her shoulder. "You sleazy little sack of shit. My husband's in the fucking hospital and you're coming on to me. I should take that tire iron over there and shove it up your ass."

The man's mouth hung open in a mask of stupid surprise. Maggie turned on her heel and walked out.

"What about my fifty bucks?" the man called out behind her.

She turned around. "Sue me."

When she got behind the wheel, she started shaking. She took a deep breath, then another. Asshole. Finally she put the car in drive and pulled out onto Route 1.

She reached down and turned on the car radio. Just AM, but maybe she could get something. The sweet sounds of *Dock of the Bay* drifted through the car like filaments of syrupy smoke. She smiled for an instant in recognition, then a sudden volley of emotions passed though her – sadness, anger, loss. For an instant, she could smell the reek of stale beer, then it was gone.

"The island..." The words, barely a whisper, passed unnoticed across her lips. Tears streamed down her face. "Gene."

Suddenly, she saw flashing lights in her rear-view mirror.

"*Shit.*" Her head was instantly clear. She pulled over to the side of the road, rolled her window down, and sat waiting, her hands on the wheel at ten and two.

A shadow fell across her arm and she looked up. He was big, about six-four, skinny and young, with that lean, big-jawed Midwestern farmboy look. A pair of mirrored sunglasses covered half his face, shadowed by the brim of his Smokey hat.

"What seems to be the trouble, officer?" She could

feel his eyes behind the large, bug-like lenses, looking her over.

"Can I see your license and registration, please?"

She produced her driver's license and the rental paperwork and sat waiting while he studied them.

"Could you get out of the car, please?"

"What's wrong, officer?"

"Please, ma'am, could you just get out of the car?" His voice was flat and inflectionless, like one of those telephone answering machines that told you the date and time of your calls. She opened the door and stepped out onto the shoulder of the road.

"Could you recite the alphabet backwards, please, ma'am?"

"Backwards?"

"Yes, ma'am. Starting from 'Z'."

When she got down to 'M', he interrupted her with a sigh. It was the first human sound she heard out of him.

"That's fine, ma'am. Do you know why I pulled you over?"

"I have no idea, officer." In fact, she had a pretty good idea. She must have been all over the road.

"You were driving very erratically."

"I'm sorry, officer. My husband had a very bad car accident. I've just come back from the hospital, and just now from the garage..." She didn't have to elaborate – she could feel the tears still drying on her cheeks. She considered telling the cop about the schmuck from the garage but thought better of it. She'd threatened him, after all, and could probably get nailed for the fifty bucks if she pushed things.

He handed her back her papers. "Where are you staying?"

"Trailer park down the road. The Ocean View."

"Why don't you get on home and get some rest, then?"

"I'll do that. Thank you, officer."

She got back in the car. As the gleaming black-and-

29

white pulled in front of her and accelerated away, her hands began to shake again. She steadied them on the steering wheel.

Loaded, Jesus Christ. She'd been absolutely shitfaced. The sensation was burned into her memory, hardwired into her nervous system, and her body remembered it like the face of an old, familiar friend. But she hadn't had a drink in over four years.

CHAPTER FOUR

One surefire way to keep Ariel out of trouble was to sit her down in front of one of the *Animal Kingdom* videos. There were eight of them, each devoted to a different family of animals. Ariel's favorite was *Fish!* – she could watch it for hours, over and over again, hypnotized by the bright colors. It was a window into a cool, blue world.

Gabe was partial to *Insects!* himself. They were so soulless, so vicious. Whatever was in their way, they devoured, dismembered or subdued, no apology, no discussion. It had a certain appeal.

He hefted the two tape boxes in his hands, and settled on *Fish!*

They sat together in the darkening gloom of the trailer, watching the video. The voice-over was soothing and mellow. The music synched perfectly with the darting motion of the fish. Gabe wondered what was going to happen. Was Dad going to die? It didn't make any sense. He just couldn't get his mind around it. He was scared, but it felt like something separate from him, like it was all happening to somebody else. Part of him was glad, too, and he pushed that part far back into a deep compartment in his mind where he wouldn't have to look at it.

He thought about Otto. He was kind of an odd guy, but Gabe liked him. He tried to imagine what it would be like to have a father like that, who wasn't drunk half the time.

They would play catch together, go to scary movies on Saturday afternoons, maybe get a dog. A dog would be cool.

"When is Mommy coming back?" Ariel asked, after they had been watching for about a half hour. She had her thumb firmly planted in her mouth, muffling her words. Her skin looked ghostly in the pale, blue light of the television.

"Take your thumb out of your mouth, Ari," he teased. "You're not a baby anymore." She hadn't been doing that very much for the last year or so and it startled Gabe to see her slide back like that.

"She'll be back soon. She just went out to do some errands and get pizza, remember?"

"Oh, yeah," Ariel said. "Is she bringing Daddy?"

"Come on, quit acting like a kid. Daddy's in the hospital, you know that. Nobody knows when he can come home."

She looked blankly at Gabe for a second, then she turned back to the television screen and stared, her eyes wide, fixed straight ahead. After a moment, her thumb found its way back into her mouth.

Nobody knows, Gabe said to himself again.

He heard a key turn in the front door and his mother walked in, carrying a flat, square box and a brown grocery bag. She put them down on the counter separating the kitchen area from the living room, tossed her purse onto the couch and sat. Ariel clambered up into her lap.

"Hey, squirt. Momma needs a hug." Ariel giggled and buried her face in her mother's shoulder. Maggie stared blankly at the images chasing each other across the television screen. Her face looked worn and haggard.

Old, Gabe thought. Something tightened in his stomach and around his eyes. *She looks really old.* He felt a fierce pulse of emotion surge through him. He had no words for it and it surprised him by its intensity. It was partly love, that old familiar connection he had with her even when she was drinking. But there was something else there as well, a kind of longing. He wanted to protect her, to shield her from

32

the world. It was a weird feeling, like a piece of clothing that didn't fit quite right.

He got up from the floor and began unpacking the groceries.

Maggie looked over at him and smiled weakly. "Thanks, Gabe," she said.

Gabe lay in bed, listening to the little sounds that fill a new place at night. Every place was different and once you got used to a place's night sounds, once you could catalog them, you were really there. In the trailer it was the intermittent hum of the refrigerator motor, the low growl of the trucks on Route 1, the distant whisper of the ocean. The sounds wove in and out of the regular rhythm of Ariel's breathing.

The smells in the trailer, too – dust, a hint of mildew, a faint remnant of that sour smell from when they'd first arrived – brought sense-memories of previous summers flooding back to him, but everything felt different now. When he thought about time, he usually imagined himself a bead on a string, past and future stretching out on either side of him forever. The image failed now, though, and he couldn't see forward at all. Everything was changing. He was in free fall.

Quietly, he got out of bed, dressed, and slipped out the front door. The night was warm. A soft breeze coming in from the ocean brought the faint smell of seaweed and rot. There were some lights down on the beach and Gabe decided to investigate. He passed the bramble and paused for a moment, but curiosity won out and he continued toward the beach.

Four pickup trucks were lined up, facing out toward the ocean. Their headlights cut through the dark, eight expanding cones of light. Down near the surf, a row of fishing poles, their heels dug into the sand, thin, taut lines stretching out into the night, glowing in the light from the trucks.

About ten men were clustered around something near the water's edge. Whatever it was, they were giving it a lot of space. The men formed a kind of semi-circle, open end facing the trucks so they could get the light. Gabe walked closer to the huddle of bodies.

In the middle of the cluster of men was a shark, about six feet long. It flopped weakly, its grey sides caked with sand. Gabe could see its gills working. The flaps of tough skin clutched spasmodically at the air. A line still stretched from the shark's mouth to one of the poles and, as Gabe eased his way into the group, somebody stepped into the circle and cut the line with a single swipe of a vicious-looking blade.

At that, the shark's motions became wilder. It rolled this way and that, kicking up gouts of sand. Then it stopped, suddenly, as if drained of energy. One of the men walked gingerly up to it and kicked it, hard. He had a beer in one hand and it spilled over his wrist and onto the sand. He danced back into the crowd to a roar of laughter from his fellows. The shark twitched again, its body arching above the sand as if a current was running through it.

Gabe looked around at the faces of the men. They were rapt and glassy-eyed, streaked with sweat, sharply shadowed death-masks in the harsh light from the trucks.

Another man danced into the center, kicked the shark with a meaty *thud*, and stepped back. Another followed suit. Gabe was both repelled and fascinated. He felt bad for the shark – it didn't seem like an evil thing at all, not like *Jaws*. He sensed that all it wanted was to go back to the ocean, to swim and eat, swim and eat. There was something perfect about it.

But the energy of the men was infectious. The semi-circle was drawing tighter. After about half the men had stepped in and kicked the dying shark, Gabe found himself stepping in to do the same. It wasn't a conscious decision – he just suddenly felt his feet moving.

The shark was still for a moment. Gabe stepped up to it and looked down at its eyes, button-black and depthless, like bits of stone.

"Don't stand there, kid," someone yelled. "He'll bite your pecker off!" There was a roar of laughter.

Gabe felt something surge through him. He pulled his leg back and kicked the shark in its midsection as hard as he could. The sense of resistance and give at the impact gave him a warm, powerful feeling. The men roared approval and he kicked it again. The shark started flopping and Gabe stepped back into the crowd. Rough hands patted him on the shoulder and someone handed him a beer.

Without thinking, Gabe raised it to his lips and took a deep swallow. Foamy bitterness filled his nose and mouth and he gagged. Tears ran down his cheeks. Coarse laughter. Someone took the can from his hands.

The last time he had beer was when he was eight or nine. It was late at night and Gabe got up to get something to eat. Gene was sitting at the kitchen table in the dark. There was a row of empty cans in front of him and the smell of beer filled the little kitchen.

Gene looked up when Gabe walked in. "Have a drink with me," he said. His voice was a little slurred.

Gabe dutifully sat down and Gene pulled a can from the plastic webbing of a six-pack and handed it to him.

Gabe was more scared than anything else and he pulled the top off the can and raised it to his lips. It was bitter and the bubbles made his eyes water, but he could feel something else sliding into him as he drank. It filled him, expanding like smoke to fill all the nooks and crannies inside of him, taking on his shape, and soon he couldn't feel it at all anymore. But he knew it was there.

It was something like that for him now. Gabe looked around at the men, wild eyes and sweating faces. Their voices seemed to vibrate a membrane that was stretched tightly inside him. There was a sudden hush. Gabe saw the blue metal of a gun-barrel flash slick, rainbow highlights in the light from the trucks.

The man with the gun walked up to the shark. Its

35

body still beat feebly against the sand. The man raised the pistol and fired. The sound was very loud. The shark jumped at least a foot in the air and Gabe saw a great, bloody chunk torn out of its side. The man stepped back into the crowd and passed the gun to the person on his left, who walked up to the shark and fired another bullet into its twitching side.

The gun passed from hand to hand. Each man walked up to the shark and fired. At some point, the gun was reloaded and it continued from hand to hand. It seemed to appear suddenly in Gabe's hand and he felt other hands patting him on the shoulder, pushing him forward. The gun was heavier than he thought it would be. He walked up to the shark. Its body was a mass of broken flesh – it wasn't moving at all anymore. Gabe raised the gun and pulled the trigger. There was a roar and a flash and a feeling like someone had just punched him in the shoulder. Gabe didn't want to look at what he had just done. He staggered back into the huddle of bodies. Somebody took the gun from his hands.

There were a few more shots, then someone said something about the police coming because of the noise. The men retrieved their fishing poles and hurried back into their trucks. They drove off down the beach, kicking up a shower of sand. Gabe was left there alone with the body of the shark. Black blood pooled beneath it into the sand.

Gabe turned and walked back up the slope of the beach. When he got to the first set of dunes, he began to run.

Gabe got up early the next morning. Maggie and Ariel were still asleep. The scene down at the beach left an imprint on him that felt like a weight on his shoulders. He pulled on his shorts and an old pair of flip-flops and went outside. He stood there in the sun for a moment. To his left, Otto's shiny, silver trailer winked at him in the bright, morning light. To his right, the strip of nearly empty beach stretched out in both directions. It seemed to keep the ocean from spilling across onto the land. He turned left.

The door to the trailer was open and Gabe hesitantly

walked up the steps. He could hear Otto's deep voice – it sounded like he was on the phone. Gabe walked in. Otto saw him, beckoned him inside with a wink and a gesture, and bent his head to the phone again.

"Yeah. Dancing Sheba. That's right, a thousand to win. I know she's twenty to one. Yeah, Wilson's riding. Yeah…Why do you sound so nervous, Vito?" He let out a booming laugh. It seemed to shake the thin walls of the trailer. "See you Tuesday." He hung up the phone. "Come on in, Gabe," Otto said. "Mary went into town to do some marketing. You ever play the horses?"

Gabe shook his head. His Dad went to the track from time to time, usually returning drunk and broke.

"There's two things you should always remember if you want to win. You know what they are?"

Gabe shook his head again.

Otto held up one finger. "Numero uno. Bet to win. Place and show bets are for little old ladies and Macy's clerks." He held up two fingers. "Numero two-o. Cheat. Bribe a jockey. Better still, bribe a stable hand to slip the favorite a few boxes of Ex-Lax. It doesn't hurt 'em and it doesn't show up on the blood tests, but it slows 'em down some."

Gabe wondered how Otto could afford to bribe anybody when he was living in a trailer park, but he didn't say anything.

"How's your Dad, Gabe?"

"How did you know?"

Otto smiled gently. It transformed his face – the hard line of his jaw seemed to soften, the steely, grey light in his eyes took on a warm glow.

"Word gets around."

"He's in a coma. They don't know if he's going to die or not."

Otto nodded sympathetically.

Gabe just stood there. He didn't know what else to say. There was a tightness around his eyes and across his forehead that got worse and worse. His fists were clenched, pressed against his sides in tight knots. He began to cry. He felt large arms encircle him and he buried his face in Otto's broad chest, his body shaking with great, shuddering sobs.

He cried until his throat hurt. Otto stood there unmoving, solid as an old building. Gabe was suddenly embarrassed and he pulled away. Otto looked down at him and smiled reassuringly. He nodded his shaggy head towards the door. "Let's go for a walk."

The walked down to the ocean. The food shacks were already open and Otto bought him some french fries in a greasy paper cone. Gabe felt their heat through the paper – it felt good against his hand.

They walked past a tangle of tire tracks in the sand. This was where the trucks had been last night. Gabe looked farther down the beach near the ocean for the body of the shark, but there was nothing there but a flat expanse of damp sand. He looked beyond it to the ocean, a wrinkled blue-gray sheet stretching out to the horizon. Far off in the distance, a small boat huddled at the boundary between sea and sky.

Gabe looked over at Otto. "I don't understand why it has to be me," he said.

Otto raised an eyebrow.

"I mean, why does *my* father have to be a drunk? Why does *my* father have to get in a car wreck and become a vegetable?"

Otto nodded. "I know what you mean," he said. "It isn't fair. But look, I want to show you something. You see that boat way out there?"

Gabe nodded.

"Watch."

The wind picked up. Gabe felt it ruffling his hair. White, puffy clouds appeared in the distance and began to move in towards the center of the horizon, faster and faster, like they were sliding down the sides of a bowl, coalescing to a point above the boat. Soon, there was a grey-black tumble of clouds, flat at the bottom and piling high into the sky.

Lightning flashed inside the cloud, bright, flickering patches of electric white against its towering sides.

Gabe looked at Otto. He appeared larger somehow, his features grim and hard, as if carved from brittle stone.

A dimple appeared on the bottom of the cloud, directly over the boat. It grew into a funnel, stretching down towards the juncture of sea and sky. It touched the water, kicking up a misty nimbus around its base, then lifted up into the sky again, receding back into the bottom of the cloud.

The boat was gone. Nothing marred the sea's flat surface. The cloud disappeared like snow melting under a lit match. Otto looked over at Gabe and shrugged.

"Shit happens," he said.

CHAPTER FIVE

Gene...dreams. It is not a sequential unrolling of events, orderly and causal. Rather, it is as if a collection of scenes from his life has been imprinted on the faces of playing cards scattered randomly across a tabletop, rectangles of bright color against a dark background, and someone has gathered them, shuffled them, dealt one from the top of the deck into his consciousness...

There was a flickering against his closed eyelids, like the flapping of a luminous wing. Gene opened his eyes. The morning sun winked through a deep, green curtain of leaves outside his window, stirring in a gentle breeze. He closed his eyes, but the strobing against his eyelids was painful and insistent. He opened his eyes again, groaned, and got out of bed Clothing was scattered everywhere, amidst a chaotic distribution of album covers, pizza boxes, and an impressive collection of empty cans and bottles.

He picked up the nearest pair of jeans and stepped into them, grabbed a t-shirt that was draped across a chair, and slipped into a pair of flip-flops. He stepped out of his room and onto the stairway landing. From where he was standing he could hear Eric and Jody in the kitchen. The words were muffled, but he instinctively knew they were talking about him. He walked halfway down the steps so he could hear them better.

"I'll talk to him," Eric said. "I know he gets a little out there sometimes."

"I know he's your friend, Eric, but it's out of hand," Jody said. "I'm not going to live with this."

Gene felt a warm flush at the base of his neck. He didn't know what was going on, but it didn't sound good. He walked the rest of the way down the steps, through the living room, and into the kitchen. They were seated at the big wooden table next to the window. The room was filled with bright sunlight. Outside, the sky was a perfect, cloudless blue. It was going to be a hot one.

"Morning," he said. Eric looked down at his hands and Jody gave him a stony glare.

The air in the kitchen was thick with the smell of bacon and strong coffee. Gene wasn't interested in food, but his eyes went to the Melita setup on the stove. He walked over and helped himself to a cup. He could feel their eyes on his back.

"Okay, okay," he said, turning around. "What did I do?"

"You're going to have to move out, Gene," Jody said.

Eric looked up quickly. Jody caught his eye and shook her head.

"No, Eric, I'm sorry. I can't put up with this anymore."

She looked up at Gene.

"You're a drunk, Gene. You probably need help, but that's not my problem. I just want you out of here."

"Jesus, lighten up, Jode," Gene said. "What'd I do this time? Fuck the cat? Shit in the bath?"

Eric spoke up.

"I didn't think it was possible, Gene, but you're just making it worse."

"Gene," Jody cut in. "It just isn't working. Every time I go to sleep I wonder if you're going to pass out on the couch with a cigarette and burn the place down. I can't invite people over – you argue with the men and borrow money from the women." She took a deep breath. "Last night when we got home, you were pissing out your bedroom window into the driveway. That was the last straw. I just can't live in this sort of environment."

He looked closely at her. She was wearing a peasant blouse and a long, loose skirt. Her curly black hair was pulled back in a thick braid. She wasn't fooling around.

"Fine," he said. He looked back and forth between the two of them. Eric had a pained expression on his face. Jody looked like she was ready for a fight. "I'll be back to get my shit."

"We'll talk later, Gene," Eric said.

"Right." Gene filled his coffee mug again from the glass pot on the stove, finishing the last of it, and walked through the screen door out into the driveway, letting it slam shut behind him. He got into his car, an old war wagon Valiant with bad valves and body rot, put a Sex Pistols tape in the deck, and pulled out. Behind him, a cloud of dust rose into the still, hot air and hung next to the house like smoke.

He took the back way into town, mostly so he could ignore posted speed limits without getting nailed. It was called Bay Road, even though the nearest bay was probably a hundred miles away. He knew all the curves, hills, and hidden driveways without having to think, so he pushed it up to seventy, enjoying the protesting squeal of tires as he took the sharp turns. He laughed out loud, a short, sharp bark, remembering the expression on Jody's face.

" 'I can't live in this sort of environment,' " he said. He laughed again and rounded another curve, and standing dead still in the middle of the road in front of him was a Golden retriever, poised for running. He barely had time to hit the brakes, and from the feel of the impact and the dull, sickening *thump*, he knew it was bad. The dog went flying, sailing through the air in what seemed like slow motion. It hit a tree by the side of the road and slid down into a limp heap on the leaf-strewn shoulder just as the Valiant screeched to a halt.

42

Gene's knuckles were white where he gripped the steering wheel.

"Shit," he whispered through clenched teeth. "God damn it." He closed his eyes and rested his forehead on his wrists. "Anarchy in the U.K." was blaring over the speakers, and he reached out and flicked it off. In the sudden stillness sounds were the wind sliding through the leaves of the low-hanging trees and the slow ticking of the cooling engine.

He got out of the car and walked over to where the dog lay. He knelt down in the soft dirt next to it. It was still alive. Its breath came in shallow gasps and its eyes rolled back and forth in quick, jerky motions. There was a pink froth around the edges of its lips where they pulled back in a grimace, exposing yellow teeth. As Gene put out his hands, it shuddered once and died. He reached down and gently pulled the collar around so he could read the tag. Skippy. There was an address and phone number.

Skippy…Jesus Christ.

He scooped the limp form in his arms and carried it to his car. He opened the trunk, laid the body on top of a case of motor oil, closed the lid, and got back in the front seat. *God damn it.* He shook his head, started the car, turned the tape back on and, dumbly, began to drive. He wasn't thinking about where he was going, but imagined that he was driving the path of least resistance, sensing hidden tugs in the curvature of the road. After what seemed like a long time, he found himself in front of Maggie's house.

He got out of the car, walked up to the wide porch, and knocked on the door. There was no answer. He knocked again, a little louder this time, and he could hear her scream "It's open" from somewhere in the back of the house. He let himself in. The shades were drawn in the living room and there was a bad, yeasty smell. There were empty bottles everywhere, clustered on the low coffee table and scattered across the stained carpet and scuffed parquet.

Gene walked back to the kitchen. Maggie was sitting at the table, smoking a cigarette, a large cup of coffee in front of her. Her blonde hair was limp and tangled and there were dark shadows under her eyes. She looked twenty-five going on forty. Still, he felt a quick tug in his chest when he saw her.

"Jesus Christ, Gene, you look terrible," she said.

"Thanks. You want the good news or the bad news?"

"I've got enough troubles—you can keep the bad news. What's the good news?"

He looked carefully at her for a long moment. He opened his mouth, closed it.

"The good news is we can probably get Bloodys at the My Place Lounge," he said, finally. "I don't think anyplace else is open yet."

"If you like Popov and V-8."

"What's not to like? Let's go."

Jack was behind the bar. He didn't look up when the door opened, continued wiping down the bar with a ragged towel. Gene thought he was kind of a spook – he had a long, droopy face and he almost never spoke. There were no customers, and the radio was playing a paralyzing muzak version of "Norwegian Wood". The lights were off and the shutters were half-drawn, sending stripes of light and shadow across the floor. The room seemed filled with haze.

"This is too depressing," Maggie said. "Let's get out of here."

"Wait a minute."

Gene walked up to the bar. Maggie stayed near the door. After a moment he returned with two lidded styrofoam cups.

"Bloodys to go," he said. They took Route 9 out the north end of town. The bank clock on the corner of Main and Pleasant read 10:15.

They drove through the hill towns of western Massachusetts, working their way north, following a parallel track to Interstate 91. Twice they stopped at local road houses. They played pinball and drank Schlitz from bottles of thick brown glass.

44

"You seem awfully quiet," she said. They were in the Dial Tone Lounge, just outside of Chesterfield. A few years back, the place had been sort of a pickup joint. There had been phones in each of the booths, and you could call up another booth if you were interested in somebody. Gene had played guitar in a band called The Scientific Americans and they had gigged here a few times. It was something, watching the scene, trying to figure out who would end up leaving together. The phones were gone now, and Gene felt a vague tug of loss.

"I'm okay," he said, but suddenly in his mind's eye saw Skippy flying through the air after the impact, limp and somehow graceful. He looked up at Maggie. "Let's get out of here."

They drove on. The day was starting to heat up and the road wound through wooded hills choked with lush, summer growth. They stopped for lunch in a dingy little health food cafe across the commons from the church in Turner's Falls, an old mill town that had slipped through the cracks when the Interstate went up. They were the only customers. On the steps of the church, a girl of about sixteen in a tie-dyed skirt and long, tangled brown hair nursed a baby and gazed expressionlessly at them.

Gene had grown up in Leverett, not far from there. He remembered back in the sixties when some guy, a junkie from Worcester with old Boston money, started a commune and built a recording studio in an old barn just outside of town. He tried to get LSD sanctioned for use as a sacrament, like peyote, but it didn't fly with the Massachusetts courts. The studio never made a dime and the commune folded, but the town still harbored a few die-hards, like bits of smooth stone left on a beach after the receding of a wave. Gene wasn't sure how they survived; the place was like a ghost town. He looked at the girl and felt it again, that pull of loss, vague and unfocused.

Maggie was talking about an affair she had with a musician who lived in the commune. One night she actually met the Man himself, the junkie from Worcester, and fucked him in the sound booth of the recording studio. Gene didn't say much. He wasn't really listening.

"Skippy," he whispered to himself.

"What?"

He shook his head.

"Nothing," he said. "Is this town dry or what? I need beer."

"There's a packy just outside town. I think it's a zoning thing." She looked out at the empty sidewalks, the boarded shops. The wind pushed a scrap of paper down the middle of the street.

They got a twelve pack of Old Milwaukee from Bob's Package Store, next to the Cumberland Farms on Route 5, and continued slowly north on back roads, sipping beers. They threw the empties in the back seat and played Rickie Lee Jones on the tape deck. Just outside of Northfield, they passed an old cemetery set back a little from the road. It was built into the side of a gentle, sloping hill, and the weathered stones leaned at odd angles.

"I think I've got family around here somewhere," Maggie said. "Let's check it out."

They stepped over the waist-high stone fence surrounding the cemetery and walked between the plots, looking at the inscriptions on the markers. There were hardly any later than 1950.

Maggie stopped in front one of the stones. Black, the inscription read. 1890-1941. There was an angel carved out of the top of the stone. One of its wings had broken off, giving it an off-balanced appearance.

"This is my blood," she said. "I can feel it."

Gene didn't say anything. She looked up at him.

"I can *feel* it," she repeated. They looked at each other for a long time. It seemed to Gene like they were frozen there, held in the hot, close smell of pollen and New England summer like bugs in prehistoric amber.

He reached out and touched her cheek. She rested her

cheek against his open palm for a moment, then he let his hand fall. He turned and walked slowly up towards the crest of the hill, following a faint trail that curved around the hillside. As he neared the top, he could hear the high cries of children and the excited barking of a dog. The sounds were muffled in the damp heat. He looked back for Maggie, but had lost sight of the cemetery rounding the curve of the hill.

He reached the crest and spread out before him was a meadow of green so bright it appeared depthless, and his eye's focus seemed to slip over it and then catch again. On the downhill side of the gentle slope there was a pond, and near the pond's edge a red and white checkered table cloth was spread, the corners weighed down with baskets of food and drink.

A couple sat on the edge of the tablecloth, holding hands and watching two children, a boy of about ten and a girl slightly younger, toss a Frisbee back and forth. A golden retriever ran between them, barking happily, leaping off the ground trying to snatch the disc out of the air. Gene caught his breath when he saw the dog.

Skippy.

It echoed in his mind as if spoken by another, and it seemed like the word itself had encoded a deep blackness in him that he had no other expression for. His gullet spasmed and he tasted bile and beer. He steadied himself against a tree and took a few deep breaths. He looked closer and, really, the dog didn't look much like Skippy at all; it had a darker coat, and reddish highlights around the chest. Still, it felt as if a giant hand had grabbed his stomach and was squeezing, twisting.

The woman called out to the children. It sounded like she said 'James,' but it could have been 'Jane.' Or 'Gene.' The boy looked back at her, then looked up the hill to where Gene was standing. He raised his hand in greeting. Gene raised his in return, but the boy was already running towards the couple on the blanket, the girl and the dog following close behind.

47

Gene walked back up over the ridge, through the cemetery and down the hill to the car. Maggie was sitting in the passenger seat. She shot him an annoyed glance as he approached.

"Jesus, it took you long enough," she said. "I was gonna send out a search party."

"There's this meadow back up there," Gene said. "There were a couple of kids—"

"What are you talking about? There's nothing back there but solid woods. We drove around the curve of the hill before we parked, and there's nothing there."

Gene looked at her for a long moment without speaking. She reached out and gently rapped his forehead with her knuckles.

"Earth to Gene," she said.

He held her gaze for a moment longer, then sighed. Why argue? Maggie couldn't find her ass with both hands and a flashlight. Drunk or sober.

"Whatever you say." He put the car in gear and pulled out into the road.

They didn't talk much after that. They drove with the windows rolled down and the music very loud, surrounding them. Gene liked the feel of the hot wind on his face. He felt detached, as if he was watching himself from a few feet away, driving, fingers tapping counterpoint on the steering wheel, taking an occasional hit of beer from the can Maggie held out to him. Something was happening inside him. He could feel it, the knots in his stomach starting to work themselves loose. They made Brattleboro by dusk and when they stopped for gas they realized they were nearly broke.

"I know someone in this town," Maggie said, "but I don't want to see him."

"We can always walk back to Massachusetts," Gene said.

She gave him a sharp look.

"This is going to be really tacky," she said.

He shrugged his shoulders. She got out of the car and

48

went to the phone booth by the side of the Esso station. She was on the phone a long time. Gene could see her hands moving as she spoke. He realized suddenly that she was quite drunk.

Finally, she hung up the phone and got back in the car.

"It's cool," she said. "Let's go."

She gave him directions as he drove. They were very complicated and after about twenty minutes, half a mile up a rutted dirt lumber road, he turned to her.

"You sure this is right?"

"Yeah, keep going."

The road kept getting worse. After another mile or so, they emerged from the woods into a wide clearing. It was completely dark by this time and the stars were out. The trees on the other side of the clearing stood out sharply in the light from the high-beams. Gene stopped the car, turned off the headlights, and looked over at Maggie. She was staring straight ahead, her eyebrows knit in a puzzled frown. Gene rested his forehead on the steering wheel, took a deep breath, and let it out with a sigh.

"Mags," he said. "How would you feel about me staying with you for a little while?"

She didn't answer. He looked over at her again. Her head was thrown back and her mouth was wide open. She snored once, softly, a gentle fluttering sound. Gene sighed again, got out of the car and stretched. He walked to the back of the car and opened the trunk. He could just make out the shape of the dog, curled up in the corner. Its teeth were visible, and they seemed to glow in the darkness.

There was a shovel and some other tools. He grabbed the shovel, walked over to a spot between two huge oaks just beyond the edge of the clearing, and began to dig. The ground was soft and moist, and gave off a rich smell as he turned it over. It didn't take long. He went back to the car, wrapped the dog in the old, grease-stained army blanket that he spread in the driveway when he worked on the car, and

49

brought the bundle back to the shallow grave. It was surprisingly heavy.

When he was finished, he smoothed the dirt over and straightened up, leaning on the shovel. He looked around the clearing. The car looked very small. He couldn't see Maggie at all.

CHAPTER SIX

The wind woke Maggie up. It sighed loudly through the thin aluminum walls of the trailer, shaking the shutters on the high narrow windows and flapping a loose length of cable on the roof with a periodic clatter. But the sky showing through the windows was a perfect, cloudless blue.

Hot one today, she thought, and felt a sudden chill. Like a goose walked over her grave, her mother would've said.

As she lay in bed, the wind subsided. She stared up at the ceiling, her mind a collage of images that moved too quickly for her to get a handle on. They mostly revolved around Gene, though, their years together. Christ, going on fifteen now. Drunk and sober, together and apart. Fifteen years.

But they'd brought a couple of good kids into the world. That meant something. Gabe was becoming a fine young man. She smiled to herself as she thought of his gawky self-consciousness, the way he flip-flopped between adult and child, gravely serious one moment, giggles and smiles the next. He'd do fine.

Ariel worried her, though. It seemed like she never stopped whining, like there was some space in her that wasn't getting filled and all she knew was that the hunger *hurt*. Maggie could relate to that one, for sure. Ariel had always been the sensitive one, too, a kind of antenna for all the raw feelings that flew between Maggie and Gene. Well, not so

51

much flew as simmered. More than once, Maggie had avoided fighting with Gene because of the effect it had on Ariel. She just bit her lip and hunched her shoulders, and Gene seemed to spin farther and farther out of reach as the weeks melted into years and Maggie didn't know any more if it was more lonely with Gene sleeping the sleep of the dead drunk beside her or filling the space with the imprint of his absence.

There weren't going to be any more fights, not for awhile. She winced as she thought of him lying in the hospital bed swaddled like a mummy, wired up like a Christmas tree. She wondered if anybody was home, if *Gene* was still in there somewhere. Hell, she'd wondered that *before* the accident.

Hey, baby, she thought, feeling like she was sending the words out into the void like a message in a bottle. *We're still here*. She almost said, *It'll be all right*, but then she laughed out loud. What a joke. Polly-fucking-anna. She laughed again as she remembered an old Mose Allison song, "I Don't Worry 'Bout A Thing 'Cause I Know Nothing's Gonna Be All Right." A-men.

She wanted to tell herself that they hadn't been all bad, though, that she hadn't pissed away her best years for nothing. And it was true. Gene could be a good man when he was sober, but unfortunately that hadn't been very often the last few years, and Maggie figured that it wasn't really so much your capacity for good that counted but what you actually did with yourself.

She was one to talk, though. Forty-three years old and she was just learning how to live in the world. It wasn't easy. Maggie thought the Twelve-Steppers were mostly a bunch of sanctimonious fuckheads, but they had that "one day at a time" thing right on the dime.

She went to a meeting in Philly after she'd been sober for a few weeks and was starting to climb the walls. It was in the basement of an old church in the west end of town, a neighborhood on the downslide from poor to left-for-dead, studded with half-burned apartment buildings, hollow, cavernous warehouses, junkyards. The cigarette smoke was so thick she felt like she could write her name in the air with her finger and the letters would just hang there.

The meeting had already started when she arrived. They were all saying something in unison and the chorus of voices had a raw power to it that made her heart beat a little faster.

"—grant me the serenity to accept the things I cannot change, the courage to change the things I can, and the wisdom to know the difference."

It sounded pretty good to Maggie. She didn't know fuck-all about serenity and even less about wisdom, but there was a spark burning hot in her that felt something like courage. She took a seat near the back and looked around the crowded room. There were all sorts of people. Some of them looked like they had just crawled in off the street, but others looked healthy and normal, like they had jobs and families, mortgages and credit cards. Not like alcoholics.

A man and a woman sat at a table in front of the room. The man introduced the woman by her first name, and then she introduced herself again, saying that she was Joan and she was an alcoholic. Everybody in the room chorused back, "Hi, Joan!" which Maggie thought was a little strange, kind of like a cross between summer camp and a television game show. Then Joan started talking.

It was a long story and would have been tragic except that it was so damn *funny*. Laughter echoed through the room as Joan detailed one tale of stupid excess after another, each building on the previous one in a kind of downward spiral. Maggie was shocked at first by the laughter, but it had a warm, guileless quality about it. Then Joan got to the part about getting sober and Maggie started to have a hard time with it. She went on and on about how grateful she was, how she was nothing without The Program. The words sounded capitalized, like there was only *one*. The "G" word came up an awful lot.

Christ, Maggie thought. This woman's sober, what, ten years, and she's still going to two, three meetings a day.

That's just switching one Jones for another. Maybe you weren't going to wrap your car around a tree in the middle of the night if you were strung out on meetings, but you were still shooting something, hooked into the dependency thing. Ten years sober and she's still self-identifying as an alcoholic, first and foremost. It made Maggie sad.

Near the end of the meeting, the person who introduced Joan asked if there were any people there for the first time. A few people raised their hand and they introduced themselves, one by one. Everybody in the room applauded each time, like just getting there to a meeting was a big deal. Maggie didn't raise her hand. She slipped out the door as soon as the meeting was over.

She went to a few more meetings, but they were the same mix of resonance and discomfort for her. She liked the stories and the fellowship, even though the coffee sucked. And she had never heard people talk about themselves quite like that, like they really checked in with what was going on for themselves on a day to day basis, something not a lot of people actually did. The flip side to that was all they ever fucking *did* was talk about themselves. Maggie had never seen a group of people so uniformly self-absorbed. And there was the self-deprecation thing: I'm a helpless worm. I'm an ineffectual turd. I can't do shit and the sooner I realize that the better off I am. It was creepy.

Nobody got well. You weren't supposed to. Once, a person she'd never seen before identified herself as a "recovered alcoholic" and the bad vibes in the room were almost thick enough to see, hanging there in the air like a blue, electric mist. She never saw the person again.

They used to say this thing, reading a passage from what they called the Big Book at the beginning of the meeting. It went something like, "If you have decided you want what we have and are willing to go to any lengths to get it, then you are ready…"

One night, Maggie heard that and looked around the room. Thick eddies of smoke drifted lazily near the ceiling, the whorls highlighted by the bare sixty watt bulb. The faces looked pasty in the harsh light. She had been coming around long enough to have heard some of their stories. Al was two years sober but couldn't stop eating, pushing three hundred pounds now and getting bigger every day. Linda over there would fuck anything that moved; get a new guy in there, under sixty and with the usual complement of arms, teeth, and testicles, and she'd be all over him during the break, trying to trip him and beat him to the floor. Frank had been coming around for six years, two or three meetings a day, and he still lived in abject terror that God was going to ride down from Valhalla in a flaming Cadillac and strike him drunk.

Maggie decided that no, she didn't want what they had. She walked out of there and never came back. She hadn't had a drink since then either. It was the longest she'd gone since she started drinking at fifteen, including the stretches of white-knuckled abstinence she forced on herself when she was carrying Gabe and Ariel. It hadn't been easy, but nothing ever was.

"Mommy?" Ariel's voice, calling from outside the door.

"Come on in, baby."

The door eased open a crack and Ariel's head poked through. She was smiling, but there were dark circles under her eyes. She was a restless sleeper, this one.

"How you doing, squirt?"

She hesitated a second, then giggled and ran to Maggie, throwing herself on the bed. Maggie put her arms around her and buried her face in her hair. The clean, pure smell of her was burned into Maggie's brain, a bright strand of fierce love braided with the fear that everything was falling apart, that Maggie just wasn't going to be able to hold it together for her. Tears came to her eyes and she had to bite her lip to keep them from flowing down her cheeks.

Ariel sensed something and looked up. Her round face looked soft and malleable, like it would take the impression of whatever passed across her consciousness.

"It'll be all right, Mommy."

Maggie laughed nervously to herself. Caretaking already. Christ, I hope to fucking God this one gets to have a childhood.

"Of course it will baby. You da best."

Ariel giggled. It was a game between them.

"No, *you* da best."

Maggie touched her finger to the end of Ariel's nose.

"No, *you.*"

There was a knock at the front door.

"Come on, Ari. Let's see who that is." She got her flannel robe from her suitcase, still half unpacked, and went into the living room. Ariel trailed close behind.

A young woman stood at the door. African-American, light-skinned, what Maggie had heard described as "high yellow" when she was growing up, but the color had always reminded her of rich, old wood. A cap of short, tight curls covered the woman's head and woven into the curls were two or three strings of small, mother-of-pearl beads. She peered at Maggie through a pair of steel-rimmed glasses.

"Hello?" Maggie asked.

"Hi. Ruby Matters." She held out her hand. Maggie shook it.

"Maggie Lambent. This is my daughter, Ariel. Say hello to Miz Matters, Ariel."

"Ruby, please. Hello, Ariel," she said gravely. She held her hand out to Ariel as well. Ariel took it, gave it a single shake, and ran giggling behind Maggie's legs.

Maggie smiled and shrugged. Ruby smiled back. "I live a few units down," she said. "I heard about your ...trouble...and I just wanted to stop by and see if there was anything I could do."

"Come on in," Maggie said. "Can I make you some coffee?"

"Thanks. Only if you're having some."

"Oh, yeah," Maggie said. "I need it."

Maggie put water on the stove and they sat at the

kitchen counter. Ariel poured herself a bowl of Froot Loops and brought it into the living room. She hunched down with the bowl in her lap and began talking quietly to a stuffed dragon the size of a small cat.

Maggie looked at Ruby again. She had a gentleness about her, but there was something underneath it that was street-smart and tough as leather, something about the way she carried herself. And she wasn't all that young either. Maggie had thought mid-twenties at first because her face was smooth and unlined, but her eyes betrayed a longer history – pain given and received, mistakes made and forgiven, a large reservoir of joy. Maggie figured she was probably pushing forty.

"So how did you find out about our 'trouble'?" Maggie asked.

Ruby shrugged and smiled. "Word gets around," she said.

Maggie didn't say anything. She wasn't sure she liked the sound of that.

"You come up here regularly?" Maggie asked after an uncomfortable pause. "I don't think I've ever seen you before. Actually, that doesn't mean anything. We usually make it up here in June and when we do we sort of keep to ourselves."

An image appeared in her mind for an instant, like a slide projected onto a blank screen. Gene, slouched in front of the television, surrounded with a litter of beer cans. Not quite passed out, but a dull, stupid glow in his eyes like the blue gas flame of a pilot light in a dark oven.

"I don't think I've seen a soul I know since we got here," she continued. "Of course, we've been a little occupied..."

Ruby nodded sympathetically. "No, this is my first summer here."

"You here with your husband?"

"I'm not with anybody right now." She seemed slightly amused.

"You're probably lucky."

There was another pause.

"So, how's *your* husband?" Ruby asked.

Maggie shook her head. "He got banged up pretty bad. He's in a coma – I have to head out to the hospital pretty soon." She shook her head. "I always thought that God was supposed to look out for small children and drunks, but He must have been asleep at the switch yesterday."

Something flashed in Ruby's eyes. She looked into the living room to see if Ariel was listening and leaned forward. "The Sky God doesn't give a *fuck* about children," she whispered. "Or drunks, for that matter. Remember that."

Maggie was startled at her vehemence. "Yeah, right, whatever..." Jesus, the Sky God no less.

Ruby leaned back, smiling a little sheepishly.

"Sorry. I have this thing about the Judeo-Christian capital G one and only God. It just seems like a male power trip. I mean, thousands of years of bloodshed in His name, mostly to preserve a political power structure. It's not so blatant these days, but it's still right there if you know where to look. Every time I read about the Middle East, I picture a bunch of white guys in suits with little Lion's Club pins sitting around a prayer breakfast somewhere deciding how it's gonna be for the hordes of Godless heathens." She shook her head. "And the Church still wants to run your sex life. It's worse than that, though. They want your soul, they really do. Not for God, but for themselves."

Maggie nodded. "I've thought a lot about this stuff. I was involved a while back with a...group...and there was a lot of God talk. I could never really get behind it – they always seemed to overdo the ego-death thing. I mean, I believe that it's good to seek a connection with a Higher Power, something larger than yourself, but there's gotta be somebody left minding the store in case there's a callback, you know?"

Ruby nodded. "Absolutely."

The teakettle began to whistle. Maggie got up and

made coffee. The two women sat in companionable silence, sipping from large, white mugs, each to her own thoughts.

"Was there a storm this morning?" Maggie asked after a while. "When I woke up the wind was howling like crazy."

Ruby frowned. "There was *something* going on this morning. I don't know if it was a real storm or just smoke and mirrors."

"Excuse me?"

"Never mind," she said, shaking her head. "You have a boy, too, don't you?"

"Yeah, Gabe. In fact, I need to find him so we can go to the hospital. He's probably down at the beach somewhere. You want to come along?"

"Sure."

The three of them walked across the dunes down to the beach, Ariel between the two women, holding a hand from each. Just before they got to the frontage road, Maggie saw Gabe and another man walking towards them along the sand. Even at this distance, Maggie was struck by the color of the man's hair and beard – pure white, almost bleached-looking.

Maggie waved at them. She turned to Ruby. "That's Gabe. I don't know the other guy."

Ruby face was grim. "I know him," she said.

They crossed the road to where Gabe and the man stood waiting.

"Hi, Mom," Gabe said. "This is Otto."

Otto held out his hand to Maggie. "Otto Nye," he said in a deep baritone, the two words running together so they sounded almost like one. Next to her, Maggie heard Ruby snort almost imperceptibly.

"Hello," she said, taking his hand. He had a strong grip, but his hand was soft and uncallussed. His eyes were a clear, depthless blue and he had the kind of rugged, generic good looks that made Maggie think of cigarette ads.

"This is my daughter, Ariel," Maggie said, putting her hand on top of Ariel's head. Ariel scurried behind her legs.

59

Maggie looked at Otto and shrugged, but he was looking at Ruby with a half-smile on his face.

"Oh, and this is Ruby Matters."

"We've met," Otto said. "Good to see you again, Ruby."

"Otto Nye?" She paused just long enough before saying his name that it sounded a little like a sardonic challenge. Otto shrugged. There was a tension between the two of them that Maggie could almost see as a physical presence hanging in the air between them. And there was some weird energy going on between Otto and Gabe, too, but she couldn't figure out what. Collusion, maybe, or some kind of power thing. Her mothers' antenna picked up on that right away. You couldn't be too careful these days.

"We gotta hit the road, Gabe," Maggie said.

"Are we going to the hospital?" he asked, making a face.

"Yes," she said, putting just enough edge in her voice so he'd know she meant business.

"He's a fucking vegetable, Mom. He's not even gonna know we're there."

She resisted the urge to raise her hand to him. "God damn it, Gabe," she said.

He looked back at her, his face a cold, impassive mask. He looked pale and drawn, though, like he hadn't slept a wink the night before. She felt something soften inside her. "We have to be there, Gabe. Maybe he'll know it, maybe he won't. But we have to go. That's it, no argument."

Otto put his hand in Gabe's shoulder. "Go on, Gabe," he said.

Gabe looked down at his feet, pushing up a small pile of sand with the edge of his flip-flop. "Oh, all right," he said.

Maggie didn't like the looks of that, acquiescing to Otto and not her, but this wasn't the time to push it. "Let's get moving, then," she said. "Nice to meet you, Otto."

She turned to Ruby. "I'm really glad you came by. See you soon."

"Definitely," Ruby said.

Maggie, Ariel, and Gabe walked back up toward the trailer park. Maggie looked back once. Otto and Ruby were still standing next to the asphalt strip of the frontage road, their heads bent in conversation.

The hospital was on the other side of Lewes from the trailer park. Maggie took Dunes Road so they could avoid town traffic. It was little-used, a strip of cracked and battered asphalt winding through the dunes and low scrub that bordered the ocean. Drifts of sand stretched across the road like pale fingers.

"So what's the story with Otto?" Maggie asked, trying to keep her tone light. Gabe was sitting in the back seat with a book.

"He's a good guy," Gabe said, with a defensive edge in his voice.

This is going to be like pulling teeth, Maggie thought.

She lined up the questions in her mind. How did you meet him? What does he do? Is his family here with him? Which trailer is he in?

But she knew the answer to that last one. He lived in that old Airstream she'd noticed earlier. She didn't know how she knew that, but she was sure of it.

She was about to start in with the questions when, just as they rounded a turn, a large dog bounded across the road. She slammed on the brakes but it was too late. There was a dull, meaty thump and the dog's body went sailing through the air like a sack of flour. Maggie's arm shot across the seat to hold Ariel back as the car screeched to a halt. The silence rushed into the car like seawater.

Ariel began to cry. Maggie looked her over quickly. "Hush, baby, you're all right. You okay back there, Gabe?"

"Good one, Mom."

She turned around. "Will you just give me a fucking break, Gabe? Please?" Ariel's crying cranked up a few notches in pitch and amplitude. "Hush, Ari, it's okay." She bent over

61

and kissed the top of her daughter's head. She looked up at Gabe again. He looked back at her challengingly at first, then nodded.

"Thanks," she said. She got out of the car to look for the dog, even though she could tell from the feel of the impact that there wasn't much point.

The car's grille was undamaged, which surprised her. Maggie didn't see the dog anywhere on the road or on the shoulder. She walked out into the scrub and looked around, the tough, low bushes scratching her legs. Nothing.

She looked back at the car. It sat there on the tarry road like a squat, metal beast. Ariel and Gabe were silhouette cutouts inside.

Skippy. The word appeared in her mind in Gene's voice, a clear, soft whisper. Although the sun was high overhead and the day's heat already radiating back from the ground with a dull, constant pressure, rippling in the near distance, Maggie felt again that chill she'd felt upon awakening. It came up like a wave from somewhere deep in the center of her, rising up from darkness, numbing her tongue and filling her mouth with cotton.

CHAPTER SEVEN

The rest of the way to the hospital, Gabe didn't say anything. He sat in the back seat with *At The Earth's Core* open in his lap, but he wasn't reading. Beachfront scenery in muted tan and pale, leached green rushed past the window. There was a throbbing ache right between his eyes, like he'd eaten a big spoonful of cold ice cream on a blistering hot day.

It was all just too much. It was like there was this engine inside him – he could almost picture its angular, metallic bulk, jets of steam shooting out into the dark recesses of a cavernous warehouse, a deafening, rhythmic pounding shaking the soles of his feet. It was maxed out – a needle on a dial somewhere was quivering up against the red area on the right hand side. Pretty soon pieces were going to start flying off in all directions.

He couldn't stop thinking about the boat and what happened afterwards. When the last of the clouds had disappeared and the unbroken sea lay open before them, Gabe turned to Otto.

"There were *people* on that thing, right?"

Otto looked down at him and nodded. He still looked fierce and glowering, but there was a light in his eye that almost twinkled.

"And they're all *dead?*"

Otto nodded again. "Look, it doesn't matter," he said. "Einstein was wrong – God *does* play dice. It was just their

63

shitty luck. Their wheel spun and landed on bankrupt. Vanna won't turn their letters any more, nobody gets to buy a vowel. If it'll make you feel any better, let me tell you about Arthur Stevens, the guy who chartered the boat. He's happily married, supposedly, but he goes to sex clubs in the West Village two or three times a month when he says he's working late. He's HIV positive and knows it, but he hasn't told anybody. So's his wife now. The other guy embezzled from the pension fund of a company that was going under – he's got about eleven million stashed away in a Swiss account."

Gabe didn't even question how Otto knew all that – it seemed perfectly natural. "So you're telling me these people *deserved* it."

"No, I'm telling you it doesn't fucking matter. It was just their turn. They might just have well been a couple of nuns out there." He paused for a moment, looking out to sea. The wind picked up, blowing his long hair behind him like a white, rippling flag. For a second, Gabe had the feeling that Otto was *posing*.

"Look," Otto continued, turning back to him. "They were fishing, right?"

Gabe nodded. "I guess."

"Okay, suppose you're a big goddamn sea bass, just swimming around near the bottom minding your own business. You've just gotten laid and you're looking to scarf down a minnow or two for lunch. Life is beautiful and simple, *capisce?*"

Gabe nodded again.

"Then this big hook comes dangling down out of the sky. The way it catches the light is so beautiful it just about breaks your goddamn heart. So you go for it – you don't have any more choice in the matter than you would if somebody came along and jammed the thing through your lip. And you get yanked out of this world faster than you can say 'coronary thrombosis.' You die."

Gabe was quiet for a long time, watching the breakers coming in, listening to their periodic, rumbling crash. It seemed like just about the most powerful thing in the world, the ocean; the sound of it seemed to tether his feet to the damp sand, mooring him to the earth.

He turned to Otto. "Show me," he said. "Show me how to do it."

He didn't know what he meant exactly, what *it* was, but Otto smiled. "There's nothing to it. Just concentrate..."

Gabe shut his eyes and tried to focus his thoughts. On what, he didn't know, but he concentrated on feeling his physical presence, the way the weight of his body felt distributed across the soles of his feet, the subtle rhythm of blood music in his ears.

"Open your eyes, Gabe. You have to be *in* the world to do this, not apart from it." Otto's whisper was insistent; sibilant and harsh.

Gabe opened his eyes. Subtle flickerings laced across the sky. The blue of the ocean seemed to vibrate, as if unseen energies lay just beneath its surface. A large wave came in and began to break, the smooth hump of water foaming white at the top, peaking, beginning to fold over. Gabe felt something rush through him and out like an icy wind and the curling wave *stopped*, an abstract sculpture hanging there in mid-air. The sun glared off its smooth, rounded surface. Gabe could practically count the suspended droplets of mist that seeded the air above the crest.

He looked over at Otto. The older man looked back at him, a smile playing on the corners of his mouth. Behind him a seagull hung motionless, wings outstretched, like it was in one of those dioramas at the Museum of Natural history in New York. There was no sound, none at all – Gabe felt like his ears were stuffed with cotton gauze. Suddenly, something in him snapped and a surge of nausea passed through him. Purple spots swam before his vision and the sounds came rushing back in to fill the void. The wave continued curling again, broke, and crashed into the damp sand. The purple spots merged together and Gabe felt himself rising to meet the sky...

Otto's face hovered over him, a dark silhouette against the sky. "Wake up, Gabe," he said. "The British are coming."

Gabe sat up. His arms were caked with damp sand. Another wave of nausea passed through him and he leaned over to the side, coughing and retching.

"Not bad for a punk kid," Otto said.

"Wha – what happened?"

"I told you. The world's just a shell – you gotta get inside of it to get on top of it."

"I don't understand." Gabe said. He felt scared, but underneath the fear was the sense that he was hooked into something powerful, something much larger than himself. Things were changing inside him.

"You will, Gabe," Otto said. "Take my word for it."

"Earth to Gabe," Maggie said. Gabe shook his head. They were already in the parking lot of the hospital.

"I don't know how much longer they're going to let him stay here," Maggie said as they walked through the lobby towards the elevators. "The doctor told me yesterday that they wanted to keep him long enough to stabilize, then send him to a special ward in a hospital in Wilmington, where they'll know how to take care of him."

"What's 'stabilize'?" Ariel asked.

"That's so we can't sue them if something goes wrong when they send him to the coma place," Gabe said. "You know, 'stable lies.'"

Maggie gave him a dirty look, but the corners of her mouth turned up a little. "They just want to make sure he's strong enough to get well, Ari."

The elevator bell chimed dully and the double doors opened with a whispery rattle. A tired looking intern in a sweat-stained surgical gown got on with them.

Everything in this place was *old*. Numbers scrolled past in a cloudy little bubble of glass set above the floor buttons. The elevator rattled and creaked as it ascended. It stopped with a shudder and they got out. Gabe looked back as the doors closed in front of the intern. He hadn't registered their presence at all – his eyes had a distant, murky look. Gabe wondered what he was seeing.

Gene was just about the same. They'd changed his bandages – his head was wrapped in a bundle of bright, white gauze. There was a space in the bandages for his eyes, but it was filled in with shadow. Gabe imagined his father's eyes open in that blackness, open and looking out. He shuddered. The machines clustered around the bed hummed and beeped in a parody of reassurance.

Gabe turned to his mother. "It's like it isn't really him, you know? Like Ariel was saying yesterday."

Maggie put her hand on his arm. "Yeah, I know what you mean. But it *is* him."

And he needs us. Gabe could almost hear the unspoken words hanging there in the room, floating above the hum of the machinery. He saw her clearly then, haggard and worn, fighting for balance. He'd wondered sometimes why they didn't all just up and leave, but he was beginning to realize that it was more complicated than that, that there were forces pulling his Mom in different directions. It was weird to think of her like that, struggling, not knowing what the right thing to do was.

Maggie walked up to Gene and bent her head over him, brushing her lips against the bandages. "We're all here, Gene," she said.

There didn't seem to be too much else to do after that. They pulled chairs around the bed, sharing the space with the machines.

Ariel began to fidget. Maggie pulled out a battered copy of *Charlotte's Web* from her shoulder bag and started reading quietly to her. It almost never failed to hold her attention and this time was no exception.

It looked to Gabe like they were going to be there for a while. He could go with the flow, sit and read the Burroughs, but the thought of just sitting there all afternoon

67

was just too much.

"I'm gonna go walk around," he said.

Maggie and Ariel looked up simultaneously, and for a second they looked almost identical – the same big eyes, the same dark, wavy hair. He had a sudden feeling that was part longing, part kinship, part something else he couldn't quite identify, and his eyes misted over for a second.

Maggie didn't seem to notice. "Okay, Gabe," she said. "Stay out of trouble. If you make it down to the cafeteria, pick me up a sandwich or something."

He nodded and walked out of the room. When he was in the doorway, he stopped and looked back. His mother and sister were pulled up close to the bed, next to the machines, bent over as if in worship.

He didn't really know where he was going and just let his feet carry him. The green tile corridors branched and branched again. Scattered here and there along the walls, patients sat in wheelchairs or lay on gurneys. Sometimes their eyes followed Gabe as he walked by, but mostly they stared off into space with an inward focus, like they were marking out time on some inner clock. That's pretty much what you do in hospitals, Gabe thought. You wait.

At intersections of the corridors, the nurses' stations were humming nodes of activity. Soon, the people in starched white behind the glass began to all look alike and he wondered if he wasn't passing the same places over and over again.

He came to a lounge and looked inside. A television faced the room from a far corner, tuned to an old black and white movie. A man and a woman stood on the deck of a boat; behind them, a skyline that looked almost familiar glittered like fairy castles, throwing a shimmering reflection in the water. New York? Chicago?

"You know I'll never leave you," the man was saying.

"And I'll never leave you," the woman replied. An odd felt hat perched on her head at a jaunty angle made her look like one of Robin Hood's merry men. Violins and muted horns swelled in the background.

Give me a break, Gabe thought.

An old man, the lounge's single occupant, waved him inside and patted the seat next to him. Reluctantly, Gabe stepped inside and sat down. For a second, Gabe wondered if this was the same guy they'd shared the lounge with yesterday and he took a closer look. It wasn't him. Old people and babies, Gabe thought. The differences all sort of mush together.

The man leaned close to him. His breath was terrible – halitosis with a hint of cloying sweetness. "The orange…never waits," he said urgently.

"I'll always love you," said the man on the television screen.

"Always," replied the woman.

"The tree line…" the old man said, wafting another cloud of foulness toward Gabe.

Fuck this, Gabe thought. Suddenly, the television switched channels. Ozzy Osborne was throwing his head back, clutching a microphone like he was about to jam it down his throat. A fuzzed out lead guitar sailed screaming notes over a pounding bass line.

The old man jumped back, clutching his chest. His eyes were wide open, looking right at Gabe. Scratchy choking sounds came from somewhere deep in his throat.

Gabe stared at him for a second, not knowing what to do, then he ran out into the hall. There was a nurses' station about twenty feet down the corridor. His flip-flops slapped against the shining linoleum as he ran up to it.

"In the lounge," he said breathlessly. The nurse behind the glass looked up from a metal clipboard. "This old guy. I think he's having a heart attack or something…"

The nurse looked him over for a moment, then she picked up the phone in front of her and pushed a button on its console. "Code Blue," she said. "Lounge B." The words echoed down the green tile hallway.

In seconds, a nurse appeared from behind one of the closed doors and ran down the hall to the lounge. Another woman brushed past Gabe following close behind, a stethoscope flapping against her neck as she ran.

Gabe just stood there. He didn't know what to do. The nurse at the station was saying something into the phone again. Gabe backed around the corner and when he was out of sight he began walking quickly. He came to a stairway marked with a big, red EXIT sign and he ducked into it.

He ran up a flight of stairs, then another, and another. He found himself on a landing between floors, looking out of a wire-covered window at the parking lot. Beyond it was the commercial strip that marked the outskirts of Lewes, and beyond that, the ocean.

He stopped to catch his breath. His head hurt something awful and he felt like he was going to throw up.

Did *I* do that? He didn't even know what he had done exactly. He'd just wanted the old guy out of his face and the stupid crap on the TV to end, and he'd *pushed*. All of a sudden Ozzy was screaming his ass off and the old guy was having a heart attack.

His eyes started misting over and the pain in his head focused to a point right between his eyes. Whimpering sounds echoed in the stairwell and he realized distantly that they were his own. He began to cry in earnest, great sobs coming from somewhere deep in his chest like the baying of some huge sea creature. He was worried that someone would hear him and come to investigate. The thought of somebody seeing him like this was almost too much to bear, but he couldn't stop.

Images wheeled through his mind. His father, sitting at the kitchen table back in Philly, his face blurred into putty by alcohol. Standing outside the Escort, the wind lifting the fine strands of his hair, a sick light burning in his eyes. *I have to go to the store.* Otto, his head thrown back like a Greek statue, looking out to sea with a stern frown. His mother's haggard face, melting into the soft, open features of his sister.

70

Slowly, his breathing returned to normal. The tear glands at the sides of his eyes ached terribly, as if someone had wrung them dry by hand. His knees felt weak.

Fucking crybaby, he thought.

"You okay?"

Gabe whirled around. Standing halfway up the stairs was a teenage girl, maybe a year or two older than him. She wore black pajamas and a wicked looking cluster of hoops in her left ear, which looked strangely naked beneath a curve of shaved scalp. Her straight hair, midnight black with a wide streak of purple, was combed over to the right like a glossy wing. She had very pale skin, almost translucent; her delicate features appeared carved from frozen milk.

Gabe felt a hot rush of blood come to his cheeks.

"Yeah, I'm okay," he stammered, trying to regain his composure. "How long have you been standing there?"

She smiled. "It's cool. Don't worry about it." She walked down the stairs toward him. "I'm Casey," she said. "Cassilda, actually, if you can believe that." He noticed a faint wheeze coming from deep in her chest when she paused to take a breath.

"Gabe. How you doing?"

"Pretty good. Just wandering around, you know? I get a little stir crazy sometimes." She banged on the window three times with the heel of her hand, hard enough to rattle the glass in its frame. She looked at Gabe with an expression of mock seriousness, one eyebrow arched. The wheeze was still there, faint but persistent. It reminded Gabe of an aging smoker – he wondered if she even noticed it.

"Yeah, I know what you mean," he paused. "What, uh—"

"What am I doing here? Cystic fibrosis, man. It's a bummer."

Cystic fibrosis. He'd heard of that. The words made him think of late-night television commercials – Sally Struthers looking chunky and pathetic, pleading for dollars in front of a cheesy-looking library set. Casey looked pretty

71

normal, though, except for the punk haircut and the unnaturally pale skin.

"That's something with your lungs, right?"

"Yeah, they just don't work too good." She said it in a very matter-of-fact way, without a trace of self-pity. "Some night they'll just fill up with goo when I'm asleep and I'll drown." She bugged her eyes and stuck out her tongue in a mock death-mask, but her slight gasp for breath when she finished talking gave the gesture a macabre twist. Gabe laughed in spite of the chill he felt.

"So what are *you* doing here?" she asked.

"My father got in a…car accident. He's messed up pretty bad. In a coma…"

She grimaced. Her face was very malleable, completely transforming with the different expressions that crossed it. It made her seem accessible to Gabe, like there was really somebody home behind the punked-out persona.

"Bummer," she said. "I'm really sorry. You here with your Mom?"

"Yeah. My sister Ariel, too."

She nodded. Her earrings jangled faintly.

They were silent for a moment. Hospital sounds echoed faintly in the stairwell – muted, unintelligible snippets from the PA system, a low, humming throb of machinery from the basement.

"What about *your* parents?" Gabe asked.

"They're in Malaysia." Casey rolled her eyes. "Anthropologists. They're always going somewhere – Easter Island, Thailand, Kenya. They used to take me along, but one time we were in the Amazon and my lungs got really bad. They had to fly in a helicopter to take me to Sao Paolo. My mom said never again."

"Wow. That must've been really cool, though, going all those places."

She shrugged. "It was okay, I guess. It was really a drag with schools and shit, though, always going someplace new. And sometimes I didn't go at all 'cause there wasn't any place and my 'rents tutored me. Man, it was like Chinese water torture. Zero slack."

Gabe grinned. "So how'd you wind up in *this* shithole?"

"We have a house in Bethany Beach and my grandparents come up a lot from D.C., so it's pretty convenient. They're trying some new drugs on me. Tests." Casey grimaced. "And my Mom has all these ideas about how being near the ocean is good for my lungs – you know, negative ions and all that crap." She shook her head. "Fucking hippie."

Gabe smiled. "Yeah, well, maybe we can get you a tofu burger in the cafeteria..."

She laughed, and doubled over suddenly in a coughing fit. It had a scary, booming hollowness to it, like she was literally coughing her lungs out. It went on and on. Gabe stood there at first, not knowing what to do, then he put his hand on her back, resting it lightly there between her shoulder blades. She shook it off with a twist of her shoulders and hunched over again, coughing into her closed fist.

Gradually, the fit subsided. She kept her eyes averted, still trying to get her breath back. Gabe noticed what appeared to be a fine dusting of freckles on the back her hand. Blood.

He was a little embarrassed, as if he had witnessed something very private. Casey seemed to share his discomfort. For the first time, her reserved cool seemed to falter.

"So what do your parents do?" she asked finally, when she regained her breath. She sat down on the steps. Her face looked even paler than before, with splotches of red standing out high on her cheeks.

"My Dad's a brain surgeon," Gabe said, sitting down next to her. "My Mom used to hire out as a mercenary soldier, but she's pretty much retired now."

Casey punched him on the arm. "Come on. Really."

"Really? Okay. Um, my Dad's an astronaut. My Mom

73

models her hands on TV commercials."

Casey punched him again, harder.

"Ouch. Okay, really. My Dad…manages a restaurant. He's a musician, too, a really good guitar player. But he doesn't play much anymore." Gabe hesitated, not sure if he wanted to say more or not. He didn't want to look at her. "Mostly he drinks," he added quickly.

"Ah."

He looked up at her. She looked back frankly – no pity, no judgment. "What about your Mom?" she asked. The wheeze when she paused for breath was very bad.

"Well, she's had a lot of jobs. Tronning, mostly, but lately she's been working as an office manager and she likes that okay."

"Tronning?"

"Oh, sorry. Waitron. It's like a PC way of saying waitress." Gabe paused a beat and they looked at each other.

"Fucking hippies," they chorused together. Casey coughed and held up her hand. "God damn it, don't make me laugh."

"You okay?"

She nodded.

"She used to drink, too," he continued. "But she's been sober for four years."

"Oh, man, is she a Stepper?"

"No, she's not so bad. She went to meetings for a while but then she stopped. She said it was 'cause the coffee sucked but I don't really know what happened. She doesn't drink any more, though. She gets pretty bent out of shape when my Dad gets really hammered." He paused, remembering again why he was there. "Or she used to, anyway."

They sat together in silence. Outside the window, a pair of gulls circled each other in lazy, looping arcs.

Gabe wanted to tell her stuff – Otto, the boat, the old guy in the lounge, but he didn't know how to start. He could picture her looking at him like he was crazy and stalking off.

He took a deep breath and let it out with a sigh. Casey

looked at him. "I was watching TV in one of the lounges upstairs a little while ago," he said. "There was this old guy in there. All of a sudden, he grabbed his chest and started, like, choking."

"Code Blue, Code Blue!" Casey said, making waving motions in the air with her hands.

"Yeah, really. It was scary – I got out of there." He looked down at his hands. "Thing is, though, I feel like I caused it." He looked up at her.

"What do you mean?"

"Well, the guy was right in my face. He was saying crazy shit and he had really bad breath. I kind of thought, 'Get the fuck away from me!' and all of a sudden the TV switched to a rock video and the guy was having a heart attack."

"Yeah, well, those old geezers don't like MTV much."

"I'm *serious*."

"Sorry," she said. "But look, what you're telling me is that you can think of something and it just happens, like on *The Twilight Zone* or something. That just doesn't make sense." She paused. "I've been to a lot of shrinks. A *lot*. Mostly they're not very smart, but I've picked up a few things. It sounds to me like you're feeling guilty about your Dad for some reason and you're doing a projection number."

"No, there's more to it than that." He told her about Otto, about the boat, about standing there in front of the huge, blue ocean holding the shimmering curl of breaking wave frozen in place like an ice sculpture.

She was quiet for a long time after he was finished, except for the slight, laboring wheeze at the end of every breath, like a period at the end of a sentence.

Finally, she shook her head. "What the fuck do I know? Maybe all that really happened. I'll tell you this much, though – I'd keep my eye out for this Otto character. I don't like the sound of him."

"What do you mean?"

"I *mean*, he sounds like a manipulative fuck, that's

what I mean. I *mean*, like whatever he's doing with you, he's working his own agenda. Just a feeling I've got."

Gabe shook his head stubbornly. She didn't get it.

"Okay, let's try something," Casey continued. "Let's suppose you really are some kind of God Squad trainee, like you really can do stuff like stop the ocean, kill people, change channels without a remote."

Gabe nodded.

Casey looked at him. "Fix my lungs." There was a challenge in her eyes, but something else there as well. "I'm serious, man. I'm gonna die before I turn twenty-five unless a miracle happens. Give me a miracle. 'Cause if you can't, all that stuff you've been telling me is bullshit, even if every word's true. Give me a miracle. Fix my lungs."

"Okay, I'll try." Gabe closed his eyes and concentrated. A picture began to take form in his mind's eye, a network of tubes, branching in fractal cascades, terminating finally in clusters of tiny, membranous bladders. He could *see* what the trouble was. The membranes were riddled with scars, tough and far less permeable than healthy tissue. The blood that coursed through her lungs came away starving for oxygen.

He didn't know what to do, though. He tried to concentrate, to open himself up and let *something* surge through him like it did down at the beach, but nothing happened. He opened his eyes. Purple splotches swam before his vision and there was a pain in his head like someone was trying to push a knitting needle between his eyes.

"I'm sorry," he croaked. His eyes stung with sweat.

"Don't worry about it," Casey said with a wry smile. "God can't do it either."

They sat silently together. Gabe felt like he was playing a game with rules he didn't understand, flailing away at shadows.

"I should be getting back," he said after a while. "Listen, do they ever let you out of this place? Maybe you could come by where we're staying sometime…"

"Yeah, I can usually talk my way into a day pass. My grandmother has to sign off on it 'cause of the insurance, but that's easy. I can also sneak out for a few hours anytime – the nurses here are dumb as rocks."

"Okay, cool. I'll talk to my Mom about it."

"Come by my room before you go back so you know where it is."

"Okay."

Gabe followed Casey up the stairs. Her wheeze got a little worse with the exertion – by the time they got to the top of the stairs, each breath was followed by a gasp, like something was being torn out of her.

"You all right?" Gabe asked.

Casey nodded curtly and pushed through the door into the corridor. She turned left and Gabe followed closely behind.

Gabe was beginning to get a sense of the hospital's floor plan. Four major wings, labeled for the points of the compass, with halls and wards branching off from these like tributaries. But the wings looked identical and nothing was labeled, so you never knew where you were.

They turned into a hall that looked exactly like the last four halls they had entered and approached a nurses' station.

"Watch this," Casey said.

When they passed the station, the nurse looked up and smiled. "Hello, Cassilda," she said.

"Hello—" Casey doubled over in a fit of coughing. It sounded worse than the first time, the huge, ripping coughs coming from deep in her chest. Between the coughs her breathing sounded desperate and labored.

The nurse rushed out from behind her booth and put her hand on Casey's back. Casey straightened up and smiled sweetly at her, gesturing with her thumb back to the nurses' station.

The nurse glared at Casey, then at Gabe. "I don't think that's very funny," she said.

Casey laughed and walked away. Gabe looked at the

nurse and shrugged apologetically, then followed Casey down the hall. When he caught up with her, they looked at each other and broke out laughing.

"Some of them are okay," Casey said. "But I really hate the ones that treat you like you're a piece of meat. That one back there is pretty new. Every time she looks at me I can hear her thinking, 'Oh, that poor girl's going to die.' I have to jerk her chain some." They stopped at a door. "Here we are. Room 322 South, my home away from home."

At the foot of the single bed stood tall, green cylinder strapped to a wheeled cart, OXYGEN printed in black stencil across the top. A clear, plastic mask dangled from the end of a flexible hose attached to one of the tank's nozzles. Seeing it there gave Gabe a chill.

There was a teetering stack of books on the table next to the bed. Gabe could read some of the titles. *The Gold Cell*, Sharon Olds. *Fools*, Pat Cadigan. *The Anarchist's Cookbook*. *All the Pretty Horses*, Cormac McCarthy. *Lost Souls*, Poppy Z. Brite. Next to the books was an equally precarious stack of CDs and a Walkman. A huge crepe paper sunflower, neon orange, nodded over everything as if in defiance of Casey's person-in-black image.

On the wall opposite the bed was a poster from a movie called *The Hills Have Eyes*. It showed a creepy looking bald guy with a chain around his neck, glowering above the tagline: 'They were a typical American family. They didn't want to kill, but they didn't want to die.' Out the window, there was an unobstructed view of the ocean.

Being there gave him a good feeling, which he didn't think was possible for a hospital room. It was like she actually lived here. "Nice place," Gabe said.

"Thanks."

They stood there in the center of the room, suddenly awkward.

"Well, I gotta go," Gabe said. "Will you be here tomorrow?"

She punched him on the arm. "Duh. I'm not going

anywhere."

Gabe blushed. "Sorry, dumb question. I'll come find you. Maybe we can do one of those pass deals."

"Cool. Hey, can I bum a smoke?"

"Uh—"

"Kidding. See you." She hesitated, then took a step closer to him and kissed him on the cheek. Gabe noticed that she had to stand up on her tip-toes to do it. He mumbled something and before he knew it, his feet had taken him halfway down the hall to the nurses' station. He looked back at the open door to Casey's room. He could still feel her lips on his cheek, and the smell of her up close, sort of warm and sweet, filled him the way clear water fills a glass.

CHAPTER EIGHT

Gene floats in a sky of black velvet, a depthless backdrop of nothing. He can sense rhythms, separate and distinct – the blood rushing in his ears, the cyclic tasks of the machines that service him, the slow unrolling of the days themselves.

He has some awareness of things around him, but it is filtered through a haze of drugs, pain, and damage into a kind of kinesthesia. The sixty-cycle hum of the hospital wiring is a kind of ultraviolet haze that he can just see at the periphery of his vision, melting to black as soon as he tries to look directly at it.

When the nurse comes in to change one of his IV bottles, Gene sees her as a blur of color approaching out of the deep black distance, resolving into the shape of a cartoon lizard, man-sized and neon orange, dressed in crisp, white linen. Its tiny, curled claws perform their tasks skillfully and quickly; hissing noises escaping from between its teeth as it works. The salt breeze breathing through the window is a low sighing, a chorus of a hundred voices.

When Maggie and the kids show up, he wants desperately to let them know he is there. But again, he feels separated from his body, looking down from a great height at a cone of light illuminating the bed, the machines, his family clustered around like supplicants.

He tries to shout but his voice is absorbed into that

blackness like water into a dry sponge and he recedes back, up, the cone of light below him narrowing down to a point, a speck, gone.

The summer Gene quit drinking, he took a job at the Jocelyn Wood Academy, teaching SAT preparation classes to rooms full of sneering, fidgeting adolescents. He saw the students in his dreams: geometrical rows of smooth, liquid faces, all with the same calculated expression of scorn and judgment. He completely bullshitted his way into the job — he'd never done anything like that in his life. The thought of slinging food in a hot kitchen all day, though, was too much. Besides, working in restaurants was slippery. What you did was hustle like a son of a bitch, drink to take the edge off, coke up to get it back. It was part of the culture.

He missed Maggie and the baby with a hot, dull ache. They'd agreed to give the separation a try, see how things went. Gene figured what the fuck, maybe things would be a little more clear if he wasn't knocking back upwards of a case of beer and a pint of Jack a day. Not to mention the coke.

The first few dry weeks were the worst. No out and out D.T.'s, but his system was shocked into complete confusion by the absence of alcohol. He would awaken out of a restless half-sleep with the sweat-drenched sheets wrapped around his waist and clinging to his thighs. Stagger into the kitchen to put the water on the stove. Lurch into the shower and stand there underneath the needle spray, not bothering with soap, not thinking about anything, until some arbitrary stimulus — a random synaptic flutter, a car horn in the street outside the open bathroom window — snapped him out of it.

He repeated this every morning until one time the water in the kettle boiled off and the aluminum bottom melted onto the heating element. The smoke detector went off with an impossibly loud shriek and Gene knocked his head against the shower nozzle. He tore the curtain aside and leaped into the hall, dripping wet, to where the detector was mounted high up near the ceiling. He beat at it with his fist until the white plastic cover flew off, then he yanked the little nine-volt battery out of its mounting. It was only when the shrieking stopped that he realized the apartment was filled with a haze of acrid smoke. He ran into the kitchen alcove. The bottom of the pot glowed dull red, and there were brighter yellow sparks winking on and off around its periphery. Fingers of slag spread out from underneath it, encrusting the heating coil. He turned off the stove, went back into the bedroom, dressed, and left for work.

The students were merciless. They tolerated no mistakes and met the smallest error with derision. Gene was pretty much on autopilot most of the time, working through the examples out of the Jocelyn Wood Workbook in long, shaky loops on the blackboard, and when he stumbled over a particularly difficult algebra exercise or circuitous logic puzzle, his mind would go completely blank. He would stand there with his back to the students for what seemed like minutes, even though it was probably only a few seconds. Then, amidst jeers and catcalls, he would recover and continue with the lecture. A couple of times, crumpled wads of paper sailed over his shoulder as he stood there and once he was hit on the head.

He didn't know how to react to these assaults. He was aware at some level of a sense of humiliation, but it was an abstract thing, and when he looked to himself for a response, for some sort of template upon which to structure his presence in the classroom, his interaction with these half-formed little beings, he found nothing. His soul felt like one of the abandoned frame houses out on the far end of Macon Street near the railroad yards, paint cracked and peeling, shutters hanging at odd, forlorn angles.

Inevitably, these musings would end with fantasies of alcohol. Tall, frosted glass of golden nectar catching the fading afternoon sunlight through the high, front windows of a tavern. Beads of condensation trembling on the sides of the glass, running down like tears. That yeasty smell, cutting through everything else, going right to the heart of his awareness, right to his center.

The students seemed identical and interchangeable, except for one girl who always sat in the same seat in the back of the room, near the window. Her name was Alexis. She seemed younger than the rest of the people in the class and she almost never spoke. She was pretty, in a dark, Mediterranean sort of way—olive skin, thick black hair cut in straight bangs that hung nearly to her eyebrows. In fact, she looked a little to Gene like one of those anonymous UNICEF poster children. But there was a glassy vacancy in her eyes that made Gene wonder if there wasn't something wrong with her, some sort of learning disability. She did very badly on the mid-term practice exam, scoring as if she had simply filled in the circles on the answer sheet at random. Gene asked to speak to her after class as he was handing back the exams.

He busied himself shuffling papers on the desk as the students filed out of the room, their voices blending into a buzzing murmur. When he looked up, she was still sitting at her desk. It was late afternoon and shafts of warm, gold sunlight stabbed through the shuttered windows, laying jagged stripes across the neat rows of desks and illuminating fat specks of drifting dust. Her hands were folded in front of her and she looked down at them. Her hair hung over her eyes and Gene couldn't see her face.

Gene got up and walked down the wide center aisle to the back of the room. He pulled the chair out from the desk in front of her and sat down facing her, straddling the chair backwards and resting his arms on its back.

"How's it going?" he asked.

She didn't look up. "Okay, I guess."

He didn't know how to do his. "How are you doing with the work? You know, you didn't do so well on the practice test."

She nodded – an almost imperceptible movement of her head.

"Everything all right at home?" There was a wall

there – Gene could almost see it.

She nodded again.

Clear as a snapshot, Gene could picture her small, grimy apartment, the smell of old cabbage seeping out of the walls like a slow, heavy gas. Her father clad in boxers and undershirt, the kind with the thin straps over the shoulders, sprawled in a battered, over-stuffed chair in front of the television. Rolls of flesh folded like smiles beneath the tight, white fabric. Bottle of cheap ouzo at the side of the chair, television turned to some raucous sport. Every now and then he lifts the bottle to his lips and drinks deeply. Her mother's presence is barely felt in the apartment, a ghost-like wisp of aura emanating from the kitchen. It was her, though, that insisted on the remedial classes for Alexis. She rarely insisted on anything, but she clung to this with a quiet fierceness until the old man gave in.

Gene wanted to reach out and shake her, to get some kind of reaction out of her besides that submissive nod. He wanted to get through to her; the need was like a hungry worm gnawing away at his insides. He could *help* her.

There was a dim, remote part of him that realized something was not quite right about that, that he could barely help himself, that the fierceness of his need only pushed back the borders of his own darkness a little ways. But the knowledge was something seen from a great distance, like viewing a map from across a room.

Alexis sat there looking down at the coarse-grained wood of the desk, scrawled and scarred with graffiti in a layered archaeology. LUIS AND DONNA 4 EVVER 83. NIXON SUCKS. GO PHILLIES. JASON 71. FUCK THIS PLACE. The silence between them stretched thinner and thinner, pulled out into a fine, trembling line that Gene finally snapped.

"Well, you just try and work a little harder and we'll see how you do on the next practice test."

She nodded. "Okay." She gathered her books, got up, and hurried out of the room. Gene sat there for a long time, looking at the closed door. Every now and then, a shape moved across the frame of frosted glass, blurred and indistinct.

He'd failed. It filled him like a dark cloud, seeping into all the hidden parts of him. He'd failed. The sun coming in through the high windows was senseless, the blue sky fouled and without mercy.

He took the long way home, driving slowly through the narrow, cobbled streets of the warehouse district. He parked in front of Three Chimes Grocery and Liquors and got out. It wasn't a conscious decision. All of a sudden, there he was, just like that.

A man and a woman stood in front of the store, off to the side of the entrance. They were definitely street – their clothing was very dirty, hanging from their thin bodies in loose folds. The color seemed to have been leached out of their skin, faded from brown to a kind of dull grey. He couldn't tell if that was its actual color or a patina of street dirt. Gene walked up to the window on the other side of the door from them and looked in. Row after row of gleaming bottles. They almost glowed with their own inner light, standing there like toy soldiers under the cheap fluorescents.

The woman walked up to him. She had a box of Bess Eaton donuts cradled in one hand and her mouth was full. More than full, it was jammed with greasy, sugary dough, two or three of the things stuffed in there. Crumbs clung to her lips and chin and when she spoke, she sprayed bits of half-chewed donut in his face. Distantly, he noticed that she had no teeth. He couldn't understand a word she said.

"Excuse me?" he asked, backing away a bit.

She said something again, spraying him with more bits of dough and spittle. It sounded like, "Do you want to buy a blow job for ten dollars?"

He looked closely at her face. Her eyes were black and depthless, and he felt like he could enter that darkness and follow it, sliding down a dark, black-glass tunnel to some light at the end, some bright source. Her eyes seemed to grow

85

larger and for a second all he could see was their dark, shiny surface.

With an effort, he shook his head. "I don't think so." Her partner stood about ten feet behind her, watching silently. "Excuse me," Gene said, and shouldered his way past her into the store. The proprietor looked up suspiciously, then relaxed when he saw Gene. I'm the right color, Gene thought.

He picked up a hand basket from a pile near the door. He grabbed a box of Triscuits, some jack cheese, a couple of cans of Campbell's Chunky Chicken, a package of four rolls of toilet paper, a six-pack of Budweiser, a pint of Jack. Just like that.

It seemed like there were two of him there in the store, one going through the motions of walking up and down the aisles, taking items off the shelf, dropping them in the basket. The other Gene hovered above the street outside, looking down into the store as into cutaway diorama, this moment a study in miniature. *No*, mutely screaming. *No*.

Gene's fingers trembled slightly as he pulled the worn bills out of his wallet. The proprietor didn't even blink. *How could he not know?*

The man slipped bills and coins out of the register in quick, brisk motions and handed Gene his change. "Thanks. Have a good day."

"Right, thanks." Gene wadded the money into a ball and stuffed it into his pocket. He grabbed the bag and walked out the door into the street. The man and woman were gone.

Driving home, he could sense the bottles of beer in the paper bag next to him on the seat, cold, sweating condensate. Waiting.

His apartment was like an oven. Gene put the bag on the kitchen counter and opened some windows. It was almost sunset; the sky in the west was streaked with red and gold clouds. It was so beautiful it actually hurt, a physical ache right between his eyes.

He stood next to the sink. The bottle of Jack was

there in front of him, the seal unbroken. He'd removed the bottles of Bud from their carton and arranged them in a row next to the Jack.

It would be easy, he thought. So easy. Just twist the caps off one by one and pour it all down the sink. Just pour it all down.

He twisted the top off the Jack and raised it to his lips. The raw smell was like a gripping hand around his heart and he closed his eyes and drank. He barely felt it going down; when he opened his eyes again the bottle was a third gone. Then it hit him, like taking a tight turn in a fast car, the rush blossoming in his stomach, his chest, rising up through him.

"Home." The single unbidden word escaped his lips as barely a whisper, yet it echoed there in the silence of the twilight kitchen.

CHAPTER NINE

Ariel had dozed off while Maggie was reading and sat in the chair next to her, curled in a ball, breathing deeply. Maggie looked at her small, expressive face, like a miniature version of her own with all the hard edges rounded off, and felt a hot tightness rise in her chest.

She's so vulnerable, Maggie thought. She doesn't deserve this mess.

She looked at Gene, at the shell of him. The machines hummed and beeped in a parody of reassurance. Maggie closed her eyes. *Let me know you're there. Anything. Let me know you're there so I'll know how to feel.*

She'd been feeling *something* since the accident, some sort of connection with him, but it was pre-verbal, her consciousness responding in a kind of tropism towards their mutual history. Somewhere in the back of her mind, she had an awareness of past events unrolling, home movies flickering against the screen of her cortex, the memory of them like the memory of a dream an hour after waking. And it wasn't always her at the center of things.

What a co', Maggie thought. Seeing someone *else's* life flash before your eyes.

She looked at Gene again. He could be anybody beneath the swaddling.

It was five after three. One of Gene's doctors was supposed to come by at three to talk to her. She hated the way doctors were in places like this. Guardians of wisdom. They hoarded their knowledge, doled it out in tiny packages as if they were protecting you from the full power of it. Maggie suspected they knew a lot less than they pretended to. She could imagine them sitting around in some doctor's lounge, or wherever they hung out when they weren't walking briskly down the tiled halls or standing around a bed with a clipboard in their hands, making rude jokes about their patients' infirmities. She'd heard one doctor talk at her AA meetings a few times and his gallows humor was pretty frightening.

At twenty after, a young man dressed in surgical greens, stethoscope dangling around his neck like a talisman, walked briskly into the room. He was a different one than the day before.

Interchangeable, she thought.

"Mrs. Lambent?" he said loudly.

She put her finger to her lips and nodded in Ariel's direction. "Can we talk in the hall?"

He nodded curtly, then glanced at the swaddled figure in the bed as if to remind himself that Gene was the subject of their conversation.

He seemed very uncomfortable and hurried, as if this business of actual contact with people's trouble and grief was something to be walked through as quickly as possible.

"Your husband is in a deep coma," he said.

"Tell me something I don't know."

He looked at her strangely.

"Sorry," she said. "Go on."

"Your husband is in a deep coma."

Jesus, Maggie thought. I fucked up his little speech and now he has to start from the beginning.

"There's some sign of mental activity, some REM sleep – that's rapid eye movement—"

"I know what it is."

"—but that's not unusual. It's very difficult to estimate the extent of the brain damage. His skull has been badly fractured—" He glanced down at the clipboard he was cradling. "—and there's been some cranial bleeding. We are still observing him very closely, his signs aren't quite stable, but there's no way of telling when, or even if, he's going to wake up. In fact, there are indications that his coma is deepening."

"You mean he could just stay like this, a vegetable?"

"That's an unfortunate term."

"It sure is."

"Look, I'm very sorry, Mrs. Lambent. I wish I could bring you better news, but the truth is, we're in a grey area here. The brain is a very complicated piece of machinery."

She just looked at him. *What is this, fucking auto shop?*

He seemed oblivious. "When it's damaged, it can't really heal itself in the usual way we think of healing. What it tries to do is find new pathways around the damaged area, sort of like the phone company re-routing after a fire or an earthquake. Sometimes it can do that and everything's fine. Sometimes it can't."

"So what you're telling me is that you don't know anything."

He looked at her for a moment, then down at his chart, then back at her. For a second, his persona faltered and he looked just like what he was – a slightly scared, young man trying to cope with uncertainty and stress, wanting to do the right thing in an impossible situation.

"I'm afraid that's about the size of it."

Maggie bit her lip. "Well, I guess that's it, then. What do we do now?"

"There are more tests we can try—"

"Tests."

"—and we'll have a better idea of what's going on. An MRI scan might turn up something. We're not at the point yet where you'll have to make a decision about…support."

"Yet."

He looked at her. "That's right. Yet."

Maggie held out her hand. "Well, thanks, Doctor...?"

He took her hand, pumped it briskly once, and let it go. "Casanova."

"You're kidding."

"No, I'm afraid that's my name."

"Well, Doctor Casanova, keep me posted."

"Of course." He seemed relieved that the conversation was over. He nodded, flashed her a brittle smile, turned, and walked away.

Maggie watched him recede down the hall with a feeling of numb detachment. She felt powerless. It was all in the hands of the doctors, or God, or that Higher Power they kept harping about in the meetings. HP, she'd called it. She had had a lot of trouble with the God thing and that was her own mental shorthand for anything outside her control. Which, right then, felt like nearly everything.

HP, she thought. Hoi polloi. Human pretzel. Hardly present.

She shook her head and looked at Ariel. Just keep it together. Keep it together for her. Honey pie.

Gabe showed up a little while later with a tuna sandwich on wheat bread wrapped in tight, shiny plastic, nestled against a white, cardboard vee.

"Thanks, Gabe." She unwrapped the sandwich and took a bite. It was like biting into a wet, salty sponge.

Ariel stirred, rubbed her eyes, and sat up. "I'm hungry," she announced.

"Here, darlin', take half my sandwich."

It was strange, the trivial domestic exchanges, right in front of Gene's inert body. She kept expecting him to participate somehow, but then he hadn't really done much of that when he *wasn't* in a coma.

"I met this girl in the other wing," Gabe said. "She's got cystic fibrosis, but she seems okay most of the time. Maybe we can have her over sometime?"

"Can she do that?" Maggie asked. "I mean, if she's

91

sick, maybe…"

"It's not contagious or anything. She can get a day pass."

"Well, all right then." Maggie was glad he'd found somebody to connect with. Besides Otto, she reminded herself. Gabe was so serious sometimes, a real loner. It worried her.

"Did the doctor come and talk to you?" Gabe asked.

"Yeah, but they don't really know anything."

They were silent for awhile.

"Does Daddy know we're here?" Ariel asked. There was a gob of tuna salad on her cheek and Maggie wiped it off.

"I don't know, Ari," Maggie said. "I'd like to think so."

"He does, sort of," Gabe said. "But it's like he's dreaming us being here."

Maggie looked at him. "How do you know that?"

Gabe looked startled. "I don't know. It just makes sense."

She looked closely at him. He had dark bruises under his eyes and he looked very pale. *This is stretching him pretty thin*, she thought.

"Well, it does kind of make sense," she said, finally.

There was a note taped to the door of their trailer, folded over with Maggie's name on the outside in a neat, looping script. She pulled it down and opened it up.

Maggie – come see me. Ruby.

Maggie was going to look her up anyway. She'd been wondering what the story was with her and Otto. She opened the door and the three of them went inside.

"Gabe, will you keep an eye on Ari for a while? Take her down to the beach or something. I've got some things I have to do."

Gabe made a face, but she could tell he really didn't mind too much.

"Thanks," she said. "I'll make it up to you."

92

Maggie sank onto the couch while Gabe and Ariel changed into their bathing suits. Just a little over twenty-four hours since we got here, she thought. Everything is so different. She didn't want to even begin to think what they were going to do when they got back to Philly. Maybe just pack up and get out. Give the West Coast a try. Her Mom had told her she could take the back bedroom at her place in Oakland, fix up the basement for Ariel and Gabe.

She shook her head. Christ, he's not even dead yet and I've already written him out of my script.

Gabe and Ariel left with a mingled chorus of "Later, Mom" and "Bye" that seemed to hang in the air after the door had shut. Maggie shook her head again and sighed.

She got up from the couch, walked over to the little sink in the kitchenette to pour herself a glass of water, and froze.

Next to the sink, in a neat row, were six bottles of brown glass, the red and white Budweiser logo pasted across their sides. At the end of the row farthest from the sink, the flat rectangular shape of a half-pint bottle of Jack Daniels. The amber fluid inside looked oily and toxic. She picked up the bottle and held it up to the light streaming in through the slats of the Venetian blinds. Brown in shadow, gold where it filtered the sunlight. She tilted the bottle and the trapped bubble of air moved along its length. The focus of her awareness narrowed down to that clear capsule of air; Gene, the kids, everything else seemed to recede further and further away, as if they were sliding down the wrong end of a telescope. They became theoretical.

She twisted the top off and the smell hit her.

No. I can't do this.

With a cry that felt torn out of her, she threw the bottle against the wall of the trailer. It shattered, leaving a star-shaped stain. She stood leaning against the sink, breathing, feeling her breath fill her and leave her, in and out, in and out.

What the *fuck* was going on?

93

One by one, she twisted the tops off the beer bottles and emptied them into the sink. The yeasty smell stirred vague, ephemeral flickers of memory – driving in Gene's old Valiant on county blacktop bumpy with frost-heave; closing down Hugo's, watching through a kinetic haze of coke and whiskey as Willie wiped down the bar and unplugged the juke; waking up next to Gene in her old apartment on the end of Pleasant Street, fucking joylessly through a blinding hangover headache, trying to push the black borders back a bit.

That was me, she thought. It came almost as a revelation. That was *me*.

CHAPTER TEN

Gabe and Ariel walked across the dunes down to the beach. They stopped at the fast-food shacks on the frontage road and looked around. Paco's Snack Shack had the best selection. There were three men behind the counter in starched white shirts and hair nets, working busily at an array of grills, fryolators, and warmers. They spoke to each other in Spanish; Gabe loved the liquid sound of their voices.

One of the men recognized Gabe from earlier that day and winked at him. It reminded Gabe of the scene with Otto on the beach and he felt a rush of panic. *What's happening to me?* With an effort, he pushed the feeling away. It surprised him a little that he could do that, just push it away, wall it off somewhere, but he was used to doing that.

"You want anything, Ari?" He nodded towards the stand.

Ariel pointed to a mound of shaved ice piled like a snowdrift inside a clear, plastic cube. "Snow-cone."

"Yeah, those are good. What flavor?"

"Cherry!"

The man behind the counter had been following their exchange and, with a metal scoop, he fashioned a large snowball from the mound and pressed it into a paper cone. He held it up and dribbled red syrup onto it from a clear, glass bottle. The red just seemed to disappear into the snow and he kept pouring; suddenly, crimson patches appeared on the sides of the ball, pushing out from inside. It reminded Gabe of the first time he saw Gene in the hospital, just the day before, the way patches of blood seemed to push up from beneath the clean, white bandages.

He fished a crumpled dollar bill from his pocket and gave it to the counter man, who handed the snow-cone to Ariel with a smile and another wink at Gabe.

Ariel took it and licked the syrup dribbling down the sides. She looked so intent, almost feral. Gabe felt a rush of love for her so strong it almost overwhelmed him. His vision blurred for a second and he blinked back tears.

"Good, huh?" he said, with an effort.

"Hmm." There were small red stains on either side of her mouth, like dimples. He wadded a paper napkin, licked the tip, and wiped her cheeks clean.

"C'mon, Ari. Let's walk."

They crossed the road and walked over the last set of dunes before the beach. A wooden footbridge arched over a shallow gully and a row of shoes and sandals were lined up on the near side. The left their flip-flops there and walked across the bridge. The wood was hot under Gabe's bare feet.

Off to the left was the bramble, its silvery green dulled by the bright sun. Gabe could picture his Place deep in the heart of the brush. It would be cool in there, the green-filtered light soft and restful. He looked down at Ariel, still concentrating on her snow-cone. He didn't want to share it. Maybe he'd make it there later.

The beach was crowded near the footbridge, the knots of people becoming more sparse the further away they got. In front of them, a group of men clustered around a volleyball net. Most of them were playing; a few others stood off to the side shouting encouragement, their fists wrapped around cans of beer. It looked like Blood Volleyball to Gabe. The net play was very aggressive – it seemed like every other shot was a spike. There was a lot of grunting, swearing, and diving into the sand.

Gabe recognized a couple of the men from the night

before, on the beach with the shark. He felt blood rush to his cheeks, and he had an urge to lead Ariel away, but then one of the men standing by the net looked at Gabe and nodded in recognition. He reached down into a styrofoam cooler, pulled a can of beer from a six-pack, and tossed it. Gabe caught it with both hands, dropping the rolled-up towel he was holding.

"Thanks," he said. The guy nodded back. Part of Gabe liked the feeling of acceptance and complicity – the killing of the shark had bonded them in some way. But another part of him held back, unsure if this was something he wanted to be a part of.

"Let's go, Ari," Gabe said, picking up the towel and taking her hand. The noises of the game receded behind them as they walked away.

"Is that *beer*?" Ariel asked.

"Yeah, don't tell Mom."

"Yuck. Are you going to drink it?"

"I don't know. Yeah, I guess so."

The dunes here came all the way down to where the beach sloped into the ocean, and they offered pockets of shelter against the wind. Gabe unrolled the towel in a small, shady hollow. The dune rose up above them. Tough wisps of grass clung to the sloping sides, thickening as they neared the top. The sat on the towel with their backs against the sandy slope, cool in the shade.

Gabe pulled the tab on the beer and white foam gushed out. Ariel looked up at him and wrinkled her nose. She got up and ran to the edge of the water, dancing back as a new wave sent a sheet of sea-foam surging up the wet, sloping sand.

Gabe raised the can to his lips and took a sip. It was very bitter, but the bubbles didn't burn as much as they had the night before, and there was a warm, subtle glow that seeped up from his stomach when he swallowed.

The bitter taste, the yeasty smell, called up vague associations, half-sensed flickers of feeling, but they surfaced and washed out of his consciousness before he could get a handle on them.

That smell. It had surrounded him as a child. He remembered snuggling up against his father's scratchy chest, breathing in the fog of beer fumes, the pure, distilled essence of love itself.

It seemed like they never stayed in the same place for very long. Even in the same town, they moved from one apartment to the next with an alarming frequency. Chaos was the normal state of affairs; they were always either packing or unpacking. He had a clear, sudden memory of one of the many places they lived in. They hadn't moved to Philly yet; they were still up in western Massachusetts. They were there for a couple of years, something of a record. It was the bottom floor of an old drafty farmhouse, a few miles outside of Northampton. Gabe remembered the winding drive into town on the back roads; the tunnel of green, leafy trees that pressed down on the car during the summer, the bleak grays, whites, and browns that saturated the landscape during the long winter. The smell of beer permeated the old car and the floor of the back seat was always littered with crumpled cans.

His father was gone most of the time, working in the restaurant or playing music somewhere. There was an old acoustic guitar on a stand in the living room and sometimes his father would sit on the battered couch and coax a few notes out of it, always at odd times, early in the morning or on his way out the door. He sang songs to Gabe, lots of them, but Gabe's favorite was "You Are My Sunshine." He didn't play it like the old-time standard, but bluesy and slow, with lots of bent notes and limber, fluid licks.

During those two years in the farmhouse, he played less and less often and at some point he just stopped. He wasn't playing club dates any more either. Gabe wasn't sure how he knew that but he knew that it was true. That's when the drinking started getting really bad, too. Then, suddenly, he was gone. Philly, his mother said, "for a new job."

Gabe and his mother stayed in the farmhouse for

another few months, but then they moved back into town. His Mom's drinking started getting bad then, too. There was a succession of anonymous men – sounds of revelry filtered through thin walls late at night meant another strange bleary face across the breakfast table the next morning. Sometimes, when they were alone, his mother would take him in her arms and rock him. There was a smell about her that he associated with sadness – alcohol, cigarettes, stale clothing. Then, suddenly, they were in a new place. Philadelphia. Dad was there. Soon, Mom was pregnant with Ariel. Things were okay for awhile.

Dinosaurs taught Gabe to read. He had a collection of glorious picture books – the How and Why Wonder series, the thin, colorful Golden books – their creamy pages alive with drawings of dinosaurs. Some dinosaurs, the leaf-eaters, were stately and full or grace; others seemed a distillation of all that was fierce and random.

Gabe sounded out the phonetics of their exotic, Latin names all by himself, when he was just barely old enough to know his alphabet – *dip-lo-do-cus, bront-a-saur-us*. He remembered sitting cross-legged on the rough, wool rug, his back against the couch, the late afternoon sun coming in low across the snowed-over cornfield in back of the farmhouse. *Al-lo-saur-us, tri-cer-a-tops*.

He had a set of plastic dinosaurs and he would arrange them on the floor in front of him, imagining them moving with fluid grace across the prehistoric Earth, thinking reptile thoughts, shallow and beautiful. Eat. Run. Sleep.

The reading opened up a whole new world for him and soon he was reading everything he could get his hands on. He just about drove Maggie crazy getting her to buy him books and he stashed them all over the house, so he was never too far from one.

"Like an alcoholic with bottles," his mother said.

The idea of just picking up a book, this…*object*, and being instantly transported to another place…it was magic of the most fundamental sort. He burned through Tom Swift and the Hardy Boys and soon, at his father's urging, he was reading Burroughs and Andre Norton. That it came from his Dad as something freely shared almost made up for everything else sometimes. The Norton, in particular, was potent stuff. There was one book he read so many times that the covers fell off and pages began to peel off from the front and back, like the layers of an onion. He practically knew the text by heart, though, so it didn't matter.

The world had been ravaged by nuclear war, civilization torn, trampled, and scattered across the ruined Earth, surviving as small, tribal enclaves. The hero of the story was a young man, a *mutant*. His telepathic powers isolated him from the other people in his mountain village; his only friend in the world was a half-feral bobcat with whom he shared a sort of mind-link. Together they set off to explore the world. They wandered through scorched deserts and blasted cities, encountering strange people and recovering bits and pieces of the old, pre-apocalypse technology. Gabe didn't remember how it ended, but the hero and his feeling of difference, of being set apart, remained in his consciousness for years.

Gabe surged ahead in school. His teachers all praised his intellect, adding a wistful caveat about his "social skills." Gabe's fellow students weren't as happy about his intellect as his teachers were. After losing several bloody, after-school encounters, Gabe realized that, like the hero in the story, he had to learn to hide his differences.

It wasn't a conscious thing, but he sensed that visibility was the best protective coloration and he became the class clown. Something wild raced through him for awhile; once, when the teacher was out of the room for a minute, he and another boy pushed a desk out the window. It smashed on the sidewalk three stories below, narrowly missing an old man walking his dog. Another time, he flushed an M-80 down the toilet in the Boys' Room. The explosion ruined the old pipes and the halls filled with foul-smelling water, closing school for the afternoon.

Often blamed, rarely caught, it seemed like he was always in the principal's office, always in detention, always waiting for his mother to come get him. And it was always her that came, never his father, and she rarely scolded.

He'd established enough of a reputation as a wildling that when he settled down to serious scholarship again, his teachers were delighted, thinking they had won some sort of victory, pulling back a difficult child from the precipice of ruin. His fellow students left him alone now, out of respect or fear. He had few friends.

He closed his eyes and spread his arms out, imagining that he was a great lizard basking in the sun. His thoughts were a simmering stew of images from the last couple of days – Casey, Otto, his Dad – but he tried to quiet them down, tried to get into that reptile brain-state. Basking. The sun resting against his closed eyelids made irregular splotches of yellow and orange that floated across the blackness like white, puffy clouds across an azure sky. The periodic surge of the ocean was the slow beating of the heart of the world. Sleep opened her arms and took him.

Gabe dreamed of Pellucidar.

He was riding across a plain of black, volcanic glass on the back of a lumbering triceratops. Cairns of shiny stones marked the path. The horizon curved up around him on all sides like a bowl, the rim fading into blue-grey haze. The hollow Earth. Directly overhead hung the sun, stationary and mercilessly hot, glaring off the obsidian plain.

He ran his hand down the lizard's flank, feeling the leathery skin. The musky smell of the animal filled his nostrils – a bit like skunk, intense but not unpleasant.

There was a sibilant whisper of air, and the feathered shaft of an arrow appeared in his mount's side. It bellowed loudly and began to run. Gabe grabbed his harness and turned around. Six riders, about a hundred yards behind him, on the backs of man-sized thunder lizards, like miniature tyrannosaurs. They were closing fast, their harnesses swaying back and forth with the monsters' gait. Even at this distance Gabe could tell that the riders were no more human than their mounts.

Another arrow whizzed past him, then another. His mount stumbled and Gabe had to grab on tight to keep from falling. He looked back again. Closer. The shriveled, man-like claws of the thunder-lizards clutched at the air. The savage cries of the riders, high and sharp, carried across the narrowing distance between them.

From above came another, deeper bellow. Gabe looked up. A pterodactyl swooped down, passing over his head and bearing down on the riders, low to the ground. At the juncture of its wings and shoulders sat a man, his long white hair and beard streaming behind him.

Otto.

He had a pistol in his hand and when he was close he began to fire. Two riders went down and the rest rushed back and forth in confusion, like ants whose nest has been disturbed.

Otto made another pass and fired again. Another rider fell. His mount bent down and bit deeply into his stomach. Entrails dangled from its jaws as it raised its head. That was enough. The remaining riders turned around and galloped off across the flat, glassy plain.

Gabe pulled the reins and his mount lumbered to a stop. The pterodactyl glided toward him. At the last minute, it flapped its leathery wings and settled to the ground without a sound, folding its wings around itself like a cloak.

Otto made a beckoning gesture, and Gabe climbed off the broad, flat back of the triceratops. He untied a saddlebag of provisions from the beast's harness, slung it over his shoulder, and walked toward the reptile-bird.

Otto motioned for Gabe to climb up behind him on the creature's back. There was a complicated harness with handholds and footholds. Gabe secured himself and tied down his bag. Without a word, Otto flicked the reins. The pterodactyl unfolded its wings, took a running step, and they were airborne.

The ebony plain fell away beneath them. From this height, Gabe could make out rippling waves in the plain, frozen into place when it cooled from an ocean of molten lava. On the upward-curving horizon, Gabe could see other features – lakes, rivers, the mottled green of jungles and forests.

The pterodactyl flew without a sound, gliding through the still, hot air. Every now and then its great wings would beat, once, twice, then stretch out again to catch the thermals rising up from the desert floor.

Otto's hair streamed behind him in the wind. All Gabe could see of him was his broad back, clad in a blue workshirt. He said something, but the words were lost in the wind.

"What?" Gabe yelled.

Otto turned around. It was a death's-head face that looked at Gabe, sunken eyes, hollow cheeks. *His father.* There was a bloody wound on his forehead and the flesh there looked dented.

"I have to go to the store," it said, in a wheezing caricature of his father's voice.

Gabe jumped back, losing his grip on the harness. He tried to regain a handhold, but he was sliding off the creature's back, tumbling, falling. The wind was a high, keening whistle in his ears and the black, glassy floor of the desert rose up to meet him...

There was a sharp poking at his side. He opened his eyes. Ariel let out a giggle. She squatted next to him, a long, gnarled piece of driftwood in her hand.

"Stop that, Ari." He shook himself, trying to clear his mind of the hold the dream still had.

She giggled and poked him again.

"How long have I been sleeping for?"

Ariel shrugged elaborately. "Not too long, I guess."

"You want to head back?"

103

She shrugged again.

"You don't know much, do you?" he teased.

Again, she shrugged, and let out another giggle.

"Okay, okay," Gabe said. "You're a little pain in the bee-hind, you know that? Let's head back." He wanted to see if Otto was around. He needed to talk.

They walked back along the beach to the footbridge. The volleyball game had dispersed, leaving a wide patch of stirred and scattered sand. There were still people around, sitting on blankets or under umbrellas in clumps of two and three, but not as many as before. Gabe and Ariel retrieved their sandals from the other side of the footbridge and walked across the frontage road and up the dunes to the trailer park.

There was a note in the kitchen.

Back soon – Mom.

The sour smell of beer hung in the air and Gabe felt something drop out of the bottom of his stomach.

She can't be drinking again.

He looked around. Scattered across the counter were six twist-off bottle caps. He looked in the trash. There was a jumble of brown glass; the yeasty odor rose up like smoke.

Great time to lose it, Mom.

Ariel had gravitated to the living room and was playing with one of her stuffed animals. Just above her head Gabe noticed a star-shaped stain that hadn't been there before. As he walked over to it, he saw jagged shards of glass scattered across the floor.

"Careful, Ariel. There's glass all over the place."

He got a broom and a dustbin and swept up most of it. The tattered black-and-white label still clung to the glass, holding several shards together. Jack Daniels. That was Dad's drink; Mom hardly ever touched the stuff, even before she went on the wagon.

He *really* needed to talk to Otto. He wasn't even sure why, exactly. He felt like he was in a car skidding on black, winter ice. Spinning out. There was just too much stuff going on.

He tossed the glass into the trash and looked back at Ariel. She was looking at him with wide eyes.

"Why don't you see what's on the tube, Ari? I have to do a couple of things and I'll come right back."

She nodded, a little hesitantly.

"You'll be okay?"

She nodded again, more sure this time.

"Okay. I'll be back."

Mary was sitting in a lawn chair in front of the Airstream, looking off toward the ocean. She turned toward Gabe as he approached.

"Hi," Gabe said. "Is Otto around?"

She looked at him strangely for a moment, then nodded her head in the direction of the trailer.

"Inside."

"Uh, thanks."

Gabe walked up the steps and knocked gently on the door. There was no answer. He pushed it open and stepped inside. There was nobody in the living room, but he heard noises coming from the back bedroom. He was about to call out, but something about the sounds made him stop. He walked a few more steps into the living room.

The bedroom door was open. Otto lay on the bed with a young girl, maybe Casey's age or a little older. Her tan legs were wrapped around his pale back, her hands tangled in his long, white hair. Otto moved against her, pushing himself into her. Her eyes were closed and her face was twisted into a grimace. Each time Otto ground against her, it forced a small gasp out from between her lips.

Gabe stood there for what seemed like a long time – he couldn't take his eyes away. Then, with a start, he backed quietly to the door and let himself out.

Mary looked up at him as he left the trailer and he looked back at her. He wanted to say something to her, but he didn't know what. She looked off again toward the distant horizon and Gabe walked back home along the sandy path, the row of trailers and vacant sites to his right and the ocean to his left, a flat plain of depthless, blue glass.

CHAPTER ELEVEN

The opening was in the old train station on Main Street in downtown Northampton. Some rich yuppie from Boston had bought the place, greased some palms in City Hall to get it declared as a historical landmark, and turned it into an art gallery. Gene used to play guitar in The Scientific Americans with Peter Moses, the brother of the guy whose work was being shown, so he managed to weasel himself an invitation, even though he'd gotten fired from the band for showing up too drunk to play too many times and wasn't on very good terms with any of them.

The first thing he looked for when he walked into the place was the bar. It was at the far end of the room, behind what used to be the ticket windows. There were tables loaded with food – celery and carrots stacked like miniature cords of wood, bowls of generic, white dip, mountains of chicken wings and meatballs in silver warming trays that infused the room with the faint smell of Sterno. A piano player crouched over a Fender Rhodes next to the bar, sending light, perky jazz chords echoing into the room. The walls and floor were partly marble and it sounded like he was playing in a bathroom the size of a football field. Steve, the artist, was standing in front of a wooden sculpture of a troll, holding forth to a small crowd of people, mostly undergraduate women from Smith. An affected air of bohemian elegance hovered around them like a mist of pheromones.

Gene saw Peter standing near one of the food tables with a paper plate balanced in one hand and a glass of wine in the other. Peter looked up and saw him at the same time, and a quick frown flitted across his face before he smiled and nodded. Gene waved, grabbed a glass of white wine from one of the uniformed waiters circulating about the room, and made his way along the walls, pretending to look at the artwork.

He didn't think it was very good, actually. Smarmy, tedious woodcuts of elves, fairies, and unicorns, the occasional oil painting of same, a few nice landscapes with the colors rendered in dreamy pastels. Steve had recently done the illustrations for a coffee-table sized edition of *The Hobbit* and his career was really starting to fly. Gene had seen the book and thought it was vulgar and insipid.

He made his way over to the bar, not so quickly as to attract attention to himself. As he pushed his way through the crowd, he saw a woman standing next to the ticket window, gazing out at the room over the rim of the glass she held up to her lips. She was very pretty – big, sad eyes with a hint of bruised shadow under them, long, brown hair cascading in ringlets over her shoulders like a waterfall. The second he saw her, Gene knew she was a drunk. He'd experienced it before, that almost telepathic connection between people who belonged to the same club.

She saw him looking at her and raised her glass, the corners of her mouth turned up slightly in an enigmatic smile. He got a Jack-on-the-rocks from the uniformed bartender behind the ticket window and stood a few feet away from her, looking out at the room. He could sense her, though, at the periphery of his vision. He looked over at her, trying to be surreptitious, and she was looking right at him. He shrugged and smiled, and walked up to her.

"Hi. How you doing? I'm Gene."

"Maggie," she said, and held out her hand. Gene took it and gave it a mock gentlemanly shake. Her grip was strong and her hand felt smooth and cool.

"You look really familiar," she said, her dark eyebrows slanting down in a severe frown that was completely endearing. "Do you play in a band around here or something?"

"Yeah. I used to be in the Scientific Americans." Her eyebrows rose in recognition. "Not any more, though – we had creative differences and I quit."

She gave him a wry look. "Yeah, I remember now. I saw you fall off the stage at Rahar's last year. You were pretty hammered."

Gene felt blood rise to his cheeks.

"And now you're blushing. Me and my big mouth. I'm sorry."

She didn't seem very sorry, though – she looked like she was enjoying herself.

"So where do you know Steve from?" Gene asked, trying to steer the conversation into safer waters.

"I'm fucking him." Gene nearly choked on his drink. "He's pretending he doesn't know me, though, 'cause he wants to put on a show for his little Smith bitches. I don't give a shit – he's not the only piece of ass in town either. You?"

This is going from bad to worse, Gene thought. "Um, his brother Peter plays drums in the Sci-Ams. I've known the family for awhile."

She nodded. "You ever meet the Rev?" Steve and Peter's father was the minister at the First Episcopal Church of Northampton.

"Yeah, the Reverend Moses. Great name – he sounds like somebody from a J.P. Donleavy book."

"He's a trip, isn't he? I was over there last Christmas. Big, old house up on Pine Street – I'm sure you've been there. We were sitting around the fireplace drinking eggnog and getting hammered and I asked the Rev how many angels could dance on the head of a pin. 'Really,' I said. 'I'm completely serious. How many?' He gives me this *grave* look, takes a sip of eggnog, and says, 'Well, Maggie, I'm not a medievalist. I can't tell you that. You'll have to ask a medievalist.' Dead silence for about five seconds, then he cracks up and knock back the rest of the 'nog." She shook her head. "Never kid a kidder."

Gene nodded, trying to stretch his facial muscles into a facsimile of a relaxed, confident grin. Maggie threw him off completely, though. He felt unbalanced and awkward, out of equilibrium. He looked down at his glass and realized it was empty.

"What are you drinking?" he asked.

"Jack Daniels and ice."

Bingo. Synchronicity. "Excellent choice."

He got another couple of drinks from the guy behind the ticket window and brought them back to where Maggie was standing. They stood there in silence, looking out at the party. Gene felt like they were in a bubble, separated from the rest of the room by a thin, transparent membrane. He wondered if she felt it too.

He was about to say something to her, really put his foot in it, when the door at the far end of the room opened and Tim Gibbon walked in.

"Fuck me with a sharp stick," Gene said.

"Excuse me?" Maggie asked, with a slightly mocking grin.

He nodded towards Tim, who was already glad-handing his way across the room. "I hate that son of a bitch." Tim was the other guitarist in the Scientific Americans, and Gene was sure he'd been the primary architect in getting him fired.

He still felt his cheeks burn when he thought about it. He'd walked into the Music Source one morning, a guitar and electronic gizmo shop where Luther, the synth player, worked. It was about a half-hour before the store was supposed to open, and the whole band was hanging out near the back of the store, sitting on Fender amp shipping boxes. This was a pretty common scene – the store served as a meeting place for the band and there was a nice, little eight-track studio in the basement that they had used to work up some demo tapes. But as soon as he walked into the store, Gene knew that something was wrong. Everyone stopped talking when he came in the door, and as he walked to the back of the shop, the feeling of dread intensified.

"Hi, guys," he said. Nobody met his eyes. Craig, who he'd started the band with two years back and who was probably his closest friend among them, looked like he wanted to say something, but Tim beat him to it.

"We won't be needing your services any longer, Gene."

It felt like a physical blow. Gene backed up a step and bumped into a shipping crate. He reached out and steadied himself. "What the fuck?"

He looked at Craig, but Craig was looking down at the floor. The only person who would meet his eyes was Tim, who looked back at him with a cold, level gaze.

"Just like that?"

"That's right," Tim said. "Just like that. You've got a drinking problem and you're not going to take us down with you."

Gene couldn't believe what he was hearing – Tim was a notorious lush himself. "Fuck you, Tim. Just 'cause you're sober this week you've got a stick up your ass. Six months ago you rolled the fucking van after you scored some Dilaudid from that club owner in Palmer, remember? Craig, what is this bullshit? We started this thing together…"

Craig looked at him finally. "I'm sorry, Gene. We've talked it over and it's a done deal. We've already had two rehearsals without you and I gotta tell you that the sound is a lot tighter." He paused. "If it means anything to you, I tried to stick up for you, but I got voted down. I'm sorry, man."

"Hey, Earth to Gene," Maggie said, putting her hand on his arm. "You all right?"

"Yeah, I'm fine." He took a big sip of Jack. It burned on the way down, filling him with heat. "I just really hate that guy."

111

"Gibbon?" she said. "Yeah, I know him, sort of. He's a pretty good guitar player but he can't sing for shit." She looked up at him and grinned. It put a demented light in her eyes that Gene really liked. She handed Gene her drink. "Hold this."

She walked up to the steam tables, took a paper plate from the stack, and heaped it high with Swedish meatballs and chicken wings, smothered in plenty of sauce. Gene had an idea what she was up to, but he couldn't believe it.

It was like watching an auto accident unfold in slow motion. Maggie worked her way through the crowd, balancing the heaping plate in one hand. When she was right in front of Tim, she turned to say something to the person on her left, tripped, and spilled the plate down the front of Tim's black suede jacket. Gene could see a circle of shocked silence form around them. Maggie affected a look of horror and began brushing at the Rorschach of gravy and bits of food, apologizing profusely. Tim pushed her away, pulled his jacket off, and stalked away holding it out at arm's length. Maggie looked over at Gene and shrugged, smiling.

Oh, man, I'm in love, Gene thought.

Maggie wove through the crowd back to Gene's side. She passed near Steve and he gave her a dirty look. Gene saw Tim leaving by the front door.

"Well, that was amusing," she said.

Gene laughed. "It sure was. I can't believe you did that."

"We aim to please," she said. "Give me back my drink."

The pianist was playing a dreadful samba arrangement of 'Up, Up, and Away.' Gene found himself tapping his foot in time to it and stopped. He looked at Maggie. "You want to blow this taco stand?"

"Sure," she said. "What did you have in mind?"

"Oh, I don't know. Maybe we could go down to Hugo's, put a bunch of quarters in the juke, lock ourselves in the bathroom, and do lines until our eyes bleed."

Maggie's eyebrow rose. "You got any coke?"

"Well, no…"

She punched him on the arm. "Asshole. Why don't we just grab a few six-packs from the stash here and head up to the railroad tracks? It's warm enough out tonight."

"Grab them from where?"

"Look behind the ticket window there. They have about ten cases of Beck's stacked up right near the door. I'll keep him occupied and you slip in the back and grab a case."

He looked at her. She was doing that eyebrow thing again, one of them level, the other slanted down at a severe angle. *This woman is truly out of her fucking mind.* "If we wind up in jail tonight, I'll be really sad," Gene said. "Besides, my partner will kill me – I'm supposed to open the restaurant tomorrow."

"Hey, I thought you were a musician. You have a real job?" She affected a mock frown. "I'm disappointed."

"Yeah, I own part of Captain Howdy's, along with my partner Eric and some mysterious friends of his from New York who I've never met. My grandmother left me some money when she died last year and I thought I ought to invest in my future."

"I've been there. The stuffed shrimp are pretty good." She wrinkled her nose. "You should do something about that name, though. It really sucks."

"Tell me about it. It's the mysterious New York partners – they own fifty-one per cent of the place and they insisted. Eric wanted to call it Hog Heaven, which wasn"t a whole lot better. My idea was Sid and Nancy's, which has a nice, homey ring to it if you don't know any better, but Eric blew the whistle on me. Captain Howdy's isn't so bad if you never think about it. I get this weird feeling of, like, dis-association, though, when I see the ads in the *Gazette*. I'm thinking, 'I can't believe that's me.' "

The pianist segued from 'Up, Up, and Away' to 'Feelings.'

"That's it," Gene said. "We really have to get the fuck

out of here. You distract the guy and I'll grab the beer. I'll meet you in the parking lot – I've got this shitbox Valiant. It's pretty hard to miss."

She gave him a mock salute. "Aye, aye, skipper. Whither thou goest."

He looked quickly at her and, for a weird fraction of a second, her face looked completely familiar, every line and shadow of it, like they had known each other for years. He could tell that she felt something too. Her mouth sort of opened a little wider and her eyes had a look to them like she was seeing something far away suddenly get closer. Their eyes held for a second longer, then Gene turned away and began to work his way through the crowd to the door.

CHAPTER TWELVE

Ruby's trailer was surrounded by an array of potted flowers and herbs, a border of life and color that seemed to encircle the squat, boxy structure with a protective aura. Paths made from small, flat stones wound through the garden. Here and there, orderly collections of sculptures and ceramic bowls gave the appearance of altars.

The door was decorated with a simple wreath – a bundle of twigs curved into a rough circle, bound with vine. Maggie walked up to the door, stepped onto the cinderblock that served as a doorstep, and knocked.

"It's open." Maggie heard a muffled voice from somewhere inside.

She turned the knob and pushed open the door. The inside of the trailer wasn't much different than hers – small kitchenette, living area, short corridor leading to a bedroom Maggie knew would be not much bigger than a phone booth – but colorful tapestries hanging from the walls gave the place a warm, cozy feel. The blinds were drawn and candles burned on every available surface, suffusing the room with a warm, flickering glow.

Ruby was sitting at a card table in front of the propane stove, her hands on either side of a large glass bowl filled with water. She beckoned Maggie over to the other chair.

"Girl, you look like you've just seen a ghost," Ruby

said, when Maggie approached. "What's going on?"

Maggie sat down. She nodded in the direction of the bowl. "What's that for?"

Ruby smiled. "Water-gazing. It's a kind of meditation technique. You focus your attention on the water and pretty soon you start...seeing things. It's pretty trippy, actually. You want to give it a try?"

Maggie laughed abruptly, almost a cough. "Shit, I'm already seeing things. I think I'm going crazy."

"Tell me about it."

Maggie shook her head. "I don't know where to begin."

Ruby said nothing, her features composed in an open, neutral expression. Reflections from the candles in the room flickered in her eyeglasses.

"I...used to drink," Maggie said, after a while. "A lot. It's been about four years since I quit, and things have gotten a lot better. But since the accident – Jesus, I can't believe it was just yesterday." She shook her head. "Since then, I've been...*thinking* about it a lot. No, it's more than that. And it's not just the drinking. It's Gene, too, our life together. I feel connected to him in a way I never did before." She paused. "I feel like he's *talking* to me – not in words, but like he's broadcasting something on some channel and I'm picking up pieces of it. I don't even know if it's directed at me. I'm just *receiving*, you know?"

Ruby nodded.

"Yesterday, coming home from the hospital, I'd been thinking about Gene and all of a sudden I was *loaded*. Not a drop in over four years and I was completely smashed. It was a good thing I got pulled over or I would've wrapped the car around a telephone pole."

"You got pulled over?" Ruby asked. "By a cop?"

Maggie laughed wryly. "Yeah, it was almost funny, actually. As soon as I saw the lights in my rear-view mirror, I was fine again. I got halfway through my B.A. and he sent me home."

"B.A.?"

"Backwards alphabet."

Ruby smiled. "You sound like you've done that before."

"Yeah, well, like I said, I used to drink." She was quiet for a few moments. In the light from the candles, it seemed like shadowy shapes were moving in the water-bowl.

"I hit a dog this morning," she continued, finally. "On the way to the hospital. I stopped and went out in the bushes to look for it and I couldn't find it anywhere. I don't know what the connection to Gene is, but I could *feel* him, like he was right nearby. We used to go on these drives together, road trips up the back roads in his drunkmobile, this car he had that looked like he'd kept it in long-term parking at the Beirut airport. We'd step out for breakfast in North-ampton, just a five minute drive down to the Friendly's on South Main, and twelve hours later we're in Vermont or Martha's Vineyard or some damn place, drunk, broke, out of gas."

Maggie laughed again. It had a brittle edge to it and the corners of her eyes hurt. "He was such a fucking idiot, you know?" A small, detached part of her noted her use of the past tense. Ruby handed her a soft, green handkerchief and she wiped her eyes and nose.

"Thanks. One time, he picked up these lobster traps somewhere. He wouldn't tell me where he got them – he must've ripped them off the back of a truck or something. He was like a little kid. He kept saying, 'What we don't sell, we'll eat. What we don't sell we'll eat.'

"So, he rents a boat up near Seabrook and he goes out into the harbor in the middle of the night and drops them off, one by one. The only problem was, he was stoned on acid and Wild Turkey and he forgot to tie buoys to the things..."

"Buoys," Ruby repeated, looking confused for a moment. Then her eyes lit up and she laughed. "I guess that would be kind of important, huh?"

"Yeah. I'll never forget the expression on his face when I pointed that out to him. It was priceless. His mouth sort of hung open and he looked really sad..."

For a second, the shadows in the water bowl seemed to take on the shape of a face – two smudges for eyes, a curved fold of darkness for the mouth.

"I..." Maggie looked at Ruby and shrugged. "I really loved him, you know? It was impossible with him, just fucking doomed, but he wasn't a *bad* person. He wasn't stupid either – he did a couple of years at U. Mass before he dropped out, and I've been around enough musicians to know that they're smart in the same kind of way that mathematicians are smart. The good ones, anyway. But there was something about him that was just, I don't know, just broken."

"Well, he's not dead yet, is he?"

"Well, no. I don't know. No..." Maggie shook her head again. "But I feel like he's gone. And I feel like what I need to do is...get free, take care of myself and my kids, get...disentangled." She took a deep breath. "Today, I came home and there was a neat, little row of beer bottles and pint of Jack lined up next to the sink. I don't know what the fuck is going on – I know I didn't buy them. I don't *think* so, anyway..."

"What did you do?"

"I poured them into the sink, for Christ's sake. That's all I need now, is to start drinking again. I'll tell you something, though, the way the glass on the bottles was kind of fogged over with a few drops beading on the surface, it looked so good I could almost taste it. And when I poured it into the sink, the smell alone almost got me high..."

Neither of them said anything for awhile. The silence rested between them like something warm and living.

"You probably think I'm out of my mind," Maggie said, finally.

Ruby shook her head slowly, smiling. "No. I really don't. I think you're very sane and you know exactly what you need to do. You're not sure how to do it, but I can't tell you that either – you got to find your own path."

"It's finding *me* right now, I think. I'm just putting one foot in front of the other. I don't have much choice."

"Honey, it's *always* one foot in front of the other. And you always have choices."

"Maybe," Maggie said. "Maybe." She paused. "So what's the story with this Otto guy?"

"I think he's an *orisha*."

"Oh. Um, okay…" Great, she thought. Another New Age spaceball.

Ruby held up her hand. "Patience. You know that Higher Power stuff you were talking about earlier?"

Maggie nodded.

"In the Yoruba tradition of Africa, there's a word for it – *da*. It's a sort of life force, the glue that holds the Universe together, and it runs through…everything. *Da* is manifest in humans as *ashe*. If you think of *da* as coming from up there somewhere…" She raised her hand toward the ceiling. "*Ashe* wells up from inside you, from your spirit." She placed her hand over her heart. "If *da* is energy, then *ashe* is power. An *orisha* is…sort of a particular personification of *ashe*. There are hundreds of them, but there are a few that are really important. They can be put to work for human affairs if they're properly honored, and sometimes they show up as humans to teach us or help us."

It sounded like bullshit mumbo-jumbo to Maggie, but when you got right down to it, it wasn't any worse than things she'd heard in AA meetings. *Our Father who art in Heaven.* The only father Maggie knew beat the shit out of her and her mother every chance he got and drank himself into an early grave, and if there *was* a Heaven he for damn sure wasn't up there.

Ruby noticed the expression on her face and stopped. "You can take this any way you want, you know," she said. "This is my own spiritual tradition and I'm not trying to shove it down your throat. If you don't believe that there's literal truth in what I'm telling you, that's fine – I'm never really sure myself where symbol and archetype end and the thing itself begins. But there's also value in it as metaphor, as another way to look at the world. Just be open to it."

The room was very quiet. Again, in the inconstant candlelight, Maggie could see shadowy shapes shifting about in the bowl of water in front of Ruby. Maybe there was something here for her; she didn't know. She looked up. She liked Ruby's face, warm and open, laugh-lines around the eyes along with that ineffable imprint you see on people that speaks of hard times lived through and left behind.

Maggie nodded. "So do you know him from somewhere?"

"I don't exactly know him, but I know who he is. *Ellegua.* The man at the crossroads, the trickster. Some Native American traditions call him Coyote."

"What does he want?"

Ruby laughed. "I couldn't tell you that. And he's got his crazy wife with him and I don't know what that's about either. But you've got his attention, I know that, you and your family. And I don't know if that's a good thing or not. Ellegua throws you a growth opportunity, you better check to see your insurance is paid up." She frowned. "I think he's particularly interested in your Gabe. He's right at the cusp, you know, between boyhood and manhood. He'd have enough to handle right now even without his Daddy in the hospital. Ellegua smells change on the wind the way a hyena smells death – it's what sustains him." She paused. "You have to stay out of it, though. Gabe's got to deal with this himself, in his own way. You can't do that for him."

Maggie shook her head. "Oh, man, I just can't hear that." She felt that sharp ache around the corners of her eyes again and this time she just let it happen. Wetness rolled down her cheeks and the candles in the room became prismatic stars.

She forced herself to breathe slowly and deeply, in and out. She focused her attention on the water bowl. Its surface was a glistening skin and the reflected candlelight rested there, flattened, stretched, exploded into gold ripples by stray vibrations. Beneath the skin shadows moved, suggesting vague shapes and changing before she could identify them. She tried to concentrate, to slow the kaleidoscopic shape-shifting, and a scene began to resolve itself. The shadows fled to the corners of the bowl, there taking on vague human shapes. The clear space in the center of the bowl coalesced into the shape of a long, high-ceilinged room. She heard a buzzing murmur of voices, low, like a wild beehive in the deep woods. There was music…

Maggie looked up at Ruby with a feeling of dislocation. She didn't know how much time had passed. "I was such an asshole," she said, and the shadows in the water bowl collapsed in upon themselves and vanished.

"Excuse me?" Ruby asked.

Maggie shook her head and gestured weakly at the bowl. "I was just…remembering something. When Gene and I first met. I was such a jerk. Very young and full of myself. Scared shitless of anything that even resembled connection. But there was something real between us, in spite of all the posing, all the drinking and using we did."

"I believe that," Ruby said. "But if you don't mind my asking, what's that connection about for you now, though?"

Maggie shook her head again. "I don't know. I guess that's what I need to figure out."

"You'll do fine," Ruby said. "If you need anything, you let me know."

"Thanks."

They were silent for awhile. Finally, Maggie pushed back her chair and got up.

"I should get going," she said.

Ruby walked up to her and put her arms around her. Maggie tensed for a minute, then returned the embrace. Ruby's body seemed a couple of degrees warmer than normal and she smelled faintly of sage. Maggie pulled back and looked at her.

"Thanks," she said again. "I'll talk to you soon." She opened the door, letting in a wave of late afternoon heat. The sun was bright and it took a minute for her eyes to adjust. She walked back to her trailer blinking back purple afterimages.

Ariel was sitting in front of the television watching cartoons. On the wall above her, the star-shaped stain stared at Maggie like an accusing eye.

"Hey, baby," Maggie said. "What's up?"

Ariel looked up, smiling. "Road Runner," she said.

"Where's your brother?"

Ariel shrugged, an exaggerated gesture that reminded Maggie of Gene.

"Did he say when he'd be back?"

Another shrug, then Ariel turned back to the television. Coyote was taking apart a crate labeled ACME Catapult. He assembled the thing, following a set of instructions that kept unfolding until it trailed behind him like another tail. Finally, it was complete. Coyote turned a wheel that pulled a complicated system of levers and springs until the basket of the catapult was cocked back as far as it would go. Suddenly, the Road Runner appeared behind him, quivering with the sudden stop. The bird said "Beep-beep" into Coyote's ear and the catapult released, flinging him into the sky. Ariel shrieked with delight as Coyote slammed into a cliff, flattening into a disc crowned with two sad eyes that blinked as it slid down the cliff face.

Maggie tore her eyes away. Coyote, huh? She had a sudden memory of waking up early as a child, before anyone else was up and the daylight was nothing more than a purple bruise coloring the sky over hills to the East. Her father's snores fluttered through the little house; the living room would be cluttered with empty bottles and cans, strewn across the carpet like casualties from a battle. She would turn on the tiny black and white set, the volume squeezed down to just above a whisper, and watch whatever she could find. If she was up early enough, she could catch Modern Farmer at six and Crusader Rabbit at six-thirty. The solitude was delicious.

122

It was the only time in that house that she felt really comfortable and safe, when she knew her father was sleeping the sleep of the dead drunk.

She felt restless and off-balance – there was still a trace of whiskey smell in the close air of the trailer, and it tugged at the corners of her consciousness. She wondered where Gabe was, a little angry that he had just left Ariel alone. He was usually pretty good about stuff like that – he took on responsibilities with a quiet gravity. She worried again that he wasn't getting much of a childhood, but there wasn't much she could do about it at this point except cut him some slack every now and then, pull back hard when he took too much, let him know he was loved.

She wondered what was going on with Otto. She didn't buy Ruby's mumbo-jumbo about *orishas* – it sounded like just another bullshit New Age riff. She'd heard a lot of them. Lost souls trying to decode the mystery of the world. But she didn't *not* buy it either. There'd just been too much weirdness going on lately. That fucking dog, the bottles.

She could *feel* Gene, reaching out to her from his damaged sleep. Hovering. Everybody was hovering. Gene, on the cusp between life and death. Gabe, between childhood and adolescence. Herself too, although she couldn't say what was ahead, and she didn't know any more what was behind. She just knew she was on the verge.

"Mommy?" Ariel asked.

Maggie realized she had just been standing there staring off into space. Maggie shook her head. "Yes, baby?"

"Are you drinking again?"

She looked at Ariel. Her little face was composed in a mask of concentration and concern. Maggie sat down on the floor next to her and put her arms around her.

"No, baby. Never."

They rocked together for a while, and the sounds from the television, a babble of explosions and frantic music, merged into a kind of cushion above which they floated. Hovering.

Otto, Maggie thought. Or whatever the hell his name is. We're going to have to have a talk.

"I have to go out again, Ari," she said. "Just next door. Will you be all right?"

Ariel's features compressed in an expression of scorn. "Of course I'll be all right."

Maggie laughed and kissed her on the cheek. "Sorry, baby. If Gabe comes back, tell him not to go anywhere."

The old Airstream threw back rippling reflections of the sky, the sun a bright, irregular blob of fire on its curved side. As Maggie walked towards it, she felt increasingly nervous. She had no idea what she was going to say. Leave my son alone. Get out of our lives. It sounded melodramatic and silly. All she knew for sure was that the man had befriended her son, Ruby's warnings and her own maternal radar notwithstanding. She should at least give him the benefit of the doubt. She stopped and took a deep breath. Just a neighborly visit.

Around the side of the Airstream, a pair of empty lawn chairs faced the ocean. As she approached the door, she could hear television babble coming from inside.

She knocked sharply. A woman answered the door. She was very beautiful, and immediately Maggie felt that combination of attraction, insecurity, and resentment she sometimes felt around very good-looking women. A closer look, though, something about the eyes, revealed that she was *old*. Just how old, Maggie couldn't tell.

The woman nodded as if she had been expecting Maggie. "Come on in," she said. "We're watching Jeopardy." She turned around to go back inside, then turned back to Maggie. She leaned close and Maggie smelled seaweed, whiskey, copper. "If you fuck him I'll break your arms," she said.

I guess this is the crazy wife, Maggie thought. A part of her withered; she debated for an instant turning around and going back to her trailer. She was shocked at her fragility and mentally stiffened her back.

"Right. Whatever," she said, and followed the woman inside. Otto was sitting on a plaid couch in front of an enormous color television. An unlit cigar stub was jammed into his beard and he had his hand buried in a large bowl of popcorn.

"Who was...Pontius Pilate," said one of the Jeopardy contestants, a frumpy looking housewife with rhinestone encrusted glasses clinging to her face like a crab.

"*Barrabas*, you fucking twit," Otto roared. "*Barrabas*." His deep voice resonated in the little room.

A buzzer sounded, a deep raspberry encoding the very essence of mockery. "I'm sorry," Alex said. "Released instead of Jesus. The thief released instead of Jesus."

The other two contestants slapped their bells almost simultaneously, but the nerdy looking young guy in the conservative suit had a slight edge.

"Who was...Barrabas."

"Thank you," Otto said, clicking off the television with the remote. "Jesus fucking Christ." He turned to Maggie and winked. "If you'll pardon the expression. I'm glad you came by. How are you doing? You've met Mary."

"Well, sort of. Let's just say she introduced herself."

Mary pointed the remote at the television and turned the volume up. The Jeopardy theme played at a deafening volume. The camera panned across the three contestants, scribbling furiously on oversized slates.

"Maybe we better go outside," Otto said to Maggie. His voice carried easily over the din.

Maggie nodded. When he door shut behind them, muffling the sound, she breathed a sigh of relief.

"Let's sit down," Otto said, pointing to the chairs. "I have to apologize for my wife. She has...bad days sometimes."

"Don't worry about it," Maggie said. "We all have bad days." Bad days, shit. The woman was bat-biting crazy.

They sat together and looked out at the ocean. The sun behind them was starting to get low in the sky, painting

125

the bottoms of the clouds red and gold.

"How's your husband doing?" Otto asked.

Maggie looked at him. "Don't you know? Don't you just know these things?"

Otto shook his head and said nothing.

She held his gaze for a long moment, then looked away. "He's...I don't know. I spoke with the doctor earlier and he couldn't really tell me anything. He's in a coma. I think he's going to die. I think he *wants* to die."

"I'm sorry," Otto said.

She looked up at him again. "You know, I don't believe you. I don't believe you're the least bit sorry."

Otto shrugged. The silence stretched between them.

"What do you want with my son?" Maggie asked, finally.

"Gabe's a fine boy," Otto said.

"Yes, he is. You didn't answer my question."

"There's nothing to say. We're friends."

"Give me a break, all right? What does someone like you get out of a friendship with a fourteen-year-old boy? There's something going on with the two of you."

"I'm not interested in his cute little ass, if that's what you mean," Otto said. "I thought that, under the circumstances, he could use a little...advice."

She looked at him for a long time. He resembled a comic artist's rendering of God. Fabio crossed with Mr. Natural. There was nothing in his features to indicate age except for a very fine tracery of laugh lines around the corners of his ice-blue eyes. They returned her gaze unflinchingly. The setting sun brushed gold highlights into his white hair and beard.

Maggie sighed. "I can't tell Gabe what friends to keep," she said. "I mean, I *would*, but he wouldn't listen to me, and I can't keep him locked up in the trailer. But I'm telling you. Don't fuck with my family. We've got enough to handle right now. Don't hurt him." She got up. "Don't hurt him," she repeated.

She turned around without waiting for an answer and walked back in the direction of her trailer. Once, she turned around and looked back. The garden chairs were there facing the ocean, angled slightly toward one another, empty.

CHAPTER THIRTEEN

Gabe walked up to the door of his trailer and stood there for a moment. He felt numb; there was nothing inside him but a great, hollow space. What he really needed was to be alone for awhile, to just sit and sort things out. From inside the trailer, he heard the sound of cartoons on the television, the laugh track blending with Ariel's high-pitched giggle. His sense of duty struggled briefly with his need for solitude. She'll be okay, he decided.

He walked out across the dunes toward the ocean. Tiny sand flies, no bigger than mosquitoes, hovered in the warm air. A locust whirred up out of the tough scrub-grass and glanced off his cheek, followed, seconds later, by another. It seemed like a greeting of sorts.

Hello, he thought. Hello, bugs. Hello, hoppers.

The image of Otto's naked, white ass pumping up and down kept intruding into his awareness; the cries of the girl, the faint *smell* in the air of sweat and something else that he couldn't identify burned right to the center of his consciousness. He felt confused and angry, betrayed some-how.

He arrived at the opening in the bramble, well hidden to the casual eye unless you knew what you were looking for. He lay down flat on his stomach and crawled into the thicket. It scratched his arms and back as he worked his way through. Soon, the green roof arched a little higher over his head and he could move without getting further scratched up. The thicket opened up ahead as well as above him and he was there. His Place.

He leaned up against a thick tangle of roots and branches and just sat there, breathing in the almost piney smell of the tough, little moisture-hoarding leaves, imagining that the green light was penetrating layers of his skin, irradiating him with warm, healing light.

He thought about his father dying, slipping away from that coma state into a deeper sleep, never seeing him again, never talking to him. It hurt terribly to imagine, and he felt a surge of anger rise in him and recede, like a wave in a narrow channel. There was a part of him that knew he would have to defer some of that, push it away for later – it was just too much to bear.

And Otto. There was some connection there. Whenever he thought about his Dad, before too long Otto's craggy face, flowing hair and beard white as raw cotton, showed up in his consciousness. And vice-versa – thoughts of Otto soon turned to thoughts of his father.

Otto lies. The words took shape in his mind as if they were spoken by someone else. *He lies.* He acts like some kind of know-it-all guru, but he's *hungry.* He's paying all this attention to me 'cause he wants something from me, 'cause he's getting off on teaching me stuff.

And it's *bullshit.* All I've been able to do so far with what he's taught me is hurt people.

I don't want it, Gabe thought. *I don't want it.*

He closed his eyes for a moment, and when he opened them again, he saw that the light had *changed.* Before it had started to take on the gold softness of late afternoon; now, even filtered through the canopy of green, it had a harshness to it that suggested the merciless glare of noon.

Gabe crawled through the bramble and when he was out, he straightened himself up, brushed the sand from his knees, and looked around.

The beach looked the same, but instead of a sheet of

aquamarine stretching out to a distant, flat horizon, the ocean curved up like the sides of a blue, china bowl until, lost in haze, it joined the paler blue of the sky. The sun hung directly overhead, bright and very hot.

His dream came back to him in a flash – strange, inhuman riders atop man-sized thunder-lizards, the sharp smell of the triceratops he rode, the feel of its muscles moving under him. The silence in the air above the glassy plain, the 'dactyl's broad pinions pumping the warm air.

That was *this* place, he realized. Pellucidar. I'm in Pellucidar.

He looked behind him. The rolling dunes were broken by a road, about where the Frontage Road ought to be. But this was hardpack dirt from the look of it, overgrown with tough grass in spots, striped with drifts of sand. Beyond the road was a series of gentle, brown hills, sparsely wooded. Here and there, small herds of animals dotted the hills. They were too far away for Gabe to tell what they were, but the quick, jerky way they moved seemed vaguely reptilian.

In the distance, the land sloped gently up, forests, hills, lakes, and rivers taking on the collapsed, miniature look they get when viewed from an airplane, until they too were lost in distance haze.

There was no sign of the Ocean View RV Park. There was no sign of civilization at all.

Fuck, Gabe thought. *I'm in trouble now.*

The absurdity of the thought struck him and he laughed out loud. It was a startling sound in the still air; something deep in the bramble scurried away with a dry rustling of branches.

Uh, sorry I'm late for dinner, Mom. I got mad and squirted myself into an alternate Universe.

He shook his head and began walking toward the road. As he walked, he began to take notice of the sounds around him – the whir of insects in the grass, the gentle sighing of the wind and the muted roar of the surf. In spite of that it was *quiet*; there was no freeway hum, no airplane buzz, no babble of a distant radio. It gave Gabe a chill.

The road wasn't much more than a strip of dirt pounded flat, a straight scar through the dunes, roughly parallel to the shoreline. Wheel-ruts and hoof prints marred its surface; dried cakes of dung by the side of the road gave off an earthy smell.

He stopped and looked around, breathed in the smell of the ocean and the dung and the dust of the road. He began to walk again. He didn't know where he was going, but walking seemed like a better idea than staying where he was. Soon, he left the bramble and the beach behind. Ahead of him, the road disappeared around a stand of trees. As he approached the turn, a man-sized lizard hopped out of the bushes and stood in the middle of the road, facing him. It balanced on two thin legs, tilting its long bony head towards Gabe. Its eyes were bits of black, polished stone.

Gabe stopped dead still and racked his brain for the creature's name, but it didn't look like anything he had ever seen in any of his books. Herbivorous, though, he decided, from the look of the jaw, wide and flat to accommodate teeth made for crushing rather than tearing. At least he hoped so.

The lizard opened its mouth and let out a piercing, sibilant cry. Gabe jumped back. The creature moved its head in quick, jerky motions, first to one side, then the other. Then, quickly as it had appeared, it hopped back into the bushes.

The encounter made him jumpy. Every rustle and stir in the undergrowth sent a jolt of caution through him.

Gabe felt like there were two people inside him. One of them was fully present, breathing in the strange-scented air, feeling his flip-flops chafe where the strap rubbed against his instep, accepting the other-worldliness of this place as something that just *was*. The other, a quiet voice from somewhere deep inside him, was frankly terrified, hanging onto rationality by a thin, frayed thread.

A plume of smoke threaded up into the sky ahead, and soon a low, stone building came into view. Several grey and black striped lizards the size of horses, with complicated looking harnesses strapped to their backs, lay in the sun in front of the building, tied to a rough, wooden rail. They were motionless as statues. Beyond the building, a wood and stone bridge spanned a wide, sluggish creek. A pier stretched out into the water, bobbing gently on wooden floats.

As he approached, the lizard closest to him jerked its head up in a sudden movement, opened its mouth, and let out a hiss. Gabe flinched inwardly, but walked past it to the entrance, a heavy, scarred door carved from a single piece of oak.

He pushed open the door. A damp, close smell, cold stone and hops, filled Gabe's nostrils. It took a moment for his eyes to adjust to the gloom. A bar ran down the length of the room; bottles of glass and bright ceramic were clustered in front of an inlaid mosaic of a stylized dragon that occupied most of the wall. A squat, gnomic man in a leather jerkin stood scowling at Gabe, wiping his hands on a rag.

Rough, wooden tables were scattered about the room. Customers sat in groups of two and three, hunched over stone mugs. They looked up as Gabe walked in, looked him over, then went back to what they were doing.

At the far end of the room, at a table near a narrow, slotted window, sat Gabe's father.

He looked at Gabe, lifted his mug in greeting, and beckoned him over.

With the detachment of dream-logic, Gabe was not at all surprised. As he sat down, Gene called out to the bartender. "Another cider, Willie."

Gabe looked at his father. He wore a leather vest over a rough, cotton shirt. A fine scar ran from above his temple down the side of his face, wrapping around his jaw like a vine.

"How you doing, Gabe?" Gene asked.

Gabe opened his mouth to say something, but his eyes filled with tears.

The bartender brought over a stone mug and set it in front of Gabe. He picked it up and took a sip. It was sweet, with an edge to it that burned his throat as it went down. He pushed the mug away.

He looked at his father again. "I'm all right, I guess. There's...a lot going on."

Gene nodded. He was silent for a long moment. Gabe saw several expressions pass across his features in the space of an instant – shame, sadness, a lost, confused look. His father's face looked open to him in a way he had never seen before – he felt like he could really see what was going on underneath.

"I don't know what to say to you, Gabe," Gene said, finally. "I've really fucked things up, and it's way too late to do anything about it."

Gabe wanted to be able to say that it was all right, but he couldn't. It wasn't all right. Nothing was all right. He nodded at the mug in his father's hand. "Why do you do that? Is it so much more important than we are?"

Gene shook his head. He picked up the mug and took a long sip, closing his eyes and making a face as he swallowed. "No, that's not it at all," he said, putting the mug down. "It's not more important. It's just...easier. The path of least resistance. I know that sounds really awful, and I'm not proud of it, but that's the way it is." He looked at Gabe.

"I love you, you know. I always have. I just couldn't handle it. Being a father and a husband. Mister Mainstream." He laughed bitterly. "I mean, you'd come home from school around three. I'd be just getting up sometimes, trying to make coffee and choke down a donut, and you'd want me to come outside in the freezing cold and play football." He shook his head. "*Football.* Jesus fucking Christ. It completely bewildered me. I wanted to be able to do it, but I just didn't know how. I *couldn't.*" His eyes were pleading.

Gabe didn't say anything. He wanted to smash his mug on the floor and walk away. He felt the anger welling up inside him and he wanted to really run with it, to let it fill him, but somehow he couldn't sustain it. Like a wave hurling itself at the shore, it rose in him, broke and receded, leaving him feeling empty and frustrated.

The silence stretched between them. "I think Mom's drinking again," Gabe said, finally.

Gene shook his head. "No. Absolutely not. We still have some…work to do, your Mom and I, and there's a lot that's out of my hands, but I know for sure that she's sober."

Gabe searched his father's face. Gene was telling the truth, at least as far as he knew it.

"She's always been stronger than me," Gene continued. "When she was first getting sober, she used to say that drinking was a form of insane delusion because you were doing the same thing over and over again but expecting different results. That may have been true for her, and that may be why she managed to quit." He looked at Gabe. "That's never made any sense to me. I *never* expected anything different. It's the same thing every time and that's *exactly* why I keep coming back to it."

The silence hung between them again, like a third presence at the table. Gene was looking off into the room, but his eyes appeared focused at a point far beyond the walls. Gabe wondered what he was seeing.

This is my only chance, he thought. For what, he wasn't exactly sure, but if there was anything he wanted from his father, this was going to be his only opportunity to get it.

He had a friend in school, Jim Dorritt, who had the perfect family. Gabe was smart enough to realize that everything wasn't always what it appeared to be, but Jim's family reminded him of something lifted right out of some cheesy, old black-and-white sitcom – *Leave It To Beaver*, maybe, or *Father Knows Best*.

Mister Dorritt was always sitting in the big chair in the living room whenever Gabe came by, a newspaper or a book open in front of him. Sometimes he'd be watching a football or a baseball game as well. It was odd – Gabe couldn't imagine watching sports without the smell of beer and whiskey hanging in the air like a charge of ozone before a storm.

He always had a friendly word for Gabe, and a couple of times had volunteered to play ball with the boys. It was so *normal.* Gabe tried to imagine his father like that, available and solicitous, Ward Cleaver vibes emanating from him like warm, soothing rays, his Mom with all her rough edges sanded smooth, some sort of Barbara Billingsley clone. He laughed.

"Something's funny?" Gene asked.

"Yeah. I was just trying to picture you and Mom acting like real parents."

Gene grinned. It made the scar on his face stand out like a piece of rope, and Gabe thought of the *other* Gene, lying in a hospital bed, floating on a sea of medication and damage, wires and tubes sprouting like kudzu from his battered body.

"That's pretty funny, all right," Gene said, but something else flashed across his face and Gabe realized that his words had inflicted some hurt. It was a revelation; Gabe had never thought that anything he could say or do would have any effect on his father at all.

He looked closely at his father. Light from the slotted window fell across his face. His eyes were moist.

He looks like me, Gabe thought. People had said that throughout the years, but this was the first time Gabe had looked at his father and really seen a part of himself. The light in the room seemed to shift subtly, and there was a feeling deep inside him of something shifting as well, a door easing open with a gentle, muted click.

Years later, he would recognize it as the seed of forgiveness planted and beginning to take root; at the time he experienced it as a gentle lessening of tension, as something that felt paradoxically like both deepening of connection and breaking away.

"I love you, too, Dad," he said.

At the other end of the room, voices raised in argument. A guttural language ripe with sibilants. Two men got up from their tables and began shoving each other. Willie ran over to them and pushed them apart, talking earnestly to both of them.

Gene smiled. "Just like home."

"Maybe for you," Gabe said. "But I should get back."

Gene nodded. "Yeah. You can't stay here. Take care of your sister. She's a little sweetie, that one."

"Yeah, she is." Gabe got up, pushing the heavy chair back. He looked down at Gene. For a second, he wanted to throw himself into his father's arms, but something held him back. He remembered a scrap of lyrics from an old country and western song, something like, *You can't get no water from a well that's gone dry.*

He pushed the chair back in.

"See you, Dad," he said.

As he walked across the long room, he could feel his father's eyes on him. When he got to the door, he turned around. Gene lifted his mug and smiled crookedly. Gabe nodded and pushed open the heavy door.

The humidity hit him like a wet slap. The creatures tied in front of the tavern lifted their heads on long, thin necks and looked at him sleepily as he walked past them. He didn't know where he was going or what he was going to do. Instinctively, he headed back the way he had come.

Soon, he was back in front of the bramble. He could feel the massive presence of the ocean at his back and he turned around to face it. It went on and on, the roughness of random waves on its surface diffusing to a smooth, featureless blue as it curved up to meet the sky. The heat of the sun pressed down hard on his head and oozed back up from the white sand all around him. He felt like he was floating on a cushion of heat. With no thought at all in his mind, he began to walk toward the water, the periodic whisper-roar-whisper of the ocean pulling him to itself as if the modulated white noise encoded a language of wordless beckoning.

Gabe walked until the blood-warm ocean lapped at his waist. A wave came in, nearly knocking him over. As it receded, a strong undertow pulled at his legs with grasping fingers. A voice echoing up from a remote place inside of him asked, *What am I doing?*, but his feet kept moving. When the next wave came in, he closed his eyes and dove right into it. The surge lifted him up, spun him around, and threw him down hard. He felt himself being pulled back and under, and he stretched his feet vainly down to try and touch the sandy bottom. Another surge knocked him sideways and spun him around again. His lungs were beginning to hurt and he paddled hard to try to orient himself. Still another surge, like a strong, swift hand in the small of his back, pushed him down. His hindbrain was beginning to panic, starved for air and disoriented way down to the lizard level, but he knew that if he gave in to that it would be all over.

He let go, giving himself to the violent surge. There was a sensation of release, of a closed fist opening.

He felt another rapid acceleration and his body burst through the surface into the air. He took a deep, shuddering breath, coughing, gasping, treading water to keep from going under again. Another deep breath, the air cold in his lungs and sweet, and he blinked open his eyes. The light had the gold softness of late afternoon, the sky a deep cyan streaked with gold clouds, and when the incoming wave pushed him up out of a trough, he saw the distant horizon, the juncture between sea and sky a singular boundary, flat as the edge of a page.

Home.

Gabe turned around and the beach was about thirty yards away. A few late afternoon stragglers still sprawled on blankets, catching the last of the sun.

He began to swim towards shore and this time it felt like the ocean was helping him, sending small surges to push him closer. When his feet touched the sandy bottom, he stopped for a moment, letting the water bob him gently up and down, then he walked the rest of the way out of the ocean.

He was very tired; his eyes felt like they wanted to droop down and close out the world. He walked past the bramble and the first set of dunes, across the frontage road and the second set of dunes, up to the trailer park.

He paused at the door to his trailer and looked over at the other end of the park. Otto's silver Airstream glowed with gold fire in the setting sun. Gabe felt a complicated mixture of emotions ripple through him – attraction, repulsion, a hint of shame. He didn't get that last one – it seemed to come from nowhere. He felt like there was something incomplete with Otto, a ledger between them that was not quite balanced. He wasn't going to deal with it now, though. All he wanted to do was inhale some food and sleep for about fourteen hours.

His mother was bent over the kitchen counter, chopping vegetables. Ariel was ensconced in her usual position in front of the television. *Star Trek* this time, the old one. Kirk was emoting onscreen, his face pulled and stretched like Silly Putty into a caricature of a grimace. He looked like he was wearing eyeliner.

Maggie turned around when he walked in. She looked at him strangely, like she was mad and sad and happy to see him, all at once, but all she said was, "Gabe, you're soaking wet."

She went to the hall closet, pulled out a towel, and brought it to him. She leaned over and kissed him on the cheek.

"Good swim?" she asked.

Gabe briefly considered trying to tell her what had just happened to him, but that would be asking for trouble. Besides, he was so tired he wasn't even sure any more.

"Yeah, fine," he said. He saw the star-shaped stain on the wall and the worry came rushing back.

"Mom—"

She saw where he was looking and shook her head. "Not a drop, Gabe. I don't know exactly what's going on, but I'm not drinking."

He knew she was telling the truth. Relief flooded through him, along with another wave of fatigue and a twinge of guilt as he thought of the beers he had on the beach that afternoon and the night before.

"Okay, Mom," he said. "That's good." Spots swam before his eyes and he stumbled.

"Are you all right?" Maggie asked.

He could barely keep his eyes open. "Tired…"

He felt her arms around him and he leaned against her. He heard words from far away. "…get you to bed…"

Suddenly, he was lying down, the softness at his back pressing him up towards the ceiling.

CHAPTER FOURTEEN

The scenes stutter past Gene's disembodied mind as if an inconstant wind were riffling pages of a book at random. He doesn't know any more if a particular sequence of events actually happened to him and he's playing it back like a home movie flickering in the darkness of his cortex, or if the scenes are hallucinatory products of drugs and damage. They seem so *real*, but it seems like they are happening to someone else.

I'm dying, he thinks. *This is what dying is like.*

He hears music, hard driving rock and roll pulsing in the darkness, muffled by the velvet sky. He feels himself moving towards it, a tropism as natural as a plant leaning towards the light.

An old Little Feat tape was in the deck, and Lowell George's sweet, hard voice winging in from Dead Rocker Heaven sent Gene's fingers tapping counterpoint on the steering wheel. The white lane markers threw a flickering reflection into the upper corner of his windshield, and he adjusted his speed so that it pulsed in time with the music. Interstate 93 stretched out before him and he imagined himself to be a bug on a long gray ribbon, the shiny silk crinkling and twisting as he began to climb up from the coastal flatlands into New Hampshire's White Mountains.

Maybe get out of this heat, he thought. His old Valiant had no air conditioning and he had heard on the radio that the temperature in Boston was expected to peak at 95 degrees. He had a sudden longing for a beer, could almost taste the cold bitterness of it, and he tried to push the thought away. Intervention, they called it at Diablo Hills. Break into the addictive thought patterns before they get a foothold. *Right.*

Thirty-six days. It had been thirty-six days since he'd driven the band's truck into a parked car in Brattleboro. There'd been the usual bottomless pitcher at the gig, then someone gave him a couple of reds, and by closing time he was coasting. When he volunteered to drive, nobody in Dropkick Puppy objected. Surprise. Mickey couldn't find his ass dead sober with both hands and a flashlight, Rock was off fucking another cocktail waitron, and Lou had scored some blotter somewhere and was carrying on a very earnest conversation with a mike stand. The judge gave Gene a choice: ninety in the county stir or thirty in a recovery program. Gene took the thirty.

At first he thought it would be a drag, hanging out with a bunch of drunks and dopers trying to get clean, but he felt at home right away. Some of the stories were pretty funny, too. It was actually something of a relief being there – he had been on the ragged edge of despair for a long time, needing to straighten out, not knowing how. He began to nurse a small, flickering candle of hope.

He'd actually gotten up the nerve to call Maggie and talk to her about it. Her response had been predictably cool. They'd been separated for about six months this time and it looked like it was for keeps. It was always hot and cold with Maggie but he missed the kids with a dull ache.

He did the thirty and was on his way up to visit his sister and try to figure out what to do next. His sister. Last time he'd seen her, about five years back, she was into crystals and drove him up a wall with the Windham Hill space-metal dulcimer crap she listened to. For the last couple of years, she'd been living in an honest-to-God geodesic dome in the woods near St. Johnsbury.

141

All that was an improvement – he still had a faint, triangular scar on his upper arm from where she'd burned him with a hot iron when he was a kid. But that was water under the bridge. She was his older sister, family, and Gene felt like he needed that just then. She wrote to him at Diablo Hills and said the trip would be very "healing" for both of them. Healing. Why not? If he could go thirty-six days without drinking or using he could do damn near anything.

The road climbed and twisted. He rounded a sharp curve, and Mt. Washington came into view. It wasn't much of a mountain by Sierra standards, but here among the weathered, rounded hills of New England, it looked majestic, rising up out of the forest like the Great Pyramid of Cheops. Even this late in June, there were still a few patches of snow clinging to its rocky peak.

Gene pulled off to the side of the road and got out of the car. He breathed in deeply and closed his eyes, letting the intense, green smell of pine fill him.

You can't fall off a mountain, he thought. The phrase just popped into his head. He thought it was from Kerouac somewhere, maybe *The Dharma Bums*. You can't fall off a mountain. He smiled and shook his head. Yeah, he thought. I can do this. He wasn't quite sure what "this" was, but it sounded right. It felt right.

Gene got off the Interstate at Franconia Notch, a collection of gingerbread houses, antique stores, and tourist clip joints. When he left the town behind the quality of the state road quickly deteriorated, until it felt like he was running a slalom course around the potholes. He missed his turn and had to double back to find it, an unmarked vein of asphalt striking off into the dense woods. The trees made a thick, green canopy over his head, shot through with splashes of gold from the afternoon sun, and the car filled with the earthy smell of leaf mold. There was another turnoff onto a dirt road – three miles of kidney-pounding washboard. Finally, just ahead through the trees he could make out a wide clearing and a squat, green-paneled dome.

Something *changed* then, the quality of the light filtering through the trees, the way the sounds of wind and birdsong brushed against his ears. It was subtle, as if he was pushing through the thinnest of membranes. He felt a brief surge of panic.

Maybe this is a bad idea.

Then he was in the clearing and the strangeness vanished. He pulled up next to an old, beat-up Datsun.

As he got out of the car, Gene's sister stepped out of a low door in the dome. He stopped and stared at her. She looked *young*. Not young like a twenty-year-old, but her long black hair was thick and glossy and the crow's feet he remembered starting to creep in around her eyes were gone.

They embraced. "Sarah," he said, stepping back from her. "You look good."

She looked into his eyes, then reached out and touched his cheek. "You look like shit." She hugged him again. "It's good to see you," she whispered into his ear.

He stepped back, not sure what to say.

"Yeah, well, it's been a hard time."

There was a long awkward silence.

"How's Frank?" Gene asked. She'd been with Frank for about ten years. Gene couldn't stand him. Hippie redneck logger type, heavy drinker. Talked a lot of new age bullshit, but Gene knew that he smacked her around when he had a load on.

"Frank's…different. He's okay."

He waited for her to elaborate, but she didn't offer anything.

"Come on," she said, a little too cheerfully. "Let me show you my home."

Gene began to get that bad feeling again. Something wasn't quite right. Then she took his hand and the feeling vanished, turned off like a light switch.

They walked towards the dome. Its hexagonal green-glass panels seemed to glow with a light of their own. There was a large garden striped with haphazard rows of corn and pole bean, sprawling zucchini plants, fat, pallid melons half buried in the moist earth. A hutch and a small run enclosed with chicken wire imprisoned several lethargic looking rabbits. A goat tethered near the garden looked at Gene with an expression of stupid cunning.

Inside the dome it was...*green*. The light was very bright, but diffuse and directionless, and the dome seemed much larger than it looked from the outside. Ivy snaked up the walls, meeting and intertwining at the top. There was a maze of open-roofed "rooms" in the interior of the dome, separated by bamboo and rice paper partitions. A loft ran around the perimeter, halfway up the curving side.

She showed Gene where he'd be sleeping – a small cubicle, about eight by six with a futon on the floor.

"Do you want to rest?"

"I'm pretty wired, actually, but yeah, I could cool out for a bit."

"Well, why don't you take a few minutes to get settled and I'll start dinner." She paused and looked at him. "I'm so happy you're here, Gene. We're together now." She put her arms around him and held him to her. He could feel her parted lips resting on his neck, the warmth of her breath. They stayed like that for what seemed like a long time. Finally, she lifted her head, kissed him on the cheek, and stepped away. "You get settled."

Gene threw his bag in a corner of the room and lowered himself down on the futon, resting his back against the flimsy wall. *This is just too fucking creepy. Is she coming on to me?* He had a sudden longing for a drink. No, that wasn't really right. This was non-verbal, a needle-sharp stab of *need* that shot from the top of his head right down to his groin.

This, too, shall pass.

Another bullshit aphorism from the treatment program. Whatever bad shit is coming down on you isn't so bad that drinking or using wouldn't make it worse. Just get through it and don't pick up. *Right.*

144

It was very hot in the green of the dome, almost like a sauna. Gene felt a light sheen of sweat filming his forehead. His clothes felt damp and clingy. He drifted off into a light, fitful doze.

He awoke to the sensation of another presence in the room. He opened his eyes and Sarah was there, sitting next to the futon in the half-dark, looking at him. He had the feeling she had been sitting in the gathering gloom for a long time.

"Almost dinnertime," she said.

"How long have you been sitting there?" he asked.

She shook her head. "Not long. Come outside with me while I cook."

She had started some coals under a grate and they were glowing red, sending a column of smoke laced with bright sparks into the sky. The clear space next to the garden was illuminated by a spotlight attached to the side of the dome; the harsh, white light cast knife-edged shadows. From outside the circle of brightness, Gene heard rustling and scurrying sounds, bullfrogs calling from the edge of a nearby pond, the ever-present drone of crickets.

"What's for dinner?" he asked.

Sarah held up a finger and smiled. She walked over to the rabbit hutch, opened it, and coaxed out a large, lopsided ball of nose-twitching fur. She sat down at the picnic table with the rabbit in her lap, cooing and stroking its fur. A long, twopenny nail appeared in her right hand and, gently, almost lovingly, she pushed it into the back of the animal's neck, entering the soft spot just at the base of the skull. The rabbit shuddered once and was still.

Sarah looked at Gene. "Rabbit," she said. Her smile was ghoulish in the harsh shadows and Gene felt something wash through him, at once blooming and withering, longing mixed with horror.

She cleaned the rabbit quickly and expertly, rubbed the pair of bloody haunches with fresh sage from the garden, and put them on the grill.

145

"Did that one have a name?" Gene asked, after a long silence.

She laughed. It was an odd sound, harsh and unmusical. "That one was called...Gene," she said. She saw the expression on his face and laughed again. "Oh, Gene, I'm *kidding*. Here, let me get you something to drink."

She disappeared into the dome and came out a moment later with a jug of Almaden red dangling from one hand. Gene's fists balled up into tight knots, his nails digging into his palms. Her smile evaporated when she saw the expression on his face.

"Oh, *shit*, Gene, I'm sorry. I forgot..."

"God damn it, Sarah, what the fuck is wrong with you?" Just the sight of the cool, green jug seemed to suck the moisture out of his mouth like a sponge. His throat was so dry it hurt.

"No, Gene, I...I'm really sorry." She looked genuinely stricken. Gene felt the hardness in him thaw just a bit.

"Look, it's...I'm still really raw around that stuff."

She nodded. "I know." She put her arms around him and held him to her. "I'm sorry, baby."

He had the sudden, horrible feeling that she was smiling as she held him. He could almost see it there in his mind's eye, a cold, Cheshire grin suspended in black velvet. They stood there together for a long time and Gene felt himself gradually filling with the smell of her – woodsmoke, sage, and a rising undercurrent of pheromones that his body couldn't ignore. He pulled back a little so that she wouldn't feel his arousal.

She drew back as well.

"Let's see about that rabbit," she said.

The smell of searing meat was making Gene's mouth water and his stomach grumble, but there was a part of him that was standing off at a distance, saying, *Fuck* the rabbit, man. Whatever kind of happy fantasies you were clinging to, Jackson, you should just kiss them goodbye and *get the fuck out of here.*

146

His sister sat there, waiting, almost as if she could hear the struggle waging inside him. After a moment, she turned to the grill and forked the smoking legs onto paper plates. Gene felt it again as he took the plate from her, that sense of blossom and collapse folded into one.

"Have you spoken with Dad?" she asked. It was always 'Dad' when they spoke of their parents, never 'Mom and Dad.' Their mother was always there in the background, but their father's mercurial presence was a light that put all else in shadow.

He shook his head. "No." The word was like a line drawn in the sand. Do not cross here. End of subject. But it triggered a complex of feelings, half-memories, sense-impressions that kept bubbling up into his consciousness. A fishing trip. His father's face huge and red against the sky. His mother and sister had stayed ashore and it was just the two of them. Gene had been very proud of that at first but everything was going wrong. First, he had snagged his thumb on a hook and cried.

"*Stupid*," his father said. "Don't you understand that you have to be careful? *You have to be very careful.*"

Then, Gene got his line caught somehow on the bottom of the boat. His father cut the line and took his fishing pole away. "Wait until you're older," he said.

The pile of empty cans in the bottom of the boat grew and his father's silence smoldered in the heat of the afternoon. Finally, after his father had yanked the little motor back to life and they were heading back to shore, he picked up a can of beer, punched two triangular holes in the top with the church key dangling around his neck, and handed it to Gene.

"Drink up, boy," he said.

The beer was bitter and cold and filled him with light. He wanted another one even before the first was finished.

Gene and Sarah ate in silence. The rabbit was delicious, seared on the outside, the flesh inside pink and warm. When they were done, they sat together in the circle of light, the night beyond black and close. Gene felt the tension between them building, shifting, felt his own boundaries becoming fluid. Suddenly, he had to get away from her. Without looking at her, he excused himself and went back inside. He could feel her gaze on his back as he walked into the dome.

He lay on the futon, trying to sort out the jumble of thoughts in his head.

I should probably get out of bed right now. Get in the car and drive. Just drive.

His father's face kept appearing in his mind, glowering, his breath raw with whiskey, and Gene kept pushing it away. He had a sudden memory of he and Sarah huddling together under the blankets as a party raged on in the living room. Loud voices, music. The door burst open and someone staggered into the room. Gene peeked out from under the blanket. His father lurched over to the window, pushed it open, and pulled down his fly. Gene could hear the faint tinkling of his piss splashing into the yard below. He ducked back under the blanket and he and Sarah looked at each other, stifling giggles.

Stay. It's all right. Stay. He knew that voice. He heard it after getting fired from the Scientific Americans for showing up at gigs too fucked up to play. *It's all right. They just don't understand your art.* He heard it when Maggie threw him out. *It's okay, she's a bitch anyway. You can do better.* Heard it when his old friends stopped calling, one by one. *Fuck it. You don't need them.*

This was different, though. It sounded almost like it was coming from outside of him, something perched on his shoulder whispering siren song into his ear. *Stay. Stay. Love here. It's okay.*

He'd learned in treatment that all it took to wedge open the door of denial was a sliver of truth, but the addict in him was strong. Gene struggled against it, but it was like swimming against a strong current. He lay back down on the futon, curled up on the cotton pad, a fetal comma. He sank into sleep like a stone.

When Gene awoke this time, he was alone. He had the feeling that not much time had passed. His head felt clear. *Checkout time,* he thought, and was surprised that no answering chorus in his mind contradicted him. He grabbed his bag and walked out into the maze of partitions.

Diffuse moonlight cast everything under the dome in pearly luminescence. The partitions reached well over his head and he tried to negotiate his way through them toward the dome's perimeter. Every time he thought he was getting close, though, the rice paper corridor he was in would make a sudden turn and he found himself being directed toward the center again. He was about to give up and just crash though the flimsy walls, when he turned a corner into a wide, open space.

It felt like he was at the center of the dome, but the space itself seemed much larger than the dome could accommodate. Distances were difficult to measure, shrouded in braids of moonlight and shadow. There was a Japanese garden, smooth, mossy rocks, a pond with fat, pale koi gliding under the surface.

His sister sat next to the pond in a half-lotus position. She was naked, her breasts heavy and full. Fleshy red and white blossoms were woven into her glossy, black hair. A lean, grizzled bobcat sprawled next to her on a rock and she rested her hand on its head, scratching softly. There was a man sitting on the other side of her, also naked, so thin that his flesh seemed stretched across his bones like paper. His head was shaved and dark eyes peered blankly out from deep hollows. Gene took a step closer.

Frank.

Sarah looked over at him. She smiled gently. "I'm strong here, Gene." A bird fluttered down and landed next to her. "Something about this space, these woods. When we moved out here from Boston a couple of years ago, I had no idea. It's a power spot for me."

Gene wanted to bolt, to turn tail and run until he dropped from exhaustion.

His feet, though, took him a step forward. She opened her arms and he collapsed into her embrace. He felt himself dissolving into her. Merging. Her lips were moist and warm on his neck and when she bit his earlobe, he cried out. He kissed her neck, ran his tongue along her jaw, kissed her lips. He felt her nails dig into his back.

He took her nipple in his mouth and bit down gently, ran his tongue around the aureole. She arched her back and let out a soft moan. He licked down her stomach, bit softly into the soft, pale skin. Ran his tongue in a circle around her navel, licking down to her warm saltiness.

When he entered her, she raked her nails across his back and he felt the cuts open, felt the hot blood bead and flow. They moved together, bucked against each other. She bit down hard on his shoulder, pulled him tightly to her. He felt his orgasm moving up inside him, spreading out from his groin. When he came it was like being gutted, torn open and filled with hot lead. He lay with his head on her shoulder, eyes closed, sweat plastering hair to his forehead, breathing hard. He looked up and saw Frank staring down at him not two feet away, eyes like glittering beads.

He turned to her. "Who *are* you?"

She smiled softly and rested her hand on his thigh. "I'm your sister, Gene. That's all." Hand softly stroking. "Your sister."

He jerked away. "I'm getting out of here."

Again that slow, knowing smile. "You can leave any time, Gene. I'm not stopping you."

He got up and lurched out of the room, staggered through the maze of flimsy partitions until he was out in the twilight. The voice pulled at him. *Stay. Stay.* He got into his car, started the engine, and backed blindly down the dirt road, barely looking in the rear-view mirror. *Stay.* Gene caught a last glimpse of his sister standing near the entrance to the dome, Frank squatting in the dirt, her hand resting on his head.

Suddenly, he felt it again, that *change*. The quality of the light shifted almost imperceptibly, the whisper of the wind through the trees seemed to catch and start again. He still felt the pull of the voice, but it was suddenly quieter, as if swaddled in cotton. He slowed down and stopped at a wide spot in the road. His fingers were frozen claws wrapped around the steering wheel. He released it and took a deep breath. Took another. Turned the car around and drove.

He saw the pool of light ahead, the glowing neon. Without thinking, he pulled into the parking lot and got out of the car. He stepped into the bar and sat down at one of the stools.

Down near the other end, two men were talking and laughing. A television hung from the ceiling, baseball with the sound off. Hank Williams was on the juke, some sad song about lost love. The bartender came over, wiping his hands on a rag.

"Draft," Gene said.

The bartender poured it and set the glass in front of him. Gene fished a crumpled bill out of his pocket and tossed it onto the bar. He picked up the glass, cool and smooth against his hand. The amber fluid was a lens; through it, everything in the room curved around to meet itself.

CHAPTER FIFTEEN

Gabe floated in a sky of crushed velvet, black as the inside of a safe. There were no features anywhere to provide a sense of perspective or scale. He felt good, though; he was warm all over, buoyed by the whisper of rushing blood in his ears and the distant beating of his heart.

He realized suddenly that he was not alone. His father hovered next to him, a blob of deeper blackness tinged with purple, barely visible against the velvet sky. He looked "down" at himself and realized that he, too, was without form. They hovered there together, he and his father, pulsing slowly, without words.

He woke to brightness against his closed eyelids and an amazing hard-on. He opened his eyes. Daylight streamed in through the Venetian blinds. There were no sounds in the trailer except the hum of the refrigerator, and he knew that he was alone. His mother and Ariel were probably down at the beach or out to the store.

He reached down and touched himself. He shivered as a wave of pleasure coursed up his body. He began to stroke himself, slowly, languidly, and more waves of sensation rippled through him. He thought of Casey, pictured the two of them in some place, details of background a dark blur. Their arms were around each other, her head on his shoulder, and she was kissing his neck, running her lips up the line of his jaw to his mouth. Their lips touched, parted, their tongues caressed. She reached down to touch him and suddenly, the pleasure converged, focused to white-hot point somewhere deep in the center of him. It was so intense that he cried out.

He lay there for a while letting the intensity of the sensations subside. The sticky fluid on his stomach felt warm at first, then cool. He had a twinge of guilt for *using* Casey that way – he'd never fantasized about a real person like that before. But he realized he *wanted* that with her, to make love to her, to become close.

He got out of bed, peeked into the hall to make sure nobody was home, and padded into the bathroom. He turned the water on very hot and hard and stood under the spray with his eyes closed.

He really didn't want to go back the hospital today. He tensed at the anticipation of that antiseptic smell filling his nostrils, and the thought of looking at the shell of his father filled him with dread. It seemed to him like his father's body and whatever else it was that made him who he was, his spirit, his soul, didn't have much to do with each other anymore. He wanted to see Casey again, though.

He felt divided – his father was business to be concluded, everything else was the future.

He dried himself off, wrapped a towel around his waist, and walked out into the living room. There was a note on the kitchen counter.

Gabe. Didn't want to wake you. Went to the hospital. Back early afternoon. – Mom and Ari.

Well, all right, he thought. He felt a small twinge of guilt, but dismissed it. He did want to see Casey, though. Maybe she could get a pass or something, come back for dinner with Mom and Ari.

He called Information and got the number of the hospital. He didn't even remember if his father's room had a phone. It would be kind of weird if it did, actually – he wasn't likely to be making any calls – but it was worth a try. Before he could punch in the number, the phone rang.

"Hello."

"You're up." Mom.

"Yeah. I just got up a little while ago."

"I'm glad I let you sleep then. How are you feeling?"

"Fine. How's Dad?"

She hesitated and Gabe could picture her biting her lip. "He's all right." She gave a brittle laugh that echoed faintly in the receiver. "'Well, not so great, actually. He had what they're calling an 'episode' in the middle of the night. Heart stopped, another couple of blood vessels in his brain popped. He's stable again now, though. I talked to Doctor Casanova about whether we want to use 'extraordinary means' or not. You know what they mean by that, don't you?"

"Yeah. Do we want to keep him alive like some kind of vegetable or just let him die." He was surprised at how calm he felt.

"That's about right. I don't know, Gabe. He's not gone yet, I can still feel him, but he's never gonna be all right. I think we have to let him die."

If he'll ever let go, Gabe thought. He had a sudden realization – it was like an instantaneous knowing – that his father was *lonely* more than anything else, floating there in velvet limbo. He wasn't actually trying to hurt them, but weaving them into his dreamlike recollections to push back his own shadows. "I guess so."

He still wanted to say something about Casey, but it didn't seem right to bring it up. He felt guilty that he even thought about her under the circumstances, his Dad near dead, his Mom hurting, his sister radiating need like a small animal giving off heat, but there was something there that felt warm and good. It even seemed like his father's condition was wrapped up in that somehow – not far behind those hazy images of pleasure with Casey was the thought of his father's body swaddled in gauze, spirit clinging to flesh by a smoky tendril.

"Gabe?"

Pause. The soft background hiss of the phone line and an almost inaudible fragment of conversation whispering in and fading out. "Yeah. I'm here, Mom."

"You take it easy today, Gabe. Go back to sleep if you feel like it. We'll be back this afternoon."

"Okay, Mom. Bye."

He thought about Otto as he finished getting dressed. He wasn't sure he wanted to see him, but there was more that he wanted to learn. He felt confused, and it was the confusion more than anything else that set his feet on the path towards the silvery Airstream. Something was incomplete; Otto held the key. Gabe's cheeks burned as he remembered walking in on Otto with the girl. He pushed away the flush of anger and betrayal that came welling up.

Mary was outside the trailer, lying in a plastic-webbed beach chair. She was wearing a very scant bikini and an enormous sun visor and her body glistened with oil. At first Gabe thought she was asleep, but as he approached she raised her hand in the air and pointed toward the open door of the trailer. *What a spook*, he thought.

Otto was sitting on the couch with a newspaper spread before him. The paper was filled with columns of figures in small type and Otto ran his fingers down them, mumbling and scrawling on a yellow legal pad by his side. Gabe craned his neck to try and see better.

Otto looked up. "Racing form," he said. "I'm leaving for Pimlico in about ten minutes. You want to come? I'll have you back by five."

"What's Pimlico?"

"Racetrack outside of Baltimore."

Gabe barely hesitated. "Sure. I have to leave a note for my Mom." He paused. "*She's* not coming, is she?" He nodded toward the door.

Otto smiled and shook his head. "Not a chance. She hates the track."

Gabe ran back to his trailer. He hesitated for a moment, pen in hand. *Mom. Went to the racetrack with Otto. Back*

155

later. He didn't think so. He thought about lying, but that didn't feel right either. Finally, he scrawled *Back around 5. Gabe.* on the shopping pad and set it by the phone.

A quiet part of him noted that his reservations about Otto seemed to vanish with the invitation, and he paused for a minute, leaning against the counter and cocking his head as if listening to a far off voice. What did he want from Otto? There was no answering voice from above, no sudden revelation. He left the trailer and walked back down to Otto's. The sun was high and he noticed the day for the first time – deep, blue sky without a trace of cloud, late morning heat relieved by a salty breeze coming in off the ocean.

Mary was nowhere in sight. Gabe imagined her in the trailer, peering out at him from behind the Venetian blinds. Otto was sitting in his truck on the other side of the trailer, an unlit cigar stub clenched between his teeth. A bumper sticker plastered to the tailgate said:

HOW'S MY DRIVING?
DIAL 1-800-EAT-SHIT

Otto held the *Racing Form* open in front of him. Gabe heard him mumbling as he walked up to the truck.

"Beautiful Dreamer, not a fucking chance. Comer in the stretch last time – last *two* times. The crowd loves that shit, but it's a sucker bet. Maybe Eggzackley, especially with Figueroa riding..." He looked up. "Ready?"

Gabe nodded.

"Good." Otto picked up a pair of wrap-around sunglasses from the dashboard and put them on. They were dark as welding goggles. "Let's hit it. Post time for the first race is twelve-fifteen."

CHAPTER SIXTEEN

I'm getting used to this place, Maggie thought, as she and Ariel got out of the elevator on Gene's floor. The smells, the noises. It's been two days and it feels like forever. She imagined a succession of days like that, stretching into the future one after another, anchored by hospital smells, hospital sounds. Maggie thought of Gene and hated him.

The nurse, a young, black woman, stopped them as they walked past her station. A plastic badge clipped to her starched, white lapel said 'Janelle' in white block letters.

"Somebody here wants to talk to you."

She nodded to the right and Maggie noticed for the first time a middle-aged man in a rumpled, charcoal suit standing in the hallway on the other side of the nurses' station. When Maggie looked at him, he stepped forward and held out his hand.

"Mrs. Lambent? Sergeant Feely."

She took his hand. He gave it a perfunctory shake and released it. His skin felt cold and dry.

"Is your husband Gene Lambent?"

"That's why you're here, isn't it?"

"I'm going to have to place him under arrest."

She stepped back a pace. "Ari, go see Janelle." She looked pleadingly at the nurse. Janelle nodded. Maggie stepped down the hall a few feet with the sergeant. "Are you fucking serious?"

"I'm very sorry for your troubles, Mrs. Lambent, but I'm just following procedure. He had a blood alcohol level of point two one. That's DUI."

Christ, point two one. That wasn't just DUI, it was the Twilight Zone. "Well, you'd better put a couple of men in there and make sure he doesn't get away."

"That won't be necessary." Completely straight face. "I also should tell you that there may be civil as well as criminal charges." His features softened a bit, as if he were doing her a big favor. What a fucking sport.

"The Liquor Barn?"

"That's right."

Maggie spread her hands. "They can sue me."

"That's the idea."

"Well, look, I really couldn't give a shit right now. Thanks for coming by."

She started to walk past him and he opened his mouth as if he were about to speak.

She stopped. "You're not going to tell me to not leave town, are you?"

He smiled for the first time and Maggie thought maybe he wasn't such a schmuck after all. "No, I guess not. Look after yourself, Mrs. Lambent. I'll be in touch." He turned around and walked down the hall to the elevators. Maggie stood there and watched him go.

It wasn't surprising, not really. It just hadn't occurred to her. She felt a rush of vertigo as she thought of court, lawyers, the dry, musty smell of public buildings. That particular vigil, if it happened, would almost be worse than this one.

She walked back to the nurses' station. Ariel was busy with a doll that Janelle had produced from somewhere. Maggie put her hand on the top of her head.

"Let's go see Daddy, Ariel."

Gene didn't look any different. Maggie tried to imagine tiny blood vessels in his brain popping, one by one, each leaking a blossom of blood into the surrounding tissue, pushing Gene closer to the edge. It was draining her, this slow fade of his. If she could do anything to hurry the process along, she would. She imagined sliding the pillow out from under his head and putting it over his face. Leaning over him, her weight pushing down on him, pushing him out of the world. It might come to that. He was killing them.

It wasn't just herself she was worried about. Gabe was going through some serious shit. She didn't understand all of it, and there wasn't a thing she could do about it – he seemed so far away from her.

And Ariel. Not as raw and primal as Gabe, there wasn't that hormonal edge, but she was very subdued. Underneath that, Maggie could sense a restless, unfocused energy that worried her. It seemed inward and corrosive.

They pulled their chairs up close to Gene's bed and Maggie pulled out her copy of *Charlotte's Web*. She began to read aloud, the machines clustered around Gene's bed whispering and beeping in the background, but Ariel kept fidgeting.

"What's the matter, Ari?" she asked finally, putting the book face down on the foot of Gene's bed.

Ariel looked up at her and shook her head. There were bruised circles under her eyes. "Nothing."

Maggie looked at Gene and mentally slapped herself on the forehead. *Stupid*. What's the matter. Her father's lying there in a coma with his skull filling up with blood and I'm asking her what's the matter.

"You want to watch TV, darlin'?"

She nodded – up once, down once.

They had the lounge to themselves this time. The shades were drawn and the room was dark and cool. Ariel turned the television on and flicked impatiently from channel to channel. Finally, she settled on a rerun of *Green Acres*. She perched on the end of the couch nearest the set and didn't seem inclined to move. Blue light from the television flickered across her face.

Maggie watched the characters stagger across the screen, buoyed by the laugh-track. She tried not to think about anything. There was a state she was trying to achieve, a kind of blankness that only seemed accessible after the seventh or eighth drink. It wasn't exactly numbness, but more as if someone had come along with a power sander and smoothed off all the rough edges in her mind. It was why she drank, trying to get to that place, but it kept slipping out of her grasp and she'd slide off the edge of her high, off the edge and down.

Christ, her throat hurt. "Don't go away, Ariel. I'll be right back." Maggie got up and walked down the hall to the water fountain. She held her hair back and bent over the gleaming basin, pushed the handle and let the water squirt into her open mouth. She drank until she could feel the water sloshing in her stomach, but her throat still burned raw.

When she looked up, Doctor Casanova was standing in front of her, as if he had appeared from thin air. She jumped back.

"Jesus, don't *ever* do that."

He frowned. "I'm sorry?"

She shook her head. "Never mind. So tell me what's going on, Doctor."

He cleared his throat. "I was just coming to see you. Your husband had a stroke last night. A mild one, actually, but there's more inter-cranial bleeding and some paralysis."

"Not so you'd notice." He looked oddly at her and she held up a hand. "Sorry. Go ahead."

He cleared his throat again. "I must tell you that there is no chance of your husband recovering normal function. Even if he comes out of the coma, he would require skilled nursing care for the rest of his life."

Maggie nodded. She felt the words drifting past her head like small clouds. Normal function. Skilled nursing.

"I need to ask you about extraordinary means."

Extraordinary means. "Excuse me?"

He gave an impatient shake of his head. "To preserve

his life. If he has another episode, should we use all available means to preserve his life or let nature take its course." It wasn't a question.

"Doctor, my husband drove his car through the front window of a Liquor Barn and sailed through the windshield like a fucking crash test dummy. You tell me what nature has to do with it."

"I'm sorry, Mrs. Lambent." He paused and took a breath. "I need for you to tell me if we should do anything to keep your husband alive."

She paused. "No." Brief, dizzying rush of vertigo. "No, don't do anything."

Suddenly, he was holding a clipboard and a pen out to her. "Would you sign here, please?"

She scrawled her name next to an 'x' near the bottom of the page.

"And here."

Another looping scribble.

"One more time, just your initials."

She felt like she was being swept away. She paused and looked down at the clipboard. The words swam before her eyes. She found the space she was supposed to initial and wrote, in careful block letters, MBL. Margaret Black Lambent. Who she was. She hadn't gone by Black in many years. Maybe she'd start using it again.

Doctor Casanova tugged gently at the clipboard and she released it. "Thank you," he said.

"So where do we go from here, Doctor?"

He shrugged. "He could stay like this for months, years even. Or he could die tomorrow. We have no way of knowing. He's in a critical period right now and I don't want to move him." His lips compressed to a tight line. "We wait and see."

Maggie ran her hand through her hair. "That's not very satisfying, Doctor."

"I'm sorry, Mrs. Lambent. The brain—"

"—is a very complicated carburetor kind of thing.

Yeah, I know. You told me yesterday."

He looked at her with an annoyed expression.

"What are you looking at?" she asked. "Am I putting you out here? Jesus, fuck, you think *you've* got problems." He pushed his lips together again, forcing the blood out of them until they were almost white. She paused and took a deep breath. "Sorry, Doctor. Go ahead."

"He's suffered some brain damage," he said, as if nothing had happened. "How much, we can't be sure without exploratory surgery, and that's contraindicated here."

"Why is that, Doctor?"

He paused. "I'll be blunt. Exploratory surgery is called for only in those cases where it might do some good. In your husband's case, it would be just...cataloging the damage."

Maggie sighed. "Cataloging the damage. That's a nice phrase, Doctor. I feel like I've been doing that all my life."

"I'm sorry there's nothing more I can tell you, Mrs. Lambent. I'll talk to you again tomorrow – maybe we'll know something more."

He put the clipboard under his arm, turned around, and walked down the hall, his heels clicking on the polished floor. Maggie stood next to the water fountain and watched him walk away; it felt like *she* was receding, the tiled walls slipping past her in a green blur.

She wanted to give Gabe a call, see how he was doing. She looked in on Ariel on her way to the phone. Still perched on the end of the couch, transfixed by the television, mouth hanging slightly open. There was an expression of such vacancy on her face that Maggie's breath caught and her eyes filled with tears.

"I'm going to make a call, Ari. Be right back."

Ariel looked up, nodded, and looked back at the television.

There was only one working pay phone on the floor and somebody was on it, involved in a long, complicated argument with somebody who sounded, from this end of the conversation, like a lawyer. Periodically, he looked up at

Maggie and glared at her, as if she were responsible for his troubles. When he was done, he slammed the receiver down and brushed past her, bumping her shoulder.

"Asshole," she muttered as she dialed their number. Gabe picked up. He sounded distracted, but that was to be expected. She told him about her conversation with the doctor. About what they were going to do with Gene. It was hard to say out loud, but it felt good to articulate it. And Gabe took it well.

He's going to *have* to be strong, she thought. This isn't over yet.

As soon as she placed the receiver on its cradle, the phone rang. On impulse, she picked it up. There was a rush of static, several sharp clicks like branches snapping in winter air, a faint voice.

"Maggie." Smeared across the static in a drunken slur.

"Who is this?" Maggie asked. But she knew who it was.

"...miss you, Maggie...ought to know..." The voice faded in and out. "...never do anything to..."

"Who *is* this? You're not funny."

The static howled like a great beast of metal and steam. Maggie slammed the receiver down and leaned against the wall, holding on to keep herself from falling. She took a deep breath, then another. More crazy shit, some crank caller, she told herself, but there was a faint, clear voice that sounded counterpoint. *Denial*, it said. *This is denial.*

She straightened up began to walk down the hall. An orderly passed her going the opposite direction, pushing a patient on a gurney. Another green-suited man pushed an IV pole on a wheeled stand alongside. Maggie caught a glimpse of a woman's face, eyes closed, beatific expression. Almost smiling. She felt the breeze of their passage and caught a whiff of something foul and septic laced with a medicinal smell.

Her memory clicked into place and she recognized the face. *Sarah.* Gene's fucking lunatic sister. Maggie had only

163

met her once, but she was crazier than a sackful of rats. She was *dead*, though, asphyxiated by a propane leak in her geodesic dome up in the New Hampshire woods. Gene had taken the news pretty hard, sinking into an even deeper drunken stupor than usual, one that lasted through that winter and into the following spring.

The gurney disappeared around a corner. Maggie stopped and leaned against the wall. Suddenly it was hard to breathe. She thought of the refrain to an old Dylan song: *Something is happening but you don't know what it is. Do you, Mister Jones?*

The hallway stretched away from her in both directions, the light from open doorways reflecting in diffuse patches on the green tile.

Be strong for Ariel, she told herself. She took a breath, steadied herself, and walked down the hall to the lounge.

A young girl was sitting on the sofa next to Ariel. She looked seriously punk – partly shaved head, lots of piercing jewelry, wide stripe of purple in her straight, black hair. She wore black pajamas and odd, Japanese slippers with a space between the big toe and the rest of the foot. Obviously a patient. Maggie got a good feeling about her right away, though. She was leaning attentively towards Ariel and they were both laughing. It gave Maggie a kind of tingle up her arms to see Ariel's face stretched into a grin like that. It had been a while.

"Hi," she said.

They both looked up.

"Hi," the girl said. She wheezed a little before she spoke and her breathing seemed labored, as if she had just walked up a flight of stairs. "I'm Casey. You must be Gabe's Mom."

"Casey. Gabe mentioned you." Maggie walked over to her and held out her hand. "I'm Maggie. Pleased to meet you."

Casey shook her hand with a gravity that Maggie

found appealing. This kid was young, maybe a couple of years older than Gabe, but she didn't project that undercurrent of silliness that a lot of teenage girls did. There was something about her presence that Maggie recognized as street. She'd probably been through some shit.

Maggie sat down next to her, sinking into the foam cushion.

"Hey, check it out, Ariel," Casey said, pointing at the television. "Arnold the pig. The guy thinks it's like his dog or something. What a maroon." She looked at Maggie and winked while Ariel giggled. Her expression became serious again. "I'm really sorry for all your troubles right now. Gabe was telling me a little about it yesterday – it sounds like a major bummer."

"Major bummer." She laughed sharply. "You could say that." Major bummer indeed. Nothing seems real.

Casey was looking at her. "Sorry," Maggie said. "Yeah, it's hard. Everything's up in the air." She paused. "You probably came looking for Gabe, didn't you?"

Casey nodded. "Well, yeah, actually."

"I let him sleep in this morning. He's been going through a lot."

Casey nodded again. "Good idea."

Maggie wanted to ask her about her illness, but didn't know how to bring it up. She stopped noticing the labored breathing after a minute or two. She wondered if Casey ever stopped noticing it.

"So, you're—"

"Cystic fibrosis," Casey said. She laughed at Maggie's surprise. "I get to recognize the uncomfortable pause, you know? Okay, here it comes, I think. Maybe we can get it out of the way and I can get treated like a fucking human being instead of a medical freak or an object of pity. Sometimes it works, sometimes it doesn't. So here goes." She took a deep wheezing breath and affected the look of a stern lecturer. "Cystic fibrosis is a genetic disorder caused by the inability of chloride ions to cross the specialized epithelial cells of salivary, mucus, and sweat glands and the pancreas. Effects include heavy production of thick mucus in respiratory tracts, which increases susceptibility to respiratory infections. Ninety percent of all patients die of chronic lung disease. The average life span of cystic fibrosis patients is twenty-four years."

Casey looked at her challengingly. Her breath was coming a little faster and her already pale skin seemed almost translucent.

This kid has some serious boundaries, Maggie thought. She didn't know what she'd done to set her off.

She nodded. "Okay," she said. It sounded completely inane to her but it seemed to satisfy Casey.

They turned their attention to the television. Arnold the Pig was dressed in a tuxedo and tails and Mr. Ziffel was trying to bring him into a fancy Manhattan restaurant. The maitre d' backed up in horror and fell over a chair. Ariel laughed shrilly.

"Jesus, what is this, the all *Green Acres* channel?" Maggie asked.

"I've got the entire cable daytime programming matrix committed to memory," Casey said. "Not much else to do here. Eleven to twelve, two episodes of *Green Acres* on the Nostalgia Channel, back to back. Then we've got *My Mother, The Car* and *Family Affair*. I just want to smack Buffy. I'm glad she oh-deed."

Maggie laughed. "I wondered what happened to her."

They watched for a while longer, Casey leaning over to whisper wisecracks into Ariel's ear. Maggie started wondering what the hell they were doing there. It was too nice a day to keep Ariel cooped up with the smell of ether and antiseptic, and it didn't look likely that Gene's condition would change any time soon. And if it did, there wasn't a whole lot they could do about it.

"Do they ever let you out of here?" Maggie asked Casey. "Gabe said something about a pass."

Casey's eyes slid away for a moment. "Yeah, I can get

out of here."

"Good. You want to come over for dinner? I'm sure Gabe would like to see you. I can get you back here afterwards, or you can crash on the couch and I can bring you back in the morning."

Casey nodded. "That would be great."

"Great!" Ariel echoed. Casey ruffled her hair.

"Why don't we blow this taco stand, then? I want to look in on my husband again first. Is there anything I have to sign for you?"

"Don't worry about it," Casey said. "I'll meet you in the parking lot."

"Okay, then. Fifteen minutes?"

Casey nodded.

"Come on, Ari. Let's say goodbye to your father."

They stood in the doorway looking at him. Maggie pushed Ariel gently on the shoulders, urging her forward. She resisted, then walked a few steps into the room.

They stood there for a minute or so. The walls of the room receded further and further away, until the three of them were dots on the surface of a vast linoleum plain. The fluorescent light spanned the sky far overhead in a bright, white arch, and the ground hummed with huge, unseen machines vibrating the soles of their feet.

Maggie realized she was praying. Three words, over and over again.

Let him die. Let him die. Let him die.

Ariel huddled close, and Maggie put her arm around her shoulder.

"Goodbye, Gene," Maggie said, closing her eyes. When she opened them again, the room was back. Nothing had changed. "Let's go, Ari."

They pulled the Escort in front of the main entrance. After a few minutes, Casey appeared, wearing black jeans, small round sunglasses, and a purple, sleeveless t-shirt with 'Fuck Art, Let's Dance' scrawled across the front. A canvas bag was slung over her shoulder. She looked nervously behind her as she ducked into the back seat.

"Everything all right?" Maggie asked.

"No problem," Casey said. "Let's rock."

CHAPTER SEVENTEEN

"Those will have to come out." The dentist's face hovered over him like a pale moon. "As soon as possible, I'm afraid. I'm going to give you a prescription for some codeine for the pain, and I want you to make an appointment with Dr. Fasten down the hall. He's a very good oral surgeon. I work with him often." He pronounced the T in 'often.'

Gene grunted assent. Speaking was painful; he could barely open his mouth more than half an inch or so. Fucking wisdom teeth.

"All right, then." Dr. Mock turned the glaring examination light off. It was as if the sun had winked out. Purple spots swam in Gene's vision. The light rocked gently on its spidery arm.

"Could I have a little more nitrous before I go?" Gene asked, moving his jaw as little as possible.

Dr. Mock snorted. It sounded like a car kicking up gravel as it pulled into a driveway. "Heh. I don't think so, Mr. Lambent. You just make that appointment."

He turned and scribbled something on a pad and handed it to Gene.

Gene grunted again and got up out of the chair. A black and white photograph of a UNICEF poster girl graced the office wall. Huge, sad eyes followed him as he walked out of the room. He got his jacket from the coat-tree next to the receptionist's desk.

"Will you be coming back?" she asked.

Gene paused for a moment. "No," he said. "No, I won't be coming back."

He filled the prescription at Serio's Drugs, right next door. Gene had to look twice at the sign – at first he'd thought it said "Serious Drugs." The pharmacist, Serio, he supposed, peered owlishly at him from behind Coke-bottle glasses before shuffling back to fill the order. Gene could hear him calling Dr. Mock's office to verify it.

Hey, come on. I don't look that bad.

"This is refillable, right?" Gene asked, when the pharmacist handed him a brown, plastic vial.

The man nodded slowly, and held up one finger.

"Ayup. Once."

"Do you think I could get it refilled, like, *now*, so I don't have to come back?"

The pharmacist looked at him for a couple of seconds, then slowly shook his head.

"It don't work like that. You take one of these every four to six hours or as needed. For pain. You bring the bottle back when you use these up, I give you some more."

He was supposed to meet Maggie for lunch at Yet Now's in Northampton. Lunch was theory. He could barely open his mouth far enough to speak, let alone eat. He was looking forward to seeing Maggie, though; it had been a few days. They were in kind of a weird space lately. Like, okay, something's happening here. What do we do now? It made them both a little cranky with each other. Not much sex lately, either.

He stopped at the Hadley Package Store and picked up a six of Narragansett. Cheap and a bit skunky, especially if you let it get warm, but Gene wasn't planning on letting it get warm. He cracked open a can as soon as he got back in the car and shook four pills into his palm. One of them got caught in the back of his throat and he had to scarf down the whole can and part of another before it finally dislodged.

170

Gene put a Human Sexual Response tape into the cassette player, turned it up loud, and pulled out onto Route 9. The pounding bass line wove in and out of the engine sounds. He finished the second beer and threw the empty over his shoulder. It landed in the back seat with a clatter.

It had snowed heavily the day before and the road was bordered on either side with irregular, grayish mounds, the landscape transformed into something moon-like. By the time he was crossing the Connecticut River, just before the outskirts of Noho, he had finished a third 'Gansett. He was starting to feel all right. Sliding into normal. Two blocks before Main he passed Captain Howdy's and waved. *Hi, Eric. If you call me on my day off, I'll break your fucking legs.*

In the parking lot Yet Now's shared with True-Value Hardware, Gene overcompensated while he was pulling into his space and gouged a long, jagged line in the side of a new Ford Tempo.

"Damn." *Serves them right for buying such a piece of shit new.* He looked around for witnesses. Not a soul, but there was another space on the far side of the parking lot. He backed out, executed a complicated four-point turning maneuver in the crowded space, and glided into the new spot.

I can really maneuver this pig when I have to, he thought. He patted the dashboard. *Good boy.*

Maggie was already in the restaurant, sipping a nasty looking brown drink though a straw. A paper umbrella sat in the ashtray in front of her and she was burning holes in it with her cigarette. On a plate next to the ashtray, an egg-roll rested between pools of mustard and plum sauce.

"What in the world are you drinking?" Gene asked.

"Long Island Iced Tea," Maggie said. "You're late. What's wrong with your mouth?"

"Fucking wisdom teeth. I can barely open it more than a quarter inch. Food is impossible."

"Wow, that was sudden."

"Most things are."

She looked at him quizzically. "What do you mean?"

171

His head felt like it was filled with sodden bread. He couldn't think. "I'm not sure," he said, after a long pause.

"Well, listen, do you mind if I order something? I'm fucking starving."

"No, don't mind me. Go ahead."

Maggie raised her finger and a Chinese midget appeared, vibrating from the sudden stop. *Damn*, they were fast!

Maggie said something to the midget in Chinese and they both laughed. The midget turned to Gene and cocked her head.

"Help you?" she asked.

"Tsing Tao. Wild Turkey, straight up."

She nodded and scurried away.

"I didn't know you could speak Chinese," Gene said.

"Chinese? What the fuck are you talking about? I ordered the Kung Pao Chicken." She peered at him. "Maybe you should lay off the Turk, Gene. Stick to beer."

"Maybe you should bite my crank."

Maggie sighed and shook her head. Gene turned away and the midget was standing right next to his shoulder, holding a tray. He jumped back.

"God *damn* it."

The midget smiled and set the drinks in front of him. "Tsing Tao. Wild Turkey." She scurried off again.

"Damn, they're fast around here."

Maggie looked at him quizzically again.

Gene looked over at the far end of the room. Three of them huddled together, heads bobbing up and down. Every now and then, one of them – their waitress, he supposed, but they all looked the same to him – gestured over in their direction.

Gene turned back to Maggie. He reached for the egg roll. "Let me give that a try."

He picked it up, trailed the end first in mustard, then plum sauce, and brought it to his mouth. He tried to open wide enough to accommodate it, but it hurt too much. He managed to get his teeth around the pointed end of it and bit off a crumb. The mustard blasted through his sinus cavities like Drano.

"Jesus." He took a long gulp from the Tsing Tao, dribbling some down his chin.

"You are just one classy guy, Gene. That's all there is to it." Maggie was shaking her head and smiling.

"What's so damn funny? I can't eat a thing. I'm fucking starving, man!"

The midget appeared again at Maggie's elbow. She slid a steaming plate in front of her and disappeared, blinking out with a faint popping sound.

Gene looked closely at the plate. Bits of chicken, cubes of vegetable matter, peanuts, and wicked-looking chili peppers in a gelatinous gravy pooling into a mound of white rice shaped like an inverted bowl.

Maggie picked up her chopsticks and deftly snatched a scrap of meat. "Mm. Good. Maybe you can sort of slide some of this through your teeth, Gene. Give it a try."

Gene picked up his chopsticks and tried to scoop up a morsel of rice, but his hand wasn't working right and one of the chopsticks fell into the sauce. He picked it up, wiped it off, and tried again. He managed to balance a few grains of rice and a piece of chicken on the end of his sticks, but as he lifted it to his mouth, the chicken fell into his lap.

"*Fuck*." He licked the remaining rice off of the chopsticks, put them down and picked up the plate, raising it to his lips and tilting. He managed to slurp down a couple of scraps of chicken and some rice, swallowing without chewing, before he felt Maggie's hand on his wrist.

"God damn it, Gene."

"What the fuck, you just offered. Isn't this family style?"

"Well, sure, but—"

"Well, *fuck* you, then." He overturned the plate on the table, pressing down on top of the mound of food. Tongues of sauce oozed out from underneath the plate, staining the

173

tablecloth. Gene picked up the shot of Wild Turkey, drained it, and slammed the shot glass on top of the inverted plate.

He glared at Maggie and stalked out of the restaurant. He could feel their eyes on his back as he walked out the door, that fucking gang of midgets. God *damn* it.

The Human Sexual Response cover of "Cool Jerk" blared out his speakers as he drove down Main, the bass crackling like burning wood. He felt like he was driving on a cushion of air. Every move economical and precise. His left was coming up, onto College and down past Rahar's. There was oncoming traffic but he estimated a two second window to make the turn safely and he took it, leaning into the centrifugal force. There was a chorus of horns behind him. Fucking pussies.

Gliding downhill. The Wild Turkey threatened to come up and he closed his eyes and swallowed. Familiar lurch when he reached the bottom of the hill. They didn't plow as well here and the road was slippery, all patchy grey slush and tire tracks. He took a sharp left onto Masonic and went into a skid. He turned into it and the car spun around in a perfect three-sixty, the street gliding by in a steady pan, slow grace and beauty like a carousel.

He stopped, stalled. Everything was quiet except the keys clicking rhythmically against the steering column. The tape was in that long blank space at the end of the album, snap, snap, crackle. Miraculously, the Valiant was still pointed in the right direction. He patted the dash. *Good boy.*

Gene's apartment house was half a block down, a rickety fourplex built during the postwar construction boom. He skidded a little again as he drove down the street, but righted himself without any trouble. He slid silently into his parking space in front of the back stairs.

His kitchen was a chaotic mess of empty pizza boxes, Chinese take-out containers, empty beer cans that had been used as ash trays. Jesus, he was *hungry*.

He opened the refrigerator. The door slammed into the wall and his Elvis magnet went skidding across the floor.

Not much in there. A few desiccated scraps of pastrami in a loose fold of wax paper. A heel of rye bread. A jar of Gulden's Brown. A can of Colt 45.

Gene looked up. Atop the refrigerator like a star crowning a Christmas tree. His blender. *Yes.*

He swept a couple of empties off the table. They skidded across the floor after the Elvis magnet. Yanked out the toaster cord. Slammed the blender down and plugged it in. Some pastrami. Colt foaming over as he ripped off the tab, get some moisture in there. Big dollop of mustard with the end of his finger. *Liquefy* the son of a bitch. Whining like a fucking dentist drill. Some bread in there too, nice liquid sandwich. Faint smell of ozone.

He lifted the pitcher off its mount and held it in front of him, sloshing the contents back and forth. Opaque, foamy brew. Gene brought it to his lips and let some trickle into his mouth. God, it was *good.*

Outside, a sparse drift of white flakes past the window. More snow. Gene opened the door and stepped out onto the landing. His breath plumed into the grey sky. He pulled his shirt off and felt the flakes touch his skin, one by one, little fingers of cold fire winking out. He floated down the stairs to his car, pulled open the door. Fold of red-checked blanket in the back seat, nest of crumpled cans. He climbed in, pulled the blanket around himself. Looking up through the back window at the grey dome of the sky. Each snowflake touching the window becoming a tiny, ragged star.

CHAPTER EIGHTEEN

Otto and Gabe drove through Lewes, passing by the hospital on the other side of town. Gabe felt cold at the sight of the building, a deep, nameless dread mixed with guilt for not being there. He had a mental image of bruised flesh peeking out from beneath folds of bright, white gauze, and pushed it away. He scanned the brick and glass facade of the building, trying to pick out his father's room. He thought it was on the fourth floor, third from the right, but he wasn't certain. He was pretty sure Casey's was on the other side, facing the ocean. Gabe looked for his mother's Escort in the parking lot, but he couldn't find it.

"That where your father is?" Otto asked.

"Yeah."

"How's he doing?"

"Not so good, I guess. My mom said he had a stroke last night. They're going to pull the plug on him."

Otto grunted and nodded. "How are *you* doing?" he asked, after a little while.

Gabe looked over at him. He saw his distorted reflection in Otto's sunglasses. He felt mixed up; part of him wanted to be there and part of him didn't.

"I'm okay, I guess." He paused. "I...I want to *know* more. There are these things that I can do, I just think of something sometimes and it happens, but I don't know how I do it exactly, or how *not* to do it." He stared out the window

176

at the low, wooden houses, the blue ocean peeking through every now and then. "I don't know what's happening to me."

Otto kept driving, looking straight out at the road ahead. After a few minutes, Gabe figured he just wasn't going to say anything.

"Everything has a cost," Otto said finally. He looked straight ahead at the road, hands on the wheel at ten and two. "That's the first thing you have to remember. Maybe the only thing. Every decision you make, every time you do anything, there's a balance sheet somewhere that gets readjusted, but you don't always know what the cost is going to be, so you have to just do the right thing." He paused again, chewed thoughtfully on his cigar stub, and looked over at Gabe. "By instinct."

Gabe felt the weight of Otto's gaze beneath the dark glasses. It reminded him of the soulless, black eyes of an insect.

After a little while, Otto turned the radio on, a Golden Oldies station with lots of commercials.

The *Racing Form* lay on the seat between them, folded in half. Gabe picked it up and opened it. A color picture of a horse filled the upper half of the front page. Beneath it, the headline read: BLACK DAY LOOMING WITH BRYAN AND PAL.

Gabe read down a couple of paragraphs. The story was about a trainer named Black and two of his horses, Bryan J and Best Pal. It was crushingly dull. Inside were a few other articles about trainers or jockeys, but mostly the paper was filled with columns of numbers and odd, cryptic notes in very small type. On the page labeled Pimlico, what Gabe assumed was Otto's handwriting wove in and out of the columns in a fluid scrawl, the spidery characters graced with strange dots and underscores. It wasn't English.

"Hey, what language is this?" Gabe asked.

Otto glanced over at the page.

"Aramaic," he said. "Do you want to stop and get a burger somewhere or eat at the racetrack?"

Gabe wasn't very hungry. "Racetrack."

"Dare to be great," Otto said.

Gabe looked down the page. The big number in the upper left corner was the number of the race, and it looked like each block of fine print was a record of a particular horse's previous performance. Gabe liked the names of the horses. Twicetonight. Minniemax. The Wicked North. Double Oh Seven. Some had a long list of races below their names, some only a couple. Timings were given for each race and at the far right, brief, cryptic comments. Grudgingly. Gamely. Wide turn. Weakened.

"So you're supposed to look at this thing and figure out which horse is going to win?" Gabe asked.

"Sort of," Otto said. "It's like trying to find your way around a room blindfolded. You listen extra hard, you pay attention to the way the air feels on your face, you move slowly so you don't hurt yourself."

Gabe looked sharply at him. *Why can't he just answer my fucking question?*

"So, you look at this thing and you try to figure out which horse is going to win, right?"

"Right." Otto grinned, a wicked leer. "What you want to look for is an overlay situation, where the odds of a horse winning are significantly greater than the odds posted. That's where you make your score."

"How do you find those?"

Otto reached up and touched his nose. "You have to sniff them out. You look at the trainer's record, how the horse has done in the last few races. Sometimes a trainer will deliberately keep a horse out of condition. It flops on a few races and gets a drop in class. Its record stinks so the posted odds make it look like a dog, but it's running against a field of stiffs so it blows them out of the water. You find one of those and you're in Fat City."

"Yeah, but how do you know when you've found one?"

"You don't." Otto rolled down the window, threw

178

out his cigar stub, and pulled a fresh one from his shirt pocket. Keeping one hand on the wheel, he ripped the cellophane wrapper off with his teeth, bit off the end of the cigar, spat it out, and closed the window again. He struck a wooden match on the dashboard and puffed the thing to life, filling the cab with foul, acrid smoke. Gabe coughed and opened his window.

"The Ten Commandments of Horse Wagering," Otto said, blowing out a smoke ring. The wind in the cab ripped it to nothingness. "Thou shalt not wager on a horse unless: It has been raced in the last twenty-one days. It came in at least third in its last race. It had a workout within five days of the current day's race. It has won at least twenty percent of its races. It was no worse than third at the quarter pole in its last race. It's coming in at no less than eight to one." He paused. "You getting all this?"

Gabe nodded.

"Good. Thou shalt not wager on any horse weighing in at more than two pounds over. Thou shalt not wager fillies against males. Thou shalt not wager on a horse moving down in class after a bad race." He took a long pull on his cigar.

"What's Ten?" Gabe asked.

"I told you that one yesterday. Bet to win. No balls, no babies."

Gabe remembered that Otto had also said to cheat if you could, to do anything you could get away with. He scanned the rows and columns of figures. Maybe Antifreeze in the Sixth.

They drove east and north on small roads, passing through towns with names like Andrewville, Adamsville, Groverdale. The countryside between towns was low, rolling farmland; the towns themselves indistinguishable clusters of gas stations, fast food franchises, and factory outlets. As they approached Baltimore, the clusters grew until they squeezed out the farmland in between.

The blocky skyscrapers of downtown Baltimore were visible and getting closer when they turned off the highway at a green and white RACETRACK sign. They negotiated a maze of surface streets graced on either side with pawn shops and check cashing storefronts, and arrived at a gate where Otto gave a uniformed attendant some money.

Beyond the gate was a huge parking lot. Bright sunlight glinted off row after row of windshields. At the other end of the lot, about a quarter mile away, several tiers of grandstands stood against the sky. Men in orange vests and peaked policeman hats directed traffic; one of them motioned Otto away from the stadium toward the far end of the lot where there were still a few spots.

Otto shut the motor off and looked over at Gabe. His face split into a wide grin.

"We're here," he said. "Do you have any money?"

"Just a couple of dollars," Gabe said, flustered.

Otto reached into his pocket and pulled out a wad of bills. He peeled two twenties off the roll and gave them to Gabe.

"Here's your stake."

Gabe hesitated for a moment, then took the bills.

"Thanks."

"Remember the Commandments. Make me proud."

"Uh, okay."

They walked toward the stadium, converging with other knots of people as they approached the gate. Otto gave the attendant some money and they pushed through a turnstile. It seemed to Gabe that as soon as the turnstile clicked into place behind him, the noise level around them went up a notch. The sound was like an ocean, surging, pulsing, a palpable presence.

An old man in a stained madras sport jacket held up a bundle of long blue cards, waving them in peoples' faces as they pushed by. He was wearing a snap-brim hat with one of the cards tucked into the band, giving him the appearance of a decrepit peacock.

"Clocker Dan, Daily Double Dan. Clocker Dan. One dollar." His nasal twang cut through the ambient noise like a hot knife through whipped cream.

As they approached, Gabe saw that his teeth were brown and crooked. A nasty looking lump crusted with dried blood sprouted out of the center of his forehead like a third eye. Every now and then, somebody stopped and gave him a bill in exchange for one of the cards. Twenty feet away, another man hawked orange cards at the passing crowd. Gabe heard "Sneaky Pete. Beat the odds," floating above the babble of voices.

Gabe turned to Otto. "If those guys really know who's going to win, what are they doing here selling these things for a buck a pop?"

Otto nodded. "Very good."

"And why is anybody buying them?"

"Excellent. You catch on fast. Your average racetrack patron is dumber than a box of dead crabs."

In front of them, a pair of whitewashed booths split the river of people into three streams.

"Programs," Otto said. "Let's get a couple."

The programs were long and thin, printed on glossy paper. All they listed was the name of the horse, jockey, and trainer for each race, and what position the horse was running in. Ads for beer and cigarettes interleaved the race listings.

"We've only got about ten minutes until post time for the first race," Otto said. "Who do you like?"

"Well, Killdozer has a cool name."

Otto shot him a caustic look.

"And has a drop in class in this race," Gabe continued. "*And* came in third the last two races."

Otto smiled and nodded approvingly. "Not bad. But look here." His tobacco-stained finger hovered over the *Racing Form*. "Those races were over two months ago, and her last two workouts weren't anything to write home about."

"Okay, who do *you* like?"

"They've been holding back Samanjanet Evening on the workouts to make her look bad. Look at these timings and compare them to her last three races."

Gabe studied the paper. After a while, he nodded. "Yeah, but she's five pounds over and her last workout was over a week ago. That's Commandments, uh—"

"Three and seven," Otto said approvingly. "But slavish obedience does not a successful handicapper make. I think the smart money here is going on Samanjanet."

The crowd thickened as they approached the betting windows. There were long lines in front of each window, displacing the crowd like piers thrusting into a flowing river.

A stale, closed-in smell hung in the air, an amalgam of unwashed bodies, sour beer, tobacco, and Lysol. The crowd pressed in on all sides, jostling Gabe with a directionless, Brownian pressure like the molecules of a gas.

The man in front of them wore a tattered baseball jacket, blue wool with yellow piping, and a U.S.S. Saratoga cap. He mumbled to himself in an unbroken string of profanity, becoming more and more agitated as they approached the window.

He turned to Gabe. "Motherfucker *walked* on me. Right out the gate, motherfucker walked all *over* me." His right hand clenched and unclenched in the air between them, something apart from both of them. His eyes held Gabe's with startling intensity for a moment, then wandered off.

Otto leaned toward Gabe. "When you get to the window, you tell the guy the amount you're betting, the number of the horse, and win, place or show. Make sure you've got all that right, because they don't give refunds."

Gabe nodded. "Isn't the guy going to hassle me about my age?" he asked.

"Don't worry," Otto said. "I'll take care of it."

"Magic?"

"Sort of." Otto flashed a roll of bills at Gabe and winked.

The line moved quickly. Over the noise of the crowd, Gabe heard an announcement saying there was one minute until post time.

The man in the baseball jacket stepped up to the

betting window. He mumbled something, thrust a handful of bills underneath the bars, and walked away clutching a bouquet of white tickets.

Otto gently shouldered Gabe aside and leaned close in to the window. He pushed some bills under the bars and scooped up a handful of tickets.

Gabe walked up to the window. The agent looked at him through the bars. His face was deeply lined, eyes sunk back into the wrinkles like glass beads.

"Uh, five dollars, number three, win." Samanjanet Evening. He pushed a folded bill underneath the bars.

The man punched something on a console in front of him and a white ticket popped out of a slot in a metal plate. He slid it back under the bars along with Gabe's change.

Just like movie tickets, Gabe thought.

"It's too late to get up to the grandstand," Otto said. "Let's watch it on closed circuit."

They pushed through the crowd to a denser knot clustered around a television set fixed to the wall about ten feet off the ground. All around them, heads craned upwards. The man next to Gabe had a goiter on his neck the size of a softball. Patches of mottled skin stood out on the taut skin like islands.

The horses are at the starting gate. The horses are at the gate. The announcer's voice crackled over the ancient PA system, ringing faintly with feedback.

The ambient noise in the stadium seemed to crank up another notch, an amorphous hum of voices blending together into one.

"I can't see the numbers," Gabe said. "Where's three?"

"Second from the rail."

The horses and jockeys looked pretty much the same to Gabe.

One of these is definitely going to win, he thought. It seemed like a revelation.

And they're off.

The crowd-voice surged. The announcer was calling the race, but the words all blurred together with the crowd-voice getting louder and louder like the voice of an animal chained and straining. The Three horse was nose-on with the Six and together they surged ahead of the pack, one, two, three lengths, their heads bobbing up and down in a rhythm synched with their jockeys' flogging. The Three horse edged ahead and the pack held in that position, frozen in relative stasis, until finally in the home stretch, another horse broke free from the trailing pack, number Two, easily eating the distance to the leaders. The jockey's switch rose and fell on the horse's flank. The crowd-voice howled and it seemed the Two was riding on the crest of that mindless white noise. The Three faltered and receded behind the Six as the Two surged ahead of both of them, sailing across the finish line with impossible grace. The crowd-voice surged once more, cresting, breaking, tailing off to a beehive murmur. There was a collective holding of breath, a kind of time-slip, as they waited for the results to flash on the tote board.

Two. Six. Four. Three.

Gabe looked over at Otto. "Shit. What was the Two?"

"Killdozer." Otto looked at his tickets, put one in his shirt pocket, and let the others flutter to the ground. Around them, other people were doing the same. Useless tickets were strewn across the worm linoleum like leafy mulch.

"You *bet* him?" Gabe asked, incredulous.

Otto nodded. "Yup. Five win."

"But I thought you said—"

"I did. Look, you're in school here, Gabe, and you've just learned lesson numero uno. Nothing is true, except what happens. Before a race, you've got all these possibilities, all these futures. Any one of them could happen. Then *bang*. The race is a sort of projection operator on a state vector in Hilbert space. The wave function collapses; oneness emerges out of the many, truth from chaos." He pulled deeply on his cigar and blew a perfect smoke ring.

184

"What the fuck are you talking about?"

Otto chuckled. "Poems are made by fools like me, but only God can quantize thee. Besides, horseplayers are slime. They'll toss you a false lead just for the fun of watching you piss away your rent money on it."

Gabe glared at him. Otto laughed again and clapped him on the shoulder.

"Cheer up, Gabe. Come on, I'll buy you some nachos."

They pushed through the crowd to the concession stand. A pair of young Hispanic women pumped bright yellow cheese over cardboard cartons of taco chips, poured beer and soda, lathered mustard over greasy links. They moved with quick, fluid grace. One kept up a constant patter as she worked; the other was completely silent.

"Two dogs, two Buds, yeah, that ought to kill the pain. So who you like in the next one? Why don't you just give *me* the money 'stead of throwing it away, right, Rita?"

Rita ignored her, scattering a handful of jalapenos over the top of an order of nachos and sliding it across the counter to a very thin middle-aged man with slicked-back hair. His eyes darted about like beads of water on a hot griddle.

"Nothing like racetrack nachos," Otto said. "It's not even food, not exactly. Look at that stuff. Penzoil."

"Next." The talkative one.

"Two nachos, two Budweisers."

"Hey, the kid isn't going to drink that, is he? You'll stunt his growth."

"No, they're both for me."

"I could use a couple myself. Okay, here you go, dos cervezas."

The food and drinks materialized in front of them, everything nestled in a folding cardboard tray. Otto picked it up and they worked back through the crowd to a row of benches just out from under the shadow of the grandstand.

Otto scooped up a gob of cheese and peppers with a

chip and pushed it in his mouth. He picked up one of the beers and drained half of it in a single gulp. He gestured to the food and looked at Gabe.

Gabe picked up a chip and dipped an end of it into a greasy pool of bright yellow cheese. It was the exact color of a brand new tennis ball. He slipped a jalapeno ring on top of that and put it in his mouth. It didn't taste like much at first, then it began to burn. He could feel blood rushing to his cheeks. It wasn't unpleasant, not really, but he wasn't sure he liked it much either. He picked up the cardboard cup and took a long sip of beer. It was very cold and felt good going down.

He looked at Otto. "So, basically, everything you tell me is bullshit."

Otto took another long pull of beer, rimming his mustache with foam. He licked his lips, looked at Gabe, and shrugged. The image of the grandstand curved across his mirrored sunglasses.

"Not really, but you have to develop your own bullshit filter, Gabe. It's part of learning who you are."

He's like a slippery eel, Gabe thought. You just can't pin him down.

They finished their nachos in silence. Otto got up to get another couple of beers. Gabe leaned back and looked up at the sky, clear and depthless blue. A few wispy cirrus clouds brushed across it. There was a slight wind coming in from the Bay, bringing with it a faint salt tang. The crowd murmur floated to him from the grandstand and he felt himself buoyed by it, lifted as if by a great, slow tide to another place.

"We've got about ten minutes until post time. Who do you like?" Otto's deep voice seemed to rumble up from someplace inside Gabe, vibrating the soles of his feet, tingling in his fingertips. He handed Gabe another beer.

"I don't know," Gabe said, taking a sip. "Skee-ball has had some good workouts recently."

"Who's riding? Manzanera? Fuck, that stiff hasn't won a race since Christ was a cowboy."

"Yeah, but look at this. She placed twice at Aqueduct since May, her timings are good, and she's coming in at five to one."

Otto scratched his beard thoughtfully.

They watched the tote board for a few minutes. Skee-ball was holding steady at five to one. Dognose was sinking fast. He started at six to one, dropped to five, and was now at nine to two.

"Dognose," Otto said.

Gabe shook his head. "Sucker bet. Lookit." He waved the *Racing Form* in the air. "Sure, he's got some good timings, but he's three pounds over and hasn't been worked out in nearly a month. The drop in class is just to rope in suckers."

Otto nodded approval. "You've got a future in this. Let's place our bets."

The line moved quickly. Gabe leaned close behind while Otto placed his bet. Ten to win on the six horse. Skee-ball. Otto pocketed his ticket and winked at Gabe as he walked away. Gabe slid ten dollars under the window to the clerk. "Ten, number four, win," he said quietly.

Dognose.

They went upstairs to the stands and watched the race from there.

The gates opened and the horses surged forward, staying together in an undifferentiated lump for the first quarter-length. Slowly, three horses eased ahead of the pack. Gabe squinted, trying to read the numbers fluttering against their flanks. One, four, seven. He looked for the Six. It had fallen behind the main pack and trailed at about two lengths. The Four pulled ahead of the other two, its head bobbing. The jockey clung to its back like a gaudy hump. The three lead horses stretched further ahead of the pack. Suddenly, another horse, the Two, broke free of the main group and started closing the distance to the leaders. The voice of the crowd surged, a mindless thing empty of reason. The Two was really moving. It passed the two trailing horses and came up close behind Dognose. Too little, though, too late. Skee-ball galloped leisurely across the finish line, dead last by eight lengths. The announcer's patter braided in and out of the roaring voice of the crowd. *And it's Dognose by two lengths. Dognose. Miami Device second. Photo for show. There is a photo for show. Please hold all tickets.*

"Yes!" Gabe shouted.

"What are you so happy about?" Otto asked. "Skee-ball's on his way to the glue factory."

Gabe showed him the winning ticket. "Dognose, dognose." He did a little dance around Otto. "Dognose, dognose."

Otto puffed thoughtfully on his cigar. It had gone out and he frowned at it. "The student surpasses the teacher. Very good."

"Dognose, dognose. Dognose, dognose."

"Quit that!"

Gabe stopped, grinning and a little out of breath.

"Hey, this isn't so hard," he said. "It beats delivering papers."

"Pride goeth before a fall, my man. You want to stay ahead in this business you have to detach from the outcome."

"You're just mad 'cause I talked you into betting on Slow-ball."

Otto didn't say anything. He struck a match and puffed his cigar back to life, raising a foul cloud that hung about his head in wispy filaments before a gust of wind blew it to tatters. He looked at Gabe, grinned, and picked up the *Form*.

"Who do you like in the next race?" he asked.

"I've got a feeling about Nova Express."

"I happen to know that that son of a bitch is medicated to the gills."

Gabe shook his head. "I don't care. I can *see* it." He closed his eyes and it ran across the back of his eyelids like a movie loop, Number Six sailing across the finish line, all alone.

CHAPTER NINETEEN

The light was turning yellow as Maggie approached the intersection. She gunned it and took the turn onto Route 1 hard, leaning into the centrifugal force. There was a chorus of horns.

Fucking wimps, she thought. *That was a precise maneuver.*

She looked over at Ariel to smile and her daughter was looking up at her, eyes wide and frightened. Casey didn't say anything, but Maggie could feel the tension in her silence.

She laughed, reached over, and mussed Ariel's hair. "Hey, now. Sorry I frightened you."

The cars in the oncoming lane were rushing by fast; she felt buffeted to the side by each Dopplered *whoosh*. The Escort was handling funny, like one of the rear tires needed air. She thought the back end was about to fishtail out from under her any second.

"Hang on just a second," she said, and pulled over onto the sandy shoulder.

"What's the matter?" Casey asked.

"I think I might have a flat." She got out of the car, walked around to the back, and kicked the tires. They seemed pretty solid. She looked at Casey and Ariel looking back at her from inside the car, Ariel's mouth hanging open a little, Casey impassive and ultra-cool.

Suddenly, Maggie felt like crying. Her eyes filled up with tears and she had to blink and squint to keep them from spilling down her cheeks. She turned away and rubbed her eyes. She felt a moment of intense vertigo and leaned against the trunk of the car to support herself until it passed. The breeze coming off the ocean felt cool against her face, lifting her hair off the back of her neck, riffling her shirt.

With deliberate steps, she walked back around to the driver's side and got in.

"Anything?" Casey asked.

"Huh?"

"Any problem? Flat?"

"Oh..." Maggie shook her head and felt a small surge of nausea with the motion. "No," she said. "No problem."

She pulled carefully into traffic and drove slowly, her hands clenched on the wheel at ten and two. They drove past the little strip mall near the trailer park where the Liquor Barn was. The window was boarded up but it appeared to be open for business.

Maggie felt another surge of nausea and had to gulp back something hot and caustic trying to bubble up from her gut. For a moment, she was filled with the taste of bourbon and beer, her nose, her mouth, her whole nervous system flooded with it.

There was a note from Gabe on the kitchen table.

"Looks like Gabe won't be back until around five," Maggie said to Casey after reading it. "I have a couple of errands to do. Can I ask you to hang with Ariel for a bit?"

"Uh, sure," Casey said. "If it's okay with Ariel."

Ariel nodded once.

"Great. You could go down to the beach or something. I'll get us some dinner. Back in a little while."

As soon as she closed the trailer door behind her, she felt like a weight lifted from her shoulders. A residue of guilt nagged at her, but she pushed it aside. To her left, Otto's Airstream was a bright smear of reflected sunlight; to her right, she could just see a patch of garden in front of Ruby's place. She got into her car and drove. She didn't think about where she was going; it felt like her hands on the wheel and her foot on the gas were pushing the car along a grooved track.

Before she realized it, she was parked in front of the Liquor Barn. Whorls in the sheet of plywood where the window had been reminded her of fingerprints. A man in a lime-green polo shirt came out of the double doors carrying a twelve-pack of Budweiser in each hand.

Maggie was thirsty.

She tried to imagine it, Gene pissed and feeling that unwelcome edge of sobriety starting to creep in through the drunken haze, punching the gas instead of the brake and sailing through the window like a ship coming into port. Or poised on one of those knife-edge moments when you realize that you could *just turn the wheel* and drive into oncoming traffic, just like that, or step onto that eleventh floor balcony, climb over the low fence and just hang there feeling the world opening up beneath your feet. Open your hands and fall into it. Just like that, you could change everything, all at once. Or maybe he just passed out, his eyes rolling up in his head and his foot like a lead weight on the gas pushing him through into the next world.

Maggie tried to imagine herself picking up a six-pack of Iron City and a bag of Cheetos, looking up, and seeing Gene's shitbox Valiant skip the curb and come barreling through the window display, sound of breaking glass slicing through the Muzak.

She got out of the car and walked through the double doors. The air conditioner was going full blast; it felt like a meat locker. A carpenter's horse stood near the window. Cases were stacked haphazardly nearby and there was a piercing whiskey smell that even the air conditioners couldn't dispel.

Maggie got a quart of grapefruit juice from the small grocery area and stood there holding it by the neck. She looked around at the rows of bottles, nodding inwardly at the familiar brand names as if to old friends.

191

Popov, she thought, and she was outside blinking the sun from her eyes, feeling the heat rising up from the parking lot asphalt like a constant pressure everywhere at once. Clutching a brown paper bag.

She drove down to the lagoon on the other side of the state beach. Not too many people came here because you weren't allowed to swim or fish, but Maggie liked it, even though it was mosquito Heaven. She parked in the almost empty lot and walked down the path to the water, the dunes rising up behind her on either side.

The breeze scalloped the surface of the lagoon in small, regular ridges. A seagull swooped down, touched the surface with one wing, and rose into the air again. Maggie shook the bottle of grapefruit juice, unscrewed the lid, and took a long sip. The cold felt good going down, but it left a burning in her throat. She unscrewed the lid from the vodka bottle. The paper seal resisted, then gave, all at once.

Maggie looked at the bottle and thought, *God damn it, Gene, you fuck.* She got unsteadily to her feet. *Don't do this to me.*

"What?" His voice. There he was, standing on the rippling surface of the pond about ten feet out. "What am I doing to you?"

"Leaving me, you son of a bitch. Taking me with you."

In the blink of an eye, he was next to her. "You have to do for yourself, Mags," he said. "Don't blame me. I can't help it. Never could. And hey, don't bogart that Popov, either." He took the bottle from her hand, raised it to his lips, and took a long pull. Maggie could see his Adam's apple moving as he swallowed. "Damn." He coughed and shook his head.

After a moment, he looked at her and grinned. "Does this mean we're alcoholics?"

She laughed and closed her eyes, blinking back tears. "I don't—"

Gene was gone. The vodka bottle lay on its side, draining into the sand. Maggie picked it up and stood there, swaying back and forth, then she threw the bottle as far as she could. It sailed end over end in a slow, graceful arc and hit the water with a splash. It bobbed there for a moment and slipped beneath the water.

Like still motion frames from a movie, a slide show. Maggie standing by the lagoon. Maggie negotiating the path between the dunes back to the parking lot. Maggie sitting poised in the driver's seat, hovering.

Floating on a cushion of air, driving down Route 1. She makes the turn into the trailer park and the Escort fishtails, sliding on a patch of sand. She turns into the skid and she's right again, she's fine, she's almost home. Crushing a bed of senseless poppies as she pulls up next to her trailer.

They look up as she enters, Ruby and Casey at the kitchen table and her daughter sitting on the floor next to the couch. Maggie opens her mouth to speak and the words float in front of her, comic book clouds of speech with no letters inside. Their expressions are identical round O's and they converge on her with gentle hands. She closes her eyes and when she opens them she is lying on her bed looking up at the purple shadows on the ceiling. The room is spinning and she grabs the side of the bed to hold on. Something cool and wet on her forehead. Ruby's face, round like a moon. Ariel, Casey hovering behind. Holding on to the sides of the bed, sliding down.

CHAPTER TWENTY

Gene was late again and Maggie was going to kill him. It wasn't his fault, though, not this time. The new dishwasher at the Golden Rooster showed up drunk as a skunk, and Lou, the floor manager, asked Gene to cover until they could call somebody in. He had that look in his eye that told Gene he wasn't really asking. The supper rush was just starting and the waitrons were running out of forks, coffee cups, and dessert plates. One of the prep cooks sliced the top of his thumb off in the Hobart and they were putting out Chef's Salads with no onions or tomatoes.

"Okay, Lou," Gene said. "But you *owe* me. I want the next two Saturdays off, man. *Nights.*"

"No problem, Gene. No problem." There was a crash as one of the busboys set another tray down at the far end of the gleaming steel dishwashing machine. The Ramones "I Wanna Be Sedated" blasted out of the small speaker set near the ceiling, so distorted it was almost unrecognizable.

"And you have to call Maggie for me. If I'm late she'll have my ass."

It took two hours for Lou to find somebody to come in and cover. The supper rush died down, and as soon as he got ahead on water glasses, Gene took off his sweaty apron and pegged it at the linen box in the corner. On his way out the back door, he called to Lou.

"Did you call Maggie?"

Lou got that far-off distracted look, like when he forgot to double-shift the bar last Memorial Day weekend.

"Yeah, sure. No problem."

But Gene had a sick feeling in his gut as he steered his old Valiant into the driveway. He opened the front door and he knew right away that he was in trouble. Maggie was sitting on the faded plaid-print sofa. It sunk down on the right where the springs were going and she was listing to the left to compensate. Her shapely, stockinged legs were crossed up high, her lips pursed in a thin, hard line.

"Where the fuck have you been? I dropped Gabe off at Debbie's two hours ago. We were supposed to catch the seven o'clock show, have a nice dinner. Now we'll barely make the nine."

"Didn't Lou call?"

"No, Lou didn't call." Shit, she had that look. Gene eyed the sofa's lumpy contours. He'd be sleeping there tonight. "In fact," she went on, "I tried to call the Golden fucking Turkey twice and I got put on hold so long I gave up."

"I'm sorry, baby," he said. "The new dishwasher showed up so drunk and 'luded out he could barely see straight and Lou asked me to cover."

"Read my lips, Gene. Just say no. Enn oh. No. It's a complete sentence."

"Yeah, well." He hung his head down, tried to get that sheepish look he knew sometimes worked with her. But he was thinking, Jesus fucking Christ. Just say no *way*. He'd been late three nights running and Lou made the casual observation that there were a lot of good people out there looking for work. "I'm sorry, baby."

Gene took her hand and gently stroked the soft part of her wrist with his thumb. He could see her coming around. The corners of her mouth started to thaw just a bit into what might become a smile. But she wasn't going to let him off that easy.

"This is the third time in the last two weeks you've let

195

me sit here cooling my heels while you've been off fucking around somewhere." She raised her hand as if to ward off his protest. "No, I know. You've always got some excuse. The car. The job. It's always something." Her mouth set into that pout again, her eyebrows slanted down at a severe angle. God, she was beautiful. "I'm your *wife*, Gene, not some little cooze you picked up at Hugo's. We've got a *kid*. You've got *responsibilities.*"

Okay, enough groveling. He looked up at her, looked her in the eye. "I'm sorry, baby. Really. It won't happen again."

She looked back at him long and hard, then the corners of her mouth started coming up again, that smile coming through. "You ever hear of the Fist of Venus?"

Gene shook his head.

"It's an exercise I read about in *New Woman*." She took his hand and led him to the couch. "Come on, I'll show you."

It turned out they didn't make the nine either.

He got up early the next morning to take the Valiant into the Co-op Garage. Ten bucks an hour and you got a bay and the use of the tools. You had to show up for two hours a month and help keep the place up, but that wasn't so bad. The Valiant had been acting funny lately – pull up to a stop sign and it would just die. But only sometimes. It had to be something electrical. Gene hated electrical problems. They were the worst.

"Don't be late picking me up," Maggie said to him on his way out. "I have to be at the clinic at noon."

The clinic. Gene didn't like the sound of that – some female thing. He was going to be on time, though. He knew he'd been pushing it lately.

As he drove by the corner of Jefferson and Third, he saw Blake hanging out in front of the Kit-Kat Lounge, waiting for it to open. They'd overlapped at Harrisburg when Gene was doing ninety for a third DUI, and stayed pretty tight for a while after that. Gene hadn't seen him for a few months, though. He pulled over to the curb.

"Hey, Blake the Snake. How's it going? Someone told me you had a job."

Blake pitched his cigarette into the street and walked up to the Valiant, a wide grin on his face. Most of his teeth were gone – the man was thirty-two years old and he looked seventy.

"Did for a while, unloading produce downtown. Temp, though. I'm a free man again, least for now."

Gene got out of the car and they leaned against the hood, shooting the breeze about wives, girlfriends, who was back in the joint, who was out – the usual bullshit. Then they were silent for a while.

Blake spoke up. "You still keep that little twenty-two pistola in the glove box?"

"Yeah, why?"

"You want to go down to Urban Gold and plink some cans, maybe a rat or two?"

The owner of the junkyard was a friend of theirs, another honor farm alumnus, and didn't mind if they did a little target practice every now and then. Gene looked through the window of the Kit-Kat at the Budweiser clock mounted over the bar. Eight-thirty. An hour plinking cans, two hours at the Co-op. Plenty of time.

"Sure, why not?"

"All right, bro." Blake rubbed his hands together. "Let's do it."

They picked up a twelve-pack of Iron City at World of Liquor on the way out, and by the time they got there they had already littered the back seat of the Valiant with empties.

They drove out to an open, flat part of the yard. Teetering stacks of old tires loomed above scattered piles of masonry and rubble. They set up pyramids of cans in front of a stained couch exploding with stuffing and springs. The bet was you had to knock the top one off without disturbing the cans on the bottom. Two bucks a pop.

Before long, Gene was getting hosed, but he kept playing, trying to get his money back. They did see a few rats and Gene nailed one, but Blake kept missing. He could plink a can dead through the O in Iron City from twenty feet, but just kicked up little puffs of dust around the fat, greasy, little furballs, who were so slow and stupid they didn't even know they were being shot at half the time. Gene figured Blake just didn't have the stomach for it.

The hour passed. Two hours. They kept playing, knocking back beer after beer and using the empties as targets.

They had the car radio turned to the oldies station. "Won't hurt the battery none to keep it on," Blake said. The last strains of "Runaround Sue" faded out, and the deejay's patter intruded into Gene's consciousness.

"*And the time now in downtown Philly is 11:55.*"

It didn't register at first, then it hit him. *11:55.*

"Fuck me with a tire iron," Gene said. "We gotta go."

Blake folded up the crumpled pile of bills and stuffed it into his shirt pocket.

"Whatever," he said, grinning.

Gene wedged himself behind the wheel and turned the key over another notch. The radio died. Nothing else happened. Not a sound. He turned it again. *Come on, baby.* Dead.

"Maggie'll fucking kill me, man." He leaned his head against the steering wheel. *Fist of Venus*, he thought stupidly. *Shit.* "She'll fucking kill me. I have to get some kind of alibi."

Then it came to him, like a bolt of lightning out of a clear blue sky. It was perfect.

"Blake," he said. "I want you to shoot me."

"What?"

"I'm serious, man. You have to shoot me. Just, like, through the arm or something. Then you take off, I'll tell the cops I was robbed and I'm off the hook. Maggie'll have to buy *this*. I've been fucking robbed, for Christ's sake. *Shot.* I could've been killed!"

198

Blake was looking at him like he was crazy. "Gene, I'm sorry, man, but you're out of your fucking mind. I'm *not* gonna shoot you."

"Look, Blake, I know I'll get a couple weeks disability for this. I'll split the check with you, fifty-fifty."

Blake thought about it for a minute. "Sixty-forty and you've got yourself a deal."

Gene shook his head. "You are one cold mother-fucker."

Blake smiled and shrugged. They got out of the car.

"Just a flesh wound. Just enough so the cops buy it." *So Maggie buys it.*

Blake held the gun limply in his hand. He began to look very pale. His eyes had that deer-in-the-headlights look, wide open and without a speck of brain. Beads of sweat popped out on his forehead and rolled down his neck.

"I don't know if I can do this, Gene."

"Oh, come on, you were such a mercenary fuck just a minute ago."

"Yeah, but I can't stand blood."

"It's *my* blood, man, not yours. Just do it."

"All right." Blake raised the gun in his shaking hand. He closed his eyes and squeezed the trigger. There was a sharp *crack*.

It didn't hurt much, kind of like a bee sting, but Gene had no idea there would be so much blood. It blossomed from a small red circle on the shoulder of his t-shirt until he was covered with it, soaked through to the skin.

"God damn it, you fucking idiot. You killed me. I'm fucking dying." He felt like he was floating. "I'm dying." His words sounded hollow, like he was shouting down a long, cardboard tube. Great, purple splotches swam in his vision. He was falling...

White light, starchy linen smell. Echoing voice from somewhere. "He's coming around." White sheets. His eyes focused. White walls. Blue uniforms. Gold buttons. *Shit.*

199

"You ready to talk to us?" the cop on the left said. They looked identical, that Mount Rushmore thing they all learn in cop school. Square-jawed, efficient.

"Oh, man," Gene said, weakly. "Did you guys get the robbers?"

Left cop laughed, a short bark. "Your friend Blake panicked when you started bleeding like a stuck pig. We know what happened."

Right cop. "You're lucky you're too stupid to kill."

Gene felt his heart hammering in his chest. His shoulder was beginning to throb underneath the thick layer of bandages. His vision blurred again. The overhead light was a bright smear and he fell tumbling into it.

CHAPTER TWENTY-ONE

"Helter Skelter is looking pretty good," Otto said.

Gabe nodded. "Yeah, but I've still got a feeling about Nova Express. Good workouts, placed or showed the last four races, all in the last two months."

Otto studied the *Form* for a moment longer, looked up at Gabe, and nodded. "All right. Let's do it."

"Wait a minute. I thought you said Nova Express was medicated to the gills."

"He can handle it. Let's go with your intuition. You want to get a look at the horses?"

"Sure."

They worked their way down to the infield. Just as they got there, the trainers were leading the horses around a dirt circle off to the side of the track. Nova Express, Number Four, was a sleek looking, black filly. She seemed to flow rather than walk. Pocket Rocket, Number Two, was a tightly wound knot of muscle.

A high, white fence held the crowd at bay. Racetrack patrons were calling to the jockeys and the horses, making no attempt to distinguish one from the other. Curses were bellowed, imprecations hurled, pleas whimpered. The jockeys took it all in with no change in facial expression. They sat atop their mounts, looking straight ahead or off past the grandstands somewhere. Gabe liked the jockeys.

"Man, they better adjust the meds on Helter Skelter,"

Otto said. "Look at that."

The Six horse's side was lathered with sweat. She reared back once and minced nervously forward. She was wearing blinders, but Gabe could imagine her eyes wide, the whites showing all around. He could *feel* her fear, a dumb, animal ache in the pit of his stomach. He turned to Otto.

"I don't like it here," he said. "Let's go back to the grandstand."

Otto looked at Gabe and raised his eyebrows. "Whatever you say."

Post time is in five minutes. Five minutes to post time. The announcer's voice rang with overtones.

"You want to get some more nachos?" Otto asked.

Gabe made a face. "I don't think so."

"Another beer?"

Gabe thought about it. He could almost feel that cold, sweet alcohol numbness sliding across the top of his brain, but there was something repellent about it as well. He shook his head. "No. I'm fine."

Otto nodded. "Let's get up to the second level, then. Bird's eye view."

After they placed their bets, they climbed up the stairs to the top tier. It was less crowded up there than down below. Knots of people clustered around styrofoam coolers on the wooden benches; lone figures huddled against the stiff breeze coming in from the bay. Gabe looked out beyond the track and he could see it peeking out from behind a cluster of low, boxy-looking buildings, a patch of greenish-blue. They walked to the bottom of the balcony and stood at the rail, looking down at the oval track.

The horses are at the starting gate. The horses are at the gate.

Gabe looked over at Otto. He had taken off his sunglasses and was looking straight ahead. His eyes were narrowed and the wind whipped his hair and beard behind him in rippling waves.

And they're off.

The horses surged forward and the voice of the crowd washed over Gabe. It was the sound the ocean makes nibbling for centuries at a rocky shore. It was the sound of turbulence at the heart of a star. It emptied his mind and filled him with nothingness the way a gas expands to the shape of its container.

Gabe wondered if his father had ever been to the track. It seemed unlikely that he hadn't.

Someone down below had released a helium balloon and it soared upwards, a speck of red scraping against the blue bowl of the sky. *Dad's soul*, Gabe thought.

The pounding of hooves was like the bass rumble of a subway train. Three horses stretched out in a line easily ahead of the tangled pack. Nova Express. Sweetwater. Pocket Rocket.

Gabe looked at Otto again. Almost imperceptibly, without sound, his lips were moving.

The horses were in the last turn before the home stretch. Suddenly, as if the other horses were standing still, Pocket Rocket surged ahead, passing first Sweetwater, then Nova Express. One, two, three lengths, its head bobbing up and down in time to the rising and falling of the jockey's switch.

Otto reached into his pocket, pulled out a cigar, and snapped it in two. A sharp *crack* echoed off the sky like thunder hitch-hiking on a nearby lightning strike. The smell of ozone came flooding in from everywhere at once. Pocket Rocket stumbled.

Gabe reached out with his mind and the world stopped.

Rippling banners atop the tote board froze in mid-curl. The voice of the crowd, cut off in an instant, reverberated in Gabe's ears.

Pocket Rocket hung suspended at an impossible angle. Gabe opened himself up and was flooded with dumb animal pain and terror. Her *leg*. Gabe could see the break in his mind's eye, clean and precise, ready to grind together into jagged splinters. He didn't know what to do but he had to stop the pain stop the brutish fear he *pushed* –

Pocket Rocket sailed across the finish line, followed two heartbeats later by Nova Express, all alone. Just like Gabe had seen it. Then Sweetwater and the rest of the pack. The subway rumble died down and the crowd voice downshifted like a huge, buried machine taking to a different task. The sun beat down and the dust hanging over the track was beautiful in the light.

Gabe looked at Otto. He had put his sunglasses back on and Gabe saw in their mirrored surface the curve of the track, the blue of the sky, the sun a smear of fire.

"I think we're done here," Otto said. "What do you think?"

They didn't speak at all on the ride home. Gabe sat as far away from Otto as he could, hunched against the door of the cab. Every now and then, Otto looked over at him through a haze of cigar smoke.

He didn't know what he was supposed to feel. It was like he was making it up as he went along. He wanted to be mad at Otto – he'd been set up – but he felt good about what he'd done. It was the right thing. And it was good to know that's where his instincts pointed. But everything felt different now, everything had changed.

They drove past the hospital. Gabe looked over at the windows glinting in the late afternoon sun like chips of quartz. *There*, he thought. *That's where my father is.* He closed his eyes and he could picture him lying in his room, the angle of the shadows against the walls, the smell of bleached sheets and ether. But something was different. He didn't feel that tug at his heart like something was being pulled out of him.

His lips soundlessly shaped the word "goodbye." He thought of his Mom and Ariel. It was all right. They'd be all right.

Otto pulled up next to the Airstream and turned off the motor. They sat there silently for a while.

"Did you really want Nova Express?" Gabe finally asked.

Otto shrugged without smiling.

Gabe looked at him for a moment longer and reached for the door handle.

"The old guy in the hospital," Otto said.

Gabe stopped. "How—"

"Never mind how I know. It was his turn. You didn't do anything."

"And this time? The horse?"

Otto nodded. "This time was different."

Gabe thought about that. "Fuck you, Otto," he said, and stepped out of the cab. "Stay away from us."

When Gabe pushed open the door to his trailer, he saw Casey and Ruby sitting at the kitchen table, talking quietly. Ariel was asleep on the couch. Casey and Ruby looked up.

"Hey! Casey—" He stopped when he saw the expression on their faces. "What's going on? Where's Mom?"

Casey and Ruby looked at each other. Ruby turned to Gabe. "Your mother—"

"She came home loaded," Casey said. "Shitfaced. We put her to bed."

He opened his mouth to speak and nothing came out. *Loaded.* In his mind's eye he saw her face, frozen as if by a camera flash, all the lines and shadows sharp as the edge of a knife. About five years ago. He'd gotten up in the middle of the night to get some juice and found her seated alone at the kitchen table with a half-empty bottle of vodka. She looked at him wordlessly as he got the wax carton of orange juice from the door of the refrigerator and poured himself a glass.

"Are you all right?" he asked.

She just shook her head. She looked so sad. It frightened him. He thought he'd completely forgotten it, but with the memory came the realization that he'd held it near to himself but hidden all this time. *Loaded.*

"Oh, man…" He sat down at the table. Casey put her hand on his arm. He looked at her and smiled weakly. "So how did you get here, anyway? I was going to call you."

"Your Mom brought me here. We were going to have dinner or something—"

Maggie appeared in the hallway, leaning against the door-frame. She was very pale and looked like she didn't know where she was. Her shirt was wet and dark and it took Gabe a moment to realize that she was covered in blood. She took two more staggering steps into the kitchen and collapsed.

Ruby ran to her. She unfolded Maggie's arm from her chest and looked for the source of the bleeding.

She looked up. "Get me scissors, something sharp."

Gabe jumped up and pulled the utility drawer out of its tracks. The contents fell to the ground with a crash. Ariel woke up and started to cry.

"Hush, Ari, it's all right," Gabe said. He handed Ruby a pair of scissors and she cut at the shoulder and sleeve of the bloody shirt.

"There's a wound here, but it doesn't look too bad," she said. "Looks like a gunshot. Does your mother own a gun?"

Gabe shook his head. "Dad used to have one but she made him get rid of it."

Ruby shook her head. "Doesn't matter." She balled up the shirt and pressed it to the wound. "Get me another couple of these. We have to get her to the hospital."

Gabe ran into the back and returned with a couple of t-shirts. Ruby grabbed one, folded it twice, and pressed it against the wound. Maggie stirred and moaned.

"You're gonna be all right," Ruby said. "Here, help me with her." She put her arm under the wounded shoulder. Gabe put his hand under her other arm and together they pulled her up to a sitting position.

Ruby took Gabe's hand and held it against the compress. "Keep pressure on this." She turned to Casey.

"Can you stay here with Ari? It'll be crazy enough there as it is."

Casey nodded and put her arm around Ariel.

"Where are her car keys?" Ruby dug into Maggie's pockets and pulled them out. She turned to Ariel. "Ari. Your Mom's going to be all right. We're taking her to the hospital now, but you can come to see her real soon." Ariel nodded numbly. Ruby turned to Gabe. "Let's go."

The compress was sticky with warm blood. Gabe had trouble keeping pressure on it and bringing his mother to her feet at the same time. Maggie moaned again, louder this time, but gave them some help as they pulled her up.

They stretched her out in the back seat of the Escort. Gabe got in there with her as Ruby started the car.

He pressed down on the compress and a well of blood pooled up between his fingers. There was so much of it.

Maggie opened her eyes and looked at him.

"Hey, Gabe…" she said weakly.

"Don't worry, Mom. You're all right."

"I didn't drink." A whisper. "Your father wouldn't let me."

The nurse in the emergency room took one look at the three of them, pressed a button on the phone in front of her, and came running up to meet them. She wore heavy eye makeup and her blonde hair was stiff beneath her nurses' hat. They stretched Maggie out on a cot. The nurse pulled on a pair of latex gloves and prodded the wound.

"Hmm. Looks a lot worse than it is." She looked up. "What happened here?"

"I don't really know," Ruby said.

She looked at Ruby with a skeptical expression and continued ministering to Maggie. Pulse. Blood pressure. Another nurse and a doctor appeared and the two of them wheeled Maggie off into another room.

"I'm going to need to ask you some questions," the

nurse said. "This her son?" She nodded towards Gabe. "Are you her son?"

Gabe nodded.

They sailed through a litany of questions. Ruby answered most of them; Gabe was in a daze. Finally, the nurse pointed down the hall. "You can sit in the Waiting Room. There's a television. Somebody will come out and talk to you soon."

They had the place all to themselves. Blue walls with green trim around the windows, an array of DMV posters about safe driving habits, coffee-table stacks of torn, faded magazines bracketing an L-shaped couch, a television bolted to the wall up near the ceiling, tuned to a game show. The sound was barely audible; the steady, electronic murmur of voices and music had a comforting effect on Gabe.

They sat down on the couch, each taking a leg of the L, and looked at each other.

"How are you doing, Gabe?" Ruby asked.

He thought about it. "Okay," he said. "I'm okay."

There was another long silence. Gabe listened to the television babble, let himself be grounded by it.

"Maybe you want to look in on your father while you're here," Ruby said.

Gabe shook his head. "No. I don't think so." He'd already said goodbye.

They didn't say anything for a while after that. Gabe wanted to be left alone and he had the feeling Ruby knew it and respected his wishes. He wondered if Mom was going to have to start going to meetings again. He didn't think so. It was crazy, but he was actually feeling all right. His father was dying, his mother was in the hospital with a gunshot wound, but it was okay. Things would work out. They'd make it.

After a little while, a doctor stuck his head in the door. A pair of wire-rimmed glasses perched askew on the end of his nose. "Gabe Lambent and Ruby Matters?"

They started to get up and the doctor motioned them down. "Sit, sit." He sat down next to Gabe. "I'm Doctor

Winsome," he said. He had a calm way about him, very unlike most of the doctors Gabe had known. "Your Mom is going to be fine. She lost a little blood, but it wasn't nearly as bad as it looked." He paused, looking puzzled. "It looks like a gunshot wound, but there's no exit wound, no bullet. Neither of you—"

Ruby and Gabe shook their heads.

"Well, the police will probably want to talk to her tomorrow," he continued. "We have to report this sort of thing. But the wound's clean, bleeding's stopped. I gave her something to help her sleep. She'll be up on her feet tomorrow. Why don't the two of you go home?"

Casey and Ariel were sitting on the couch playing cards. Ariel dropped her cards in front of her, ran to Gabe, and wrapped her small arms around him. It felt like she was trying to burrow her way inside him. He stroked her head and murmured into her hair, stuff like "it's okay" and "there, there." He looked up. Casey was looking at him with a questioning expression.

"She'll be all right," he said. "They're keeping her overnight, but they're letting her out in the morning."

Casey nodded. "Good. Man, that was something. The two of you should take a look at yourselves. You look like you've been in a war."

Ruby's sky-blue shirt was streaked with blood. Gabe's own hands were sticky with it.

"I'd better go home and change," Ruby said. "I'll be back." She let herself out the door.

Ariel stepped back from Gabe. "We made salad. I set the table. We're having burgers."

"Good deal, Ari," Gabe said. "I'm going to take a shower."

He got some clean clothes from his bedroom, took them into the bathroom, stripped down, and stepped into the shower. The hot water felt good against his skin. He watched it swirling down the drain, faintly pink at first from his

209

mother's blood. Gabe closed his eyes and let the spray beat against his face. His mind felt completely blank. He was coasting.

CHAPTER TWENTY-TWO

Maggie didn't know where she was at first, but the soft metal sheen of the bedrail in the dim light, the half-open curtain surrounding the bed, the stench of disinfectant were unmistakable. *Hospital.* She tried to move and two things happened – a bolt of pain lanced from her left shoulder so sharply it made her gasp, and a rush of nausea washed over her and receded, leaving in its wake the taste of vodka and bile.

Oh, God. I fucked up.

There it was. Four years, right down the tubes. God damn it. Despair was pushing at a corner of her mind and then she remembered. Back in the dunes, Gene tilting the bottle back, its slow graceful arc before it hit the water.

She moved again, a little more gingerly this time, and it wasn't so bad. She reached across with her right hand and carefully felt near the source of the pain. The soft bulk of a bandage.

So. Inventory. She'd gotten herself hurt somehow and she was in St. Paul's Presbyterian. She had a fleeting memory of wispy clouds scrawled across a blue sky, teetering stacks of old tires, snatches of rock and roll, the smell of burning rubber and garbage. A freeze-frame snapshot of one of Gene's drinking buddies from the bad old days, eyes like black stones in the bottom of a muddy river and mouth twisted in an idiot leer.

211

Gene was nearby. She could feel his presence the way a bird knows South when the nights start getting cold. Up above her head somewhere, a little to the left.

She listened to the darkness. The night sounds of the hospital edged into the silence. Distant motors starting and stopping, the soft whir of ventilation, footsteps in the hall outside the room approaching and receding. Beneath everything the sixty-cycle hum.

Carefully, Maggie unlatched the bar on the side of the bed and slid it down. It rattled against the bedframe and the noise seemed very loud.

She eased her legs over the side of the bed and slowly pulled herself to a sitting position. The pain wasn't too bad if she moved carefully, but she had to fight back another wave of nausea.

Deep breath. Another. Her forehead was clammy, cool with drying sweat. She slid her hips along the bed until her feet touched the floor, then she slowly let them take her weight. Not too bad. She felt a breeze on her back through the open gown.

Maggie stood next to the bed, breathing, letting her body get used to being upright. The longer she stood there, the easier it was. Her mind was completely blank except for the pressure of Gene's presence like a small tumor nestled in her brain, deep beneath the convoluted surface.

When she was ready, she stepped away from the bed and pulled back the curtain. Three other beds, surrounded by pale, green curtains hanging like luminous aurorae in the dim light. At least one of them was occupied.

She walked to the closed door at the end of the room, a rectangle composed of thin lines of light. She eased it open and looked out. It took a couple of seconds for her eyes to adjust to the brightness.

There was a nurses' station at the far end of the hall. Two nurses stood with their backs to Maggie, heads bent over a clipboard. A quiet burst of laughter drifted down the hall. Maggie looked to her left. A red EXIT sign and beneath it, in black stencil, STAIRS. She slipped out of her room, closed the door behind her, and ducked into the stairwell.

She tensed, expecting any minute to hear footsteps clatter down the hall, voices raised in challenge.

Nothing but the sough of wind in the stairwell, a lonesome whisper.

She started to walk up the stairs and felt another wave of dizziness. *Breathe*, she told herself. *In, out.* She leaned against the banister, felt her gown clinging with sweat to her back. She started up the stairs again, slowly, one at a time. She closed her eyes, reaching out to feel that pressure. He was close. She must have done the rest on autopilot, because the next thing she knew she was there in the darkened room with him, her back to the closed door, listening to the sound of his ragged breath filling the shadows.

She opened her mouth and said his name.

"Gene."

The word seemed to hang there between them in the darkness.

Maggie walked toward the bed. The machines were gone and she felt sad for him, truly alone now, abandoned even by his glass and metal ministers.

She looked down at his bandaged face. Slowly, only distantly realizing she was doing it, she adjusted her breathing so that it settled into synchrony with his. *In.* Her chest rose. For the first time in a while, she felt her wound, a throbbing pressure in her shoulder. *Out.* Tension leaving her shoulders, soft whisper of escaping breath. *In, out.* It was so simple, breathing.

She eased the pillow out from beneath his head, cradling him so that when the pillow was free, she could let him down gently. She looked at him for a moment longer, then just as she was about to place the pillow over his face, she felt him pass through her as if they were both made of smoke; for an instant, they were together, completely. She *was* Gene. Then the moment was gone and she wasn't sure if it had really happened. He shuddered once, and then he was gone. The smell of shit drifted up from his still form. A parting gift. Maggie almost smiled in the darkness.

CHAPTER TWENTY-THREE

Gene wasn't surprised when his mother called to tell him Dad was on his last legs. It had to happen sooner or later. The cancer had taken him at seventy years, stocky and mean as a snake, and shaved the life off him a layer at a time until there was nothing left. That's what Gene was told, anyway. He hadn't seen him in over fifteen years.

"You should come home," Gene's mother had said. Her voice sounded small and distant over the phone. "Let it go, Gene. Come home and say goodbye to him."

He was almost there. He needed to stretch the trip out a little, give himself time to think, so for the last leg he got off the Interstate and took the back way into Leverett – Route 5 into Chicopee and then up through South Hadley and over the Holyoke Range. The road wound through the western Massachusetts hill towns in lazy loops and curves, a sharp contrast to the straight, Euclidean scar of the Interstate. It was autumn, the fullness of the leaf season, and the trees were splashes of color – bright red, flaming yellow – reaching up to the crisp, blue sky on either side of the road.

It felt like his old Valiant had become a time machine – most of the towns along the way pretty much fell through the cracks when the Interstate went up and hadn't changed at all since the last time he'd been through. As Gene drove, he felt his father's presence like a weight, getting heavier the closer he got to home.

He pushed the images away but they kept returning – fragments of conversation, ghost-flicker recollections of his father's face, the raspy feel of his father's cheek on his own.

He was a son of a bitch, there was no question about that. Gene couldn't remember hearing a positive word out of him since he was fourteen. There was some trouble with the police when he was a teenager, but it was just kid stuff – a little dope, some stealing. His father really took it to heart, though. There was one time Gene got caught smoking dope with a couple of friends in the old abandoned felt factory on Route 47. His father picked him up at the Hadley Police Station and they were driving home. It was late winter and all the trees were covered with a white crust of snow. Without warning, his father smacked him hard across the face with the back of his hand.

"How can you do this to me?" he said. The whiskey smell hung between them.

Gene looked over at him. His father's eyes were fixed on the road ahead. He was serious. How can you do this to me.

He was a son of a bitch, all right.

And Gene was driving up through the landscape of his childhood to watch him die.

Suddenly, Gene wanted a drink with an almost overwhelming fierceness. There was a sound in the car, a soft moan, and he realized with a start that it was his own voice.

Two months, he thought. Two months. Two months.

The feeling passed and he loosened his grip on the steering wheel. His fingers tingled with returning blood.

He took Route 63 north into the hills, bypassing the congestion around Amherst. Leverett Center had hardly changed at all. There were a few new houses on the south end of town and a video store had opened up in Don Wilson's old Gulf station.

There was a feeling about the town, though, of a generic New England postcard that had started to discolor with age and curl up around the edges. The Town Hall was badly in need of a new coat of paint and the Commons was overgrown. It clashed against the pure, simple colors of childhood memories. White and green. White for the perfect, Colonial houses and the picket fence in front of the LaFlamme place; green for the slow, syrupy heat of New England summer. White for the quiet blanket of winter's first snow; green for the sharp, clean smell of pine. As Gene drove past Dad's old store he realized he had been holding my breath and he let it out in a rush. He could still see the outline of the letters in the window.

HARDWARE
APPLIANCES
WE FIX ANYTHING

A sign proclaimed that Walgreen's was Coming Soon.

We fix anything. Gene snorted and shook his head. There was a tightness in his forehead and the corners of his eyes. He turned onto Rattlesnake Road *nearest rattlesnake probably two thousand miles.* Made that steep climb *how many times down this hill on scooter bicycle skateboard jumpstart that old junker Dodge.* Crested the hill *blue sky framed by gold red yellow trees.* Sharp right turn up the twin-rutted driveway *home.*

He pulled up next to a fairly new Camry – his mother's, he assumed, although he'd never seen it – and walked up the flagstone path to the front door. They'd had the place painted recently and the familiar shape of the house looked strange under the new colors. Light blue with red trim. It didn't look bad, but Gene kept expecting to blink his eyes and see the house restored to its old, weather-beaten grey and white. The front door was open and he walked on in.

The first thing he noticed was the smell of the place, a signature like none other that identifies home – wood, dust, upholstery, a touch of mildew, an overlay of cooking smells. On top of that melange of scents floated something unfamiliar, a faint sweet-sour whiff. Gene knew what it was, though. The sickroom smell. If he'd walked in off the street a perfect stranger he would've known someone in that house was dying.

His mother was in the kitchen. It's how he pictured her when he thought of her, standing alone in the kitchen in her faded, red-checked apron. It was kind of corny, an image right out of a Rockwell painting, but it got him every time. There was an array of pots and pans on the stove, wisps of steam curling up from half-closed lids. She didn't hear him come in and he just stood there for a handful of heartbeats, looking at her. Then she looked up at him and jumped back.

"Gene," she said, putting her hand to her chest. "You startled me." She looked older, a little more bent over. Gene could still see a young woman, though, in the lines around her eyes, in the wry half-smile on her face. She put down the ladle she'd been holding, walked over to him, and they embraced. She felt frail and small, as if her bones were hollow as a bird's. She stepped back.

"You look good." She patted his stomach. "Not what anyone would mistake for a starving artist, either." She looked closely at his face. "Staying off the booze, too, I see. Good." She patted him again. "Good."

Gene felt a warm flush on his cheeks. He always felt so exposed with her. "You look good too, Mom."

She tilted her head to the side. "I've raised you to the polite lie," she said with that half-smile. "That's good. But it's been a hard year and I know it shows."

"No, I mean it, Mom. You look good."

"How are you and Maggie doing? And my grand-children?"

"We're...working things out. Everybody's fine."

She put her arms around him again. "Welcome home, son," she said. "Let's go look in on your father."

They made their way through the darkened house. The shapes looming in the shadows were familiar yet strange. Here, the china cupboard that had graced the hall was now against the south wall of the living room. There, an old sagging bookcase he remembered had been replaced by a modern-looking stereo cabinet. They walked down the hall to the back bedroom. Gene's heart was pounding in his chest. When they reached the door, his mother turned to him.

"Don't be too surprised by what you see." She opened the door halfway, looked in the room, then turned around and motioned him in.

His father lay there, sunken into the big, wide bed like a wedding cake ornament half-buried in frosting. He appeared to be asleep. His eyes were closed and the room was filled with the rattling sound of his breath. He looked like an outline of the man who had been Gene's father, a stick-figure drawing. Mottled skin strewn with liver spots stretched tightly across his forehead and cheekbones and hung in bruised, puffy folds under his eyes. Gene felt hot tears form in his own eyes and start to spill down his cheeks. His vision blurred and he blinked several times. When it cleared, he saw that his father's eyes were open and he was looking at him. Gene's breath caught in his throat. His father motioned weakly for him to come closer. Gene took a couple of small steps toward the bed. His father's bony hand snaked out and grabbed Gene's wrist with a surprisingly strong grip, then relaxed. His eyes fluttered closed. His breathing was deep and regular.

Gene's mother touched his elbow and gestured towards the door. "He's like that," she said when they were back in the hallway. "In and out. Some days he's talking, even gets up and walks around a bit. Usually, though, there's just not much strength in him. I had him in and out of the hospital for the last few months, but Doctor Ross says there's nothing more anyone can do and I wanted him home for...you know." She looked away and bit her lower lip. She took a breath as if she was about to speak, then let it out in a long sigh. Finally, she looked up.

"There's something you should see," she said.

She led Gene through the house to the back porch, a screened-in addition to the house that overlooked a gently

219

sloping hill leading down to a small pond and the woods beyond. It looked like somebody had opened a junkyard back there. The hill was covered with appliances of every description, in various stages of decrepitude.

Washers, dryers, dishwashers. Stoves, refrigerators, water heaters.

They were stacked drunkenly atop one another, leaning precariously with the grade of the hill. A couple of narrow paths meandered through the mess down to the water, and in the pond itself a mossy jumble of rust-streaked shapes pushed up through the algae-covered surface.

Gene looked at his mother. "What—"

Her eyes were fixed on the piece of apron she was wringing between her hands. "When he first got sick, they just started...appearing." She looked up at him. "Every day, one or two more. I've never seen anybody pull up with a truck or anything. They just...appear."

Gene almost wanted to laugh. There wasn't anything mysterious about it. Some redneck shitkicker who couldn't put two and two together thought Dad was still in the business and was dropping stuff off for resale. At the same time, though, a small voice deep inside him said that that wasn't quite right.

Gene put his arm around her and they stood there looking out over the yard. The sun was setting and the appliances cast long, purple shadows. The wind gently pushed the blades of a fan perched on top of an old refrigerator and a rhythmic squeaking filled the dusk.

Gene got up early the next morning and stepped out onto the porch. Down near the pond he saw a bone-white meat freezer the size of a coffin. He didn't think it had been there the night before.

He opened the screen door and walked out into the yard. There were old, rounded refrigerators with rust-pitted chrome fixtures and sleek new microwave ovens, waffle irons and Cuisinarts. It looked like a seconds warehouse for a TV game show.

Gene spent the rest of the day doing odd jobs around the house. Every now and then he took a break, stepped out back, and looked over the mess in the yard. There didn't seem to be much he could do about it, though. He thought about getting Mom a dog. He thought about calling the police. But he also thought that things were difficult enough right then, and he decided that whatever he was going to do could wait.

A couple of times he felt it again, that chemical fire of need racing through his system. Burning throat, a feeling of *wrongness* at a cellular level that only alcohol could make right. When it happened, he breathed slowly and deliberately, tried to empty his mind, and waited for the feeling to pass.

He changed the oil in the Camry, fixed the leaky pipe under the kitchen sink, and raked the front lawn. He didn't look in on his father at all, and he could feel his mother's eyes on him in silent reproach as he went about his tasks.

He called Maggie at home and they talked for a bit, but Gene was distracted. He didn't tell her about the stuff in the yard. He wanted to, but it just sounded ludicrous. She could tell something was wrong, though, and asked a couple of times if everything was all right. He kept dodging and by the time they hung up she was mad and hurt and Gene felt like a jerk.

He stood there looking at the phone resting on its cradle and felt a rush of love and longing for Maggie that brought tears to his eyes. *Soul mate.* Hot and cold, up and down, crazier than shit half the time, but there it was. They were bonded. He wondered if he'd ever see her again.

Now where the hell did *that* come from, he thought.

Gene and his mother ate dinner in uncomfortable silence. She could still make a serious pot roast, but he didn't have much of an appetite. After he moved the peas from one side of his plate to the other for the third time, she spoke up.

"I don't like the way he's been with you any more

221

than you do, you know."

Gene knew what was coming. He's your father. Forgive and forget. What a crock.

"But he's your father. I don't expect you to forgive him, but you have to say goodbye to him." He looked up. His mother's eyes were sharp and clear. "For you, Gene. You have to say goodbye."

"Why have you stayed with him all these years? You know what he's like..."

She shook her head. "Me and him, it's just different with us, that's all. It's just different."

Gene didn't understand, not really. They finished the rest of their meal in silence.

Before going to bed, he opened the door to his father's sickroom and stood there looking at him for a long time.

This man, his father. Dying. His withered, bony frame propping up the sheets, tent-like. The rise and fall of his chest. Gene imagined that he could feel his father moving slowly through him toward death. He didn't know what he felt. He wanted to say something to him, to walk over and touch him, but he couldn't. Gently, he shut the door and went to bed.

Gene woke up in the middle of the night to bright moonlight streaming through the curtains in his old room. He got up and walked over to the window. His father was standing out there in the yard, his robe hanging limply on his bony shoulders, like somebody had just made him out of clay and put him there.

Gene put on a robe, went downstairs, and walked out into the yard. His father looked at him, his eyes glittering in the moonlight. Gene imagined he saw light from the Other Side flickering there, getting closer. He turned away and together they looked out at the shadowy machine shapes.

After a little while, his father pointed at a patch of grass near his feet. It shimmered like heat haze, then began to sparkle. The sparkles started whirling around faster and faster, then coalesced into a solid shape. An electric mixer. Hamilton Beach. The curved blades caught the moonlight, and the smooth, white bowl seemed to glow with a pearly light of its own.

Gene looked up at his father. His father looked back, almost apologetically, his lips stretched tight across his bony skull in a death's head grin.

Miracles, Gene thought, and shook his head. "Let's go back inside, Dad. It's getting chilly."

He put his arm around his father's shoulder.

"Lean on me," he said.

Gene looked up and the house was gone, vanished as if it had never existed. Just the tall grass, blue in the moonlight, waving gently in the breeze. Beyond that, the woods, deep in shadow. And beyond the woods, low to the horizon, the sky held a suggestion of light. Not daybreak, but a phosphorescent glow pushing up from behind the fringe of trees like a corona, warm and cool at the same time. Gene felt it pulling at him with wordless promise.

Gene and his father began to walk together, uphill through the tall grass, toward the light.

CHAPTER TWENTY-FOUR

When Gabe got out of the shower, Ruby had returned and dinner was ready.

"You okay?" Casey asked. "You were in there a long time."

"Yeah, I'm okay," Gabe said. "Hungry."

The four of them sat at the small table and began passing food around. There was very little conversation during the meal. Gabe felt a tension stirring between Casey and himself. It wasn't a bad thing – it was sort of a cross between anticipation and anxiety. He wondered what was going to happen between them and he knew that she wondered the same thing. Once, their knees touched under the table and they both jerked back.

It must have been obvious that something was going on. Ariel kept looking back and forth between the two of them, and every now and then, when she thought nobody was looking, Ruby's face creased in a grin.

When they were done, Gabe cleared the table and Ariel got a quart container of chocolate ice cream from the freezer and four spoons.

"I can stay in Maggie's room tonight if you like," Ruby said, digging into the ice cream.

Gabe felt a quick flush come to his cheeks. His kneejerk reaction was that he didn't want to be treated like a kid. But he wanted some time with Casey and he wasn't about to leave Ariel in the trailer alone, even asleep. What if she woke up and nobody was around? She'd freak. Things were hard enough. He wondered how much of this Ruby had figured out. Plenty, he decided, recalling her quiet smiles during dinner. He didn't want to seem too eager, though.

"You don't have to do that," he said. "We're okay."

Ruby looked at him. "Yes, you are," she said. "It's really no problem, though."

"Okay, then," Gabe said. "Thanks. That would be great." He looked at Casey. She was looking right at him, a slight smile on her face. She turned to Ariel.

"How you doing, squirt? You tired?"

"Nope." She shook her head emphatically.

"I could have told you that," Gabe said to Casey.

They finished the ice cream and retired to the couch. Casey turned on the television with the remote and they channel-surfed for awhile. A Mannix rerun. Trauma Team, one of those docudrama shows, this one about paramedics. A news special about cross-dressers.

Gabe was acutely aware of Casey's presence. The tension between them felt real enough to touch; it was pulling them together and keeping them apart at the same time. Once, their eyes met and Gabe saw a flush creep up her pale cheeks.

In spite of her earlier denial, Ariel conked out after about twenty minutes. Gabe turned to Casey.

"You want to go for a walk?"

She nodded. "Sure."

Gabe turned to Ruby. "We're, uh, going for a walk."

"So I heard. Have a good one."

Gabe got some candles and matches from the kitchen drawer. As an afterthought, he pulled a blanket from the top shelf in the hall closet, folded it into a square, and tucked it under his arm.

They walked across the dunes toward the beach without talking. The moon was out, bathing everything in bluish light. It hung low in the sky, its reflection on the ocean

225

a bright, ragged scar. As they crossed the access road, Casey reached over and took his hand. Hers was dry and cool. Their fingers intertwined. Gabe felt his heart pounding in his chest.

They reached the opening to his Place. "Careful," he said, as he got down on his knees. "Don't scratch yourself."

He crawled through the path in the bramble. In spite of the moonlight, the path was dense with shadow. He could hear her following close behind him. Once, he heard a muffled curse.

"You all right?" he asked.

"Oh, fine. Just blood and pain."

Soon the roof of the bramble opened up over his head and he stopped. He unfolded the blanket, set a pair of candles deep in the sand next to it, lit them, and reached for her hand. They sat close together on the blanket, their knees touching.

"How you doing?" Casey asked. "It's really good to see you."

He laughed. "Oh, yeah. Hello, and all that." He shook his head. "I'm okay, I guess. Pretty good, actually, everything considered."

"You seem…different. Older."

He nodded. "A lot's happened." He looked up at her. Her face was golden in the candlelight. He leaned toward her and brushed his cheek across hers, gently at first, then again with a little more pressure. He felt her hand on the back of his neck. He put his arms around her and kissed her neck, her lips. Her mouth opened and their tongues met, caressed. She took his hand and brought it to her breast. He held it there, feeling the round, warm curve. He rubbed his thumb gently over the nipple and it stiffened under his touch.

She tugged at his shirt and he pulled back and raised his arms, letting her pull it off him. She took her shirt off and suddenly it seemed like they were both ripping articles of clothing off, flinging them into the close walls of the bramble, rolling on their backs in the enclosed space, giggling. When they were both naked, they lay close to each other on the blanket without moving. For the first time in a while, he was aware of the wheeze in her breath, a small gasp punctuating each inhalation. He felt a rush of feeling that he had no words for and his eyes filled with tears.

He put his hand on her hip and let it slide gently down the length of her thigh. "God, you're beautiful," he said.

She chuckled. "I bet you say that to everybody."

"Nope, there's never been anybody. Just you."

She put her arms around him and pulled him close. They stayed like that for awhile, then she began to move against him. He eased his thigh between hers and felt her bush slide against his skin, friction and moisture.

"Wait a minute," she said. She reached over to her pants and pulled a foil-wrapped condom from her wallet. "Be prepared." She unwrapped it and unrolled it over his cock. "Oh, man, are you prepared." She squeezed gently and he thought it would be all over right there. But she lay back, pulled him close, and eased him inside her.

It wasn't anything like his fantasy. He had time for that thought before it was swept away by raw physicality. He felt something take over him, at first pulling him along, then pushing…then *he* was pushing, higher and faster and it was all over so *soon* he was draped against her, his head nuzzling the crook of her neck, breathing hard and covered with sweat.

"How do we know how to do that?" he asked.

She chuckled, and it felt to Gabe like it was reverberating from somewhere inside him.

"Okay, this time you're bringing me with you."

The second time was slower and calmer. Gabe felt like he stayed in his body, connected with Casey, the bramble around them, the night outside. Near the end, she cried out and pulled him into her even more deeply. Her intensity startled him for a moment, almost frightened him, then he let himself ride with it. Free fall. He was in free fall. When he came this time, it seemed to happen from a deeper part of

227

him, and he felt like he was really with her, the two of them together fused into something that was larger than each of them alone. Afterward, they lay together on their sides, arms around each other, legs entwined. They slept.

When Gabe awoke, the candles were almost completely gone. The flames sputtered and flickered in twin pools of wax. Gently, he disentangled himself from Casey and sat up. She stirred and moaned faintly, then settled down again. He looked at Casey's face, relaxed in sleep, and felt it again, that rush of something that he had no words for, part sorrow, part joy.

His whole body felt tingly and alive. He pulled on his pants and crawled out of the bramble. It was still night, but a bruised, pinkish glow was beginning to push itself up from the juncture of sea and sky. He walked down to the beach, down to where the waves sent irregular, foamy sheets up across the wet sand. The foam seemed to glow with a light of its own. Out a little ways, he could see the breakers curling, spilling, crashing down, sending clouds of spray up into the air.

He reached out with his mind, like he did the first time on the beach with Otto, like he did at the track yesterday. (Yesterday? It seemed so long ago). He *pushed*, trying to find that space between heartbeats where it would all just stop for him, where it would hang there crisp and clear like a photograph and he could slide into it...*and he couldn't do it.*

He tried again. Nothing. The more he tried to remember what it was he had done, the more elusive it became, until he didn't even know anymore what it was he was trying to do. Whatever it was he'd had, it was gone.

The eastern sky was beginning to lighten up for real now, red near the horizon brushing the bottoms of a few wispy clouds, purple fading to deep, starry blue overhead. Gabe turned around and walked back up to the bramble.

Casey grinned sleepily at him as he crawled into the open space. "Good morning."

"Hey." He lay next to her and put his arms around

her. "Maybe we should head back up to the ranch. They're probably wondering about us."

Casey grinned. "Ruby isn't wondering about anything – she set us up. Besides, they're both probably sawing wood. But yeah, I want to wash some of the sand out of my crotch." She poked him in the ribs, then pulled back and looked at him. Her eyes had a soft look to them, but serious, almost grave. "This is good," she said. "This is a good thing."

Gabe nodded. "Yeah. It is."

The uphill walk didn't seem to bother her. When they got to the trailer, Gabe saw patches of color on her cheeks, but she was barely winded.

There was something on the kitchen table, a vague shape in the half-dark. Gabe turned on the light. It was an old electric mixer, the kind they don't make any more, all porcelain white and chrome silver. Gabe reached out and felt the raised letters across its base. Hamilton Beach. He looked at Casey and shrugged.

"You hungry?" he asked.

She nodded. "Yeah, I could eat something."

"How about some pancakes?"

She nodded again. "Sounds great."

Gabe got eggs and milk from the refrigerator, flour and baking powder from the cupboard. He cracked the eggs into the bowl, measured in the milk and flour, added a good pinch of baking powder. He plugged in the mixer and turned it on low, watching the blades catch the light in a silvery blur. Slowly, carefully, he lowered the spinning blades down into the mix.

EPILOGUE

Otto packed the last of the breakables in cardboard boxes and sat down heavily on the couch, next to Mary. A map of the United States was spread on the coffee table in front of her. "It's time, baby," he said. She sat immobile, staring off into space.

"Mary," he said. "It's time." Still no response.

Otto reached into his pocket and pulled out a straight razor, the blade protected in a black plastic casing. He unfolded the blade and reached for her hand. She offered no resistance. Quickly, he drew the blade across the top of her thumb, just deep enough to draw blood. She winced, but didn't pull away. Otto held her hand over the map, and when the first drop of blood beaded and fell, he drew it back.

There, a star-shaped splash of red, nested among the snaking arterial roads. Otto peered at the map and nodded. "Well, all right." He turned to Mary. "Look alive, we've got some driving to do."

<u>Also available from Apodis Publishing</u>

Stumble Down the Mountainside
Ian Donnell Arbuckle

Lithium has just graduated college and wants nothing more than to sleep in late on summer mornings and occasionally hit his younger brother with a stick. One morning, he wakes up to find the rest of humanity gone, destroyed in a man-made apocalypse -- but somehow his family is untouched. Drug-addled Mom; his brothers, suicidal Brat and jelly-spined paranoiac Grant; his Dad the zombie. Lithium begins to feel like the center of a brand new rarity: the dysfunctional family. He is the tormented middle child, but he's the last middle child on Earth. As far as he is concerned, that means he gets to write the rules from here on out.

9780973804713, $11.95 USD

Sleeping With Gods
Michael Fontana

After a suicide attempt, 19 year old Mark finds himself living in a rooming house, hardly anything to his name except a seemingly endless supply of Pepsi. Told by his therapist to socialize, he befriends his housemate Daniel, who tries to introduce the intimacy-fearing Mark to the world of women. Then Mark meets Leah, a girl with her own troubled past. In his remarkable debut novel, Michael Fontana weaves together the lives of two lost souls.

9780973804744, $13.95 USD

Also available from Daniel Marcus

Binding Energy
Elastic Press (www.elasticpress.com)

In these nineteen stories Marcus maps out possible futures and theoretical pasts, crisscrossing reality with fantasy, and weaving intricate storylines in the process. His characters are frightened and fragile, facing brave new worlds whilst retaining their humanity. If you want to know what the future really looks like, then look here.

9780955318160, £5.99 GBP

Burn Rate
Apodis Publishing

Ross and Lori Williamson are living the Boomer version of the American Dream. Ross is a Silicon Valley entrepreneur, battered but still standing after the Internet collapse. Lori has quit her upscale corporate law job to make pottery, study martial arts, and start a family. Unable to conceive, they hire Annie Day as a surrogate to bear their fertilized egg to term. Annie has a few skeletons in her closet, including an ex-boyfriend desperate for cash and on the run from the Italian and Russian mobs.

9780973804737, $14.95 USD

CPSIA information can be obtained at www.ICGtesting.com
Printed in the USA
LVOW061627280911

248288LV00007B/8/P